<u>GAGE</u>

THE HUSTLE CHRONICLES PREQUEL

BLACC TOPP

Published by: BlaccStarr Media Group & amp; InkSlinger Publishing Written by: BlaccTopp

For information contact:
BlaccStarr Media Group
P.O. Box 9451
Port St. Lucie, FL 34985-9451

www.novelistblacctopp.com
Instagram: NovelistBlaccTopp
Facebook: Dean Swift
Twitter: NovelistBlaccTopp

ACKNOWLEDGEMENTS

This novel is dedicated to those Swift Boys. My Father Rufus Swift and my uncles Eugene Swift, Otha Lee Swift and Charlie Boy Swift. You men were beasts in your time and I'm proud to carry the last name Swift. I am proud to have been privy to the stories of how our family came to be. Salute to you all and I love you!!

CHAPTER 1

Nathaniel Gage stood in the center of the small, nondescript bedroom and undressed slowly. Tears stained his cheeks as a band of crickets ceremoniously chirped the soundtrack to his pain. "Well, do you want this fifteen cents, or don't you nigga?" The woman asked.

Nathaniel didn't bother to answer. He watched the moonlight dash into the room, only to be veiled in darkness by passing clouds. A sliver of light still remained and washed across the drunken harlot's face. He imagined that the light had literally washed her, but he had no such luck. She reeked of alcohol and the rancid odor of her stench filled the room. She ripped the dirty sheets from her body to welcome him into her bed. The smell that had invaded his nostrils seemed to embed itself on the fibers of his tongue, swirling and swishing in his mouth until he felt as if he might vomit. He felt the urge to purge himself of the boiled egg sandwich that he'd eaten earlier that day. Wafting from the hairy catastrophe between her legs were the remnants of too many drunken lovers and not enough hot baths. Nathaniel slid into bed and pulled the covers up to his chest. She propped herself up on one elbow and stared at him. Her breath was hot and rank, emitting a sweet, yet rotten, putrid funk. She had very few teeth in her mouth. Most of them had been knocked out by the angry white men that she'd bedded and robbed, or from the lack of proper care. They were a dull shade of greyish brown and again Nathaniel felt the food in his stomach churn.

"You ready to service me nigga boy?" She asked.

Nathaniel turned his head toward the window to escape both her breath and her lustful gaze. "Gimme a kiss," she said.

"No, let's just get this over with!" He said tersely.

"Have it your way nigglet," she spat and stroked his flaccid penis until it was hard.

Nathaniel cursed his young manhood for cooperating with the haggard drunk. He refused to look at her as she climbed on top of him and guided his cock into her semi-wet snatch. He closed his eyes tighter, so tight in fact that he felt as though the blood vessels in them might pop. She bounced on top of him vigorously to a rhythm that only she could hear. She bent over until her face was nearly touching his own and attempted to kiss him repeatedly, but Nathaniel kept turning his head.

"Open your fucking mouth!" She screamed.

As soon as Nathaniel's lips parted, he felt the familiar feeling of her slimy tongue probing the recesses of his mouth. Nathaniel tensed his body and tried to think of

2

happier times before his body was used as a human sex receptacle, but it was to no avail. He could only think of the woman grinding on top of him, soiling his fifteen-year-old soul. Finally, he heard the beginning of her descent. It was a slow, yet deliberate and guttural moan that filled the small room. She cursed unthinkable obscenities at him as she bucked and thrashed against him, assaulting his pelvis.

"Fuck me white boy! Fuck me good yella nigga!" She rolled over, and collapsed next to Nathaniel, leaving his midsection wet with her malodorous juices.

She stood, walked to the dresser across the room and lit the wick of an oil burning lamp. Her features were dark and evil as her eyes burned into Nathaniel's flesh. She picked up one of the stale cigarettes on the dresser and bent over to light it with the lamp's flame. Nathaniel wished that her entire face would catch fire. She turned to face him again. He watched in horror as she reached down between her legs with her free hand, and scooped a finger inside of her moist snatch in an attempt to see if he'd ejaculated. There was none, like most times and it angered her when he didn't.

"Oh, I ain't good enough for your little yella nut boy?" She asked, inhaling her cigarette, blowing ringlets into the darkness. "I oughta make you do it again. What kinda man don't bust a nut when he's fucking a beautiful woman?" She asked no one in particular.

"Probably because I ain't no man. I'm fifteen years old. I don't wanna do this no more."

"You sassin' me boy? You'a do whatever I tell you to do. I oughta beat the freckles off your yella ass, but I'm tired," she scoffed.

"Why do you hate me?"

"I don't hate you, boy. I love you. This here is just grown folks' business. This is called being grown and getting you a little experience. Wouldn't you rather be fucking a woman with some experience, rather than one of them little trollops that don't know what they're doing?" She asked.

"I'd rather not be doing this at all. The bible says a man and a woman shouldn't lay together until they're married. And you 'specially ain't s'posed to lay with kin."

Delores Gage crossed the room and hissed in Nathaniel's face, "Stop being a little bitch boy! When your pappy died you promised me that you'd be the man of the house! Well, a man's job is to make sure that the woman of the house is happy! Don't be preaching to me boy. It's your job to make sure that your mama is happy! Don't you wanna make mama happy?"

"My pappy? My pappy? Mama, really? Rufus Gage lay right here in this bed 'fore he died and told me he wasn't my pappy. He say some white man you was screwing in town my real pappy. He say he loved me the same as I was his own, so don't make him no never mind who my real pappy was. I 'spect he turning over in his grave knowing how the house he built with his own two hands being done by you!" Nathaniel spat.

Delores slapped Nathaniel with such force that he fell from the bed, but he sprang to his feet. Standing on the opposite side of the bed from his incestuous mother with his fists balled up, he mentally dared her to strike him again.

"I want you outta my house Nathanial Gage and don't you ever darken my door again!" Delores screamed.

"My pappy say this here my house! He wrote it on a piece of paper he called a deed. He say if'n you started in on me I'd always have somewhere to go! You need to leave Delores, I don't want you in my pappy house, in my house. Now git!!" He barked.

"Who gonna take care of you if mama leave baby?" She pleaded.

"I'm grown, remember? I 'spects I take care of everything around here anyway while you're gallivanting around with them white mens, so I'm sure I be fine."

Delores dressed slowly, forcing tears from her eyes as she did. She looked at him through wet eyes, hoping to gain his sympathy. However, there was no sympathy in his eyes when he looked back at her, only unbridled hatred. Rage seethed in the young man for the woman who brought him into the world, but had defiled his innocence. She tossed the few belongings that she owned into a pillow case and moved toward the front door. Her feigned sadness gave way to anger as she realized that her son was serious. "You'll need me again you yella bastard! Nobody will ever love you boy, because you're worthless! You're a cracker to the niggas and you're a nigga to the crackers, so who's gonna love you 'sides me?" She barked.

5

Nathaniel slammed the rickety wooden door in her face and watched from the window as she disappeared down the red, clay dirt road. He watched until her body became a mere speck of darkness beneath a full moon heavy and ready to give birth to new possibilities.

Chapter 2

Nathaniel walked through downtown Marianna, Arkansas half expecting to see his mother Delores out on the corner hooking, but he didn't. Instead he saw black people shuffling toward their prospective jobs. Many of them were elderly black people who cleaned for the well to do white people in town. Others worked in the fields of Marianna on former slave plantations. Cotton was one of their main staples in the small town and their sparse population of 4,300 kept the country town bustling, especially with a makeup of 80% black and 20% white. Even with such a small concentration of white people in the town, they still controlled every aspect of life in Marianna. The blacks were relegated to the *bottoms*. The *bottoms* was an area on the southern end of town lined with shotgun shanty houses made from salvaged wood and collected, often stolen pieces of tin. Many of them still had dirt floors and their residents still cooked on open fires in kettles. Many of the homes, if they could even be called homes, were former slave quarters and the poor citizens of Marianna were just happy to have somewhere to lay their heads. Nathaniel considered himself lucky, because Rufus Gage had worked hard for the land that Nathaniel now owned. Rufus' entire family had been owned by the Gage family and after slavery ended, Rufus' father stayed on to tend the fields of the plantation. When Joseph Gage died, he left the plantation to his son Philip Gage. After his father's death Philip saw the opportunity to live a life that he'd always wished for. He wanted the city life and he would never have that in Marianna, but he'd always dreamed of going to New York City. He'd heard stories of bright lights, big city living and carriages that moved on their own with no horses. He was far less adamant about the upkeep of the old plantation and considering that he and Rufus had grown up together, it was he who signed over the deed to Rufus Gage. The land wasn't much in the way of lavish plantations, but it was profitable nevertheless and Rufus made it his own. Unlike the plantations of other parts of Arkansas, the Gage plantations' big house wasn't big at all. It was a one story wooden house with three very small bedrooms. It did however, have indoor plumbing and a wood burning stove. Rufus had inherited not only the name of his family's former master, but also the land that his family had slaved on. He in turn had passed that land on to the boy that he had affectionately given the name Gage.

Nathaniel straightened his tie and wiped the dust from his leather shoes on the back of his tweed slacks. When he entered the Lee County Bank, the whites inside stopped and looked at Nathaniel Gage as if he'd assassinated Abraham

Lincoln. "Are you lost boy?" A fat white woman asked, staring at Nathaniel over horn rimmed glasses.

"No ma'am, I wanted to ask 'bout maybe startin' up me a saving account."

"If you can count nigger, I'm assuming that you can read too boy!" She hissed.

"Yessum, I can read."

"Then how come you didn't bother to read the sign on that door that said this bank don't cater to coloreds?" She wondered.

"My money spend just like white folks money!"

"Is there a problem here Martha?" An elderly white man asked.

"Yes Mr. Lund. I told this here nigger that we didn't want his money and now he's sassin' me!" She said.

"That true boy? You sassing this here white woman?" Mr. Lund asked.

"No suh, I's just trying to find a way to bank my earnings. I didn't come in here fuh no trouble suh." Nathaniel stared at the ground.

"Well, let me be the first to tell you boy. You're going to find plenty of trouble if you don't get your black ass out of my bank. Take your coon ass down to the bottoms. Maybe one of those slimy niggers down there can help you, but we don't mix good white citizens' money with dirty nigger money!" Mr. Lund spat.

Nathaniel turned on his heels and left the bank. Although he hadn't witnessed it first hand, he'd heard of boys not much older than himself being found hanging from trees in the back woods of Marianna, Arkansas. He walked through town with his head held low, feeling even lower. If the white people wouldn't allow a black man in their bank and if they wouldn't allow him as a young man to save money, then how was he supposed to someday have a family? Maybe he would start his own bank. Yeah, that would teach them. He pulled the deed from his pocket and read it slowly. Who was he fooling? He had a fifth grade education and he was fifteen years old. The chances of him starting a bank; hell any business, was slim to none.

He trudged to the *bottoms* and wandered into Lenny's Juke Joint. It wasn't more than a gutted barn that had been converted into a party palace. It was a little before dark when Nathaniel wandered into Lenny's to the sound of guitar licks and piano riffs. He walked to the make shift bar and ordered three shots of whiskey.

"You a little young to be drinking ain't you boy?" The bartender asked.

"Don't worry 'bout how old I is. I gots money and I aim to spend it. Or is you too good to take my money too?"

The bartender didn't exchange another word with Nathaniel. He sloppily poured the drinks, spilling a little bit onto the wooden bar. The sound of the lead guitar wafted through the air as riotous patrons danced in the middle of the dusty, dirt floor. Nathaniel downed the three shots back to back and beckoned to the bartender.

"Hey man, how much for the bottle?" He asked.

"It's a whole dollar." He looked at Nathaniel skeptically.

"Leave it," Nathaniel said, leaving a crumpled dollar on the bar. He poured a shot from the bottle and downed it quickly. He was just about to pour another one when a young woman joined him at the bar. She touched his hand, stopping him from pouring more liquor. "You're drinking kind of fast, don't you think you should slow down?" She asked.

"I think you should mind your own damn business!"

"Just because you drunk don't give you no cause to be rude. I'm Juanita." She extended her hand. Nathaniel shook it, introduced himself and apologized. He explained to her how bad his day had been and how the white people had broken his spirit.

"Nathaniel, that's just one obstacle honey. If you're really persistent you can do anything that you put your mind to. When I was nine years old my pappy left us and it broke my mama down, but she was always there for me. She used to tell me that I could be anything I wanted to be. I went all the way to the 10th grade before my mama took sick and I had to get a job to help take care of home. One day I'm going to be rich Nathaniel. You watch and see!" She said excitedly.

"I believe you Juanita. I don't think I's smart enough to get rich. I just wanna have me a family and work my land."

"One gone be rich, one ain't. Shit I don't think neither one of you niggas gone be shit!" A large black man spat. He stood behind the pair huffing and puffing, glaring at Nathaniel.

"Walter Polk, don't come over her starting no trouble now! Me and Nathaniel is having us a private conversation," Juanita said.

"Yeah, well did you tell this little, frail, half yella nigga that you's my woman?" Walter Polk's chest heaved as he spoke. He was one of the biggest men that Nathaniel had ever laid eyes on and he was terrified. The buttons of his shirt held on for dear life, trying to contain the massive, hairy chest that hid beneath it.

"I ain't your woman Walter. We had a go and that was that, but I don't belong to you!" Juanita spat.

"You 'longs to me 'til I say different, now grab yo' thangs, we's leaving!" Walter Polk shouted. He grabbed Juanita by her arm and attempted to drag her out of the juke joint. Nathaniel gripped the neck of the bottle and leapt from his seat.

"She said she ain't your woman, so I reckon you oughta leave her be," Nathaniel said. He was surprised at the authority in his own voice. He wasn't sure if it was the liquor giving him the courage, or plain stupidity.

"And what you gon' do if I don't little, high yella nigga? Sit you little ass down 'fore you make me mad boy."

Nathaniel made a move toward the man who was four times his size, but before he reached him, a woman leapt onto his back and slit his throat from ear to ear. Walter Polk released Juanita's arm and fell to his knees, holding his throat. Nathaniel watched as the massive man slipped into darkness. The music stopped and gasps of horror filled the room. Delores Gage stood over Walter Polk's dead body holding a bloody straight razor.

"We're even now boy! My debt is washed away. I don't owe you shit no mo'!" She hissed. Delores disappeared through the rear of the barn to never be seen again by her son, or anyone else for that matter.

The bartender came from around the bar with his shotgun in hand. "See what you done, done boy? These white folks already don't want me open and now I gots to explain a dead nigga in the middle of my establishment. Get your ass outta here and don't never come back and take this tramp with you. She might can sang, but she ain't worth the damn trouble!"

"Lenny we leaving, but I wanna be paid what I'm owed for singing in your place!" Juanita snarled.

"You can consider that your pay for cleaning up this boy's mess, now get on outta here! Start your own goddamn juke joint and kill whosonever you want. Now get on outta here!!"

CHAPTER 3

"**W**hat did that woman mean she don't owe you nothing else? Who is she?" Juanita asked.

"She's my mother and it is a very long story that I don't want to go into tonight. Can I walk you home?"

"Yeah, that would be nice," Juanita obliged.

They walked in silence for a long while before Juanita took Nathaniel's hand in her own and turned to him. "Maybe we should consider what he said Nate."

"Consider what?" Nathaniel asked.

"Maybe we should start our own juke joint? I mean Lenny's was a nice place, but people complained that the band played the same music and that Lenny watered down the drinks. All we have to do is find a place and make it our own."

Nathaniel didn't know how to take the things that she said. On one hand he liked the fact that she used words like we, us and our, but they had just met. "All that sounds good, but where we gon' find liquor? What we know 'bout running a bar?" He asked.

14

"I've been watching Lenny in that joint for about a year and a half. I know where he gets his liquor. I know most of the band and my sister is the waitress. I got an auntie who cooks for the white folks and I'm sure she'd be up for some extra money cooking for us. I can sang most nights and when we get some real money, we can even bring in some talent like Ethel Waters, or Ma Rainey!" She said excitedly.

"Hold on now Nita! You mighty excited for something that ain't even happened yet. I don't even know your last name. I don't know how old you is, or nothing."

"My last name Mention and I'm eighteen years old. Haven't you ever been excited about things to come Nate?" She asked.

"Okay, so we business partners now? You think when you find you a man he gonna take kindly to you having a man as a business partner?"

"Don't be silly Nathaniel Gage, you gon' be my man. So unless you gon' be mad at yourself, then that's a worry we won't have," Juanita said

"You know I'm only fifteen years old. What a grown eighteen year old woman gonna do with a boy who look like me?"

"You don't give yourself enough credit Nathaniel. I'm gon' do whatever you want me to do."

"I just wants you to be a good woman to me Juanita. I done had enough madness in my life to never need no mo', so long as you can treat me right, I'll do the same," Nathaniel told her.

"I'll never do you wrong Nathaniel Gage, but if you ever put your hands on me, I'll leave and you'll never see me again. I watched my daddy beat my mama until she was black and blue and when that no account nigga left, she still pined for him like he was Jesus Christ himself. I promised myself that I'd never live that way."

As if ignoring her plea, Nathaniel skipped to an entirely different subject. "You know; I believe I have just the place for our juke joint."

"And where is that?"

"Meet me at the Gage house. Do you know where that is?" He asked.

"Yeah, I know where it is. That's the place past the old cotton mill right?"

"Yeah, that's it. Meet me there in the morning and I'll show you," he said.

"Okay, I'll meet you there. This is my house right here. You wanna come in for a spell?"

"Naw, I best be gettin' home. It ain't safe for a man to be walking these Marianna streets late at night. I see you in the morning," Nathaniel kissed Juanita on the cheek and scurried off down the dirt road toward his house. Every crackle of a branch, and every bark of a dog caused Nathaniel to jump. Crickets chirped from beyond the fields and from somewhere in the distance Nathaniel heard the sound of horse hooves drawing close. Nathaniel ran off the road and hid in the high grass of the ditch line. He could hear the angry white men as they passed on their horses.

"Why are we even concerned about a dead nigger sheriff? That's one less coon for us to hang," one man said.

"I could give two shits about a dead nigger Tom. I'm going down here to save face and get me a bottle of that good hooch this nigger Lenny keeps in the cellar," he said.

Nathaniel didn't dare move while they passed. He barely breathed as he lay there still until he was certain that they were gone. He wondered if the bartender/ bar owner had blamed him for Walter Polk's death. If he had, they would most certainly come for him. Maybe in the middle of the night like the Klan did to their victims. Nathaniel sprang to his feet and ran nonstop the entire mile to his house. He burst through the door and lay on the living room floor. He lay perfectly still, staring at the ceiling, afraid to move for fear that someone might see his shadow and come for him. He thought of Rufus and what he must think of him, lying on the floor, cowering in fear. He waited for the first torch to come crashing through his window, but it never came. Instead what came was the overwhelmingly welcomed exhaustion and the sleep that followed.

CHAPTER 4

The sound of the deep, throaty roosters pulled Nathaniel from his deep sleep. He was still laying in the same spot where he'd collapsed the night before and his body ached. The wooden floor was unrelenting and unforgiving. Nathaniel stumbled to his feet and dusted himself off. He peered out of the window and saw a one horse carriage racing the dust trail that tailed it. He looked at the small wooden cuckoo clock on the wall. It was 7:40 am and Juanita was due there in twenty minutes. It must've been her. It had to be her. She was early, but that didn't bother Nathaniel, because he was anxious to share his plan with her. He rushed to the bathroom and threw some water on his face. Then he took the dingy face towel from the sink, wetted it and wiped his teeth. He ran his hand across his kinky, red hair and smiled at his reflection in the tarnished mirror. He heard a knock at the door and a huge smile spread across his face. He couldn't wait to see Juanita again. Her complexion was darker than his, but not so dark that she looked greasy. He hated that, but in all actuality he hated white people *and* black people. Delores Gage had been right, the whites didn't accept him, because as they'd stated on more than one occasion, one drop of nigger blood tainted a man, or woman and the blacks didn't accept him because they *knew*. It seemed that everyone knew of his less than honorable origins. Everyone except Nathaniel Gage himself. Juanita was different. She didn't seem to care about his mixed breed status. At least that's what she made Nathaniel believe. He walked to the door with a goofy smile still plastered across his face, until he saw the dull shine of the Sheriff's badge attached to the shirt of Wilbur Buchanan.

"Morning suh?" Nathaniel said.

"Your mammy here boy?" The sheriff asked, ignoring Nathaniel's greeting.

"No suh, she ain't here."

"What happened down at Lenny's last night?" Buchanan asked.

Nathaniel hesitated. He didn't give a damn about his mother, but he didn't want her to die at the hands of an angry white mob either.

"Before you answer boy, just know that I already know what happened. I'm giving you an opportunity to clear your name. If you lie to me, I will haul your black ass in and have you swinging from a tree before nightfall," Buchanan said.

"No suh, I wouldn't dream of lying to you suh. I went down to Lenny's to have me a little taste and I's talking to a little lady when this big nigga name Walter assaulted the guhl. I asked him tuh let her go, but he wouldn't. I's just gone scare him a bit with a bottle of rye I had, but before I could, my mama came up behind him and cut his throat. She left and I ain't seent her suh."

"If'n she comes back here boy, you tell her that I said she needs to turn herself in. If I find her first, she'll meet the end of a rope," Buchanan said.

As Buchanan turned to leave, Nathaniel spotted Juanita emerging from the woods that lined his property. He wasn't sure why she was coming from the woods, but she was a welcomed sight. Sheriff Buchanan ambled toward his horse drawn carriage, struggling to heave his beefy frame onto the rickety wood. "Yah! Yah!" He said once he was settled comfortably.

"What Sheriff Buchanan want Nathaniel?" Juanita asked.

"He askin' after my mama. He say if'n she don't turn herself in and they find her, they gone hang her."

"Oh, my sweet Jesus! You need to find her and tell her, so she can get a trial. She was just protecting her son," Juanita said.

Nathaniel shrugged his shoulders. He didn't give a damn one way, or another. Maybe she deserved it, maybe she didn't, but he wasn't getting involved.

"I ain't telling her shit. She grown. 'Sides, she don't deserve my help and I ain't liffin' one finger to help her black ass! You want some coffee? I gots me some bacon I cured myself and I can go grab some eggs from the hen house for breakfast."

"That sounds fine, mighty fine Nate. I can cook if you want. I love to cook. 'Sides if you gonna make me your woman, you need to be fed right?" Juanita asked.

Nathaniel smiled at her and walked out of the house toward the hen house. The closer he got to the hen house the more agitated they seemed. As he stepped in, he grabbed the Winchester rifle from the wall. Between the black bears and coyotes, Nathaniel had lost a few of his prized hens and roosters and if he shot one of them, he'd just skin it, cure it and sell it to the unsuspecting white people as deer meat. It was neither though. It was Delores Gage, crouched down between the coop and the back wall.

"Nathaniel, that you?" She whispered.

"You can't be here Delores. Sheriff Buchanan done already been here looking for you. He find you on this property after I done told him I ain't seen you and he'll lynch us both!"

"I did what I did for your little ungrateful high yella ass and this is the thanks I get?" She barked.

"You did what you did to clear your dirty mind. I want you gone by the time I come back, or I'm goin' to the sheriff myself."

"I'm still yo' mama nigga, so don't forget that! You just gone let them white people hang me Nathaniel?" She asked.

"My mama died the night she came into my room and made me a man before it was time," Nathaniel sneered.

He filled the basket with eggs and walked toward the door, but stopped short. He looked back and smiled at her. "I hope when they hang you, it's the same white men who you gave your body to for a nickel a pop."

By the time Nathaniel made it back to the house Juanita already had the thick cut bacon frying in the black, cast iron skillet. The aroma of fresh brewed coffee from his glass percolator filled the room and Juanita was rolling dough to make homemade biscuits. She poured Nathaniel a cup of coffee, placed it on the table in front of him and went back to her biscuits. She poured some of the bacon grease onto the metal baking pan, swished it around, laced the pan with biscuits and placed it in the oven.

"You like your bacon real crispy, or a little soft?" She asked.

"I don't care one way or another Nita."

Juanita poured herself a cup of coffee and joined Nathaniel at the table. "So, if we're going to be together, you're going to have to tell me why you and your mama are at odds Nathaniel," she said.

Nathaniel took a deep breath and started to recall the horrid story of his often tumultuous relationship with his mother. He gave her detail after incestuous detail. He even told her that he blamed himself and that he felt guilty, because his manhood had risen to the occasion, something he felt he should have had control over. Nathaniel also told Juanita that realistically, he didn't know if he could ever love, because a boy should never be thrown into that sort of madness. He explained that his mother had made him quit school in the fifth grade, because real men didn't add, or subtract; they provided for their families. She said that no school could teach him how to be a man. Nathaniel looked deep into Juanita's eyes, but it was more like he was looking through her into some faraway place.

"I never saw it coming. The first time, I mean. She was drunk and she kissed me. I tried to pull away, but she scolded me something fierce and I let her have her way with me," he explained.

"It's not your fault Nathaniel, so don't you never blame yourself for her foolishness," Juanita assured him. She walked to the oven and removed the biscuits. Then she fried some eggs in the same skillet that held the leftover bacon grease and made Nathaniel a large plate. He dove into the food, not caring how hot it was. Between bites he smacked and nodded his head, devouring the food as if he hadn't eaten in months.

"Mm mm mm, Nita that was mighty tasty, mighty tasty! I feel like I can work now. Lemme show you where we can put this here juke joint." He took her by the hand and led her to the barn to the east of his home. It needed a little paint, but Juanita could see the potential in it. It was a sturdy spacious barn. Sure it smelled like dirt and hay, but the space was perfect. "

So, what you think?" Nathaniel asked.

"I think we can make a real nice speak easy outta this place Nate. Downstairs we can have music and dancing. Over here we can put some card tables and crap tables. Back here in this corner," she said, moving toward the rear of the barn, "we can put the bar! You see all that space up top? We can have some working girls up there."

"What? Like a ho' house? I don't know 'bout that part Nita." Nathaniel shook his head.

"We already doing wrong by having gambling and booze Nate. Ain't no sense in not taking advantage of it all. We'll be rich in no time!" Juanita said, twirling around in a dusty circle.

She grabbed Nathaniel's face and buried her tongue deep within his mouth. She let her tongue swirl around his. Nathaniel let his hands glide over the thick material of her dress and felt the familiar stirring in his loins that had caused him so much grief.

"If'n we gone do this I wanna do it right Nita. Let's get married!" He suggested.

"A boy gots to be eighteen and a girl sixteen with her parent's blessing. We still gots three full years 'fore I can marry you Nathaniel Gage!"

"That don't stop us from practicing. You can move here with me. Hell, we can live like we's married. Onliest thang marriage is, is a piece of paper and a ring." He shrugged.

"So you want to play like married folk, but we ain't?"

"You just said I ain't old enough yet Nita. What I 'sposed to do?" He asked.

"I guess you right Nathaniel. I'ma go home and pack my things and I'll be back."

*****

A couple of days later Juanita returned with a carriage packed with all her things being pulled by a mule. The mule trudged slowly toward the house in no particular hurry. No matter how many times Juanita cracked her cat-o-nine tail, he never changed his pace. They both unpacked her things and chatted all the while.

"You know, I was thinking Nathaniel. Those six small houses that you have out back, we could rent those out to the band and whatever girls we find to work the bar. That way we get some of the money back that we're spending to pay them."

"I don't even know how much to charge for no rent Nita," Nathaniel admitted bashfully.

"I think with the size we can charge about $15 a month. That's $90 a month, not to mention the profit from booze, gambling and girls."

Nathaniel had no concept of what money could do, or its value. He could add and subtract a little bit, but he knew for certain that he'd never had $10 at one time let alone $90. Juanita was smart and she had a plan. Maybe they would be rich together after all.

CHAPTER 5

It took less than a month to get everything into place just the way Nathaniel and Juanita wanted it. They had all of the cottages rented out and the club was coming along nicely. Juanita and Nathaniel stood back from the barn to survey the crudely painted sign that hung from the door. JUANITA'S SPEAK EASY was doing pretty good business. After only a week of being open, they had been doing close to $25 a day."

Well, baby girl we're doing pretty good so far, but where are we going to keep this money? They ain't gone let us keep it at the bank," Nathaniel said.

"Come with me Nate. I have an idea."

They walked to the house and once inside Juanita pulled out an old pillow case out and dumped all of their earnings inside. She pulled up one of the boards from the floor and placed the pillow case inside.

"There you go baby. If they won't allow us to use their bank, we will just make our own bank. I have a surprise for you Nate. Sit down and close your eyes," Juanita said.

Nathaniel did as he was told and heard Juanita scurry off to the other room. When she returned, she instructed him to open his eyes. On the table in front of him was a baby's rattle with a baby blue bow on it. He stared at it for a long while until it finally dawned on him what it was that Juanita was trying to tell him. He looked up at her slowly through tear filled eyes.

"That's right baby, you gonna be a pappy!" Juanita said.

Nathaniel couldn't believe what he was hearing. Hopefully he would have a son to carry his name for an eternity.

CHAPTER 6

Juanita couldn't be happier. Since they'd opened the juke joint, business had boomed. So much so, that Lenny's had closed down. Juanita had been able to convince all of the old crew to come work for them and Lenny had reluctantly given her his liquor connection. She'd given birth to their first child, Otis and at the rate that they were having sex, it wouldn't be long before she got pregnant with her second. Although they weren't married, she'd given Otis the Gage name. Nathaniel had proven to be a fantastic father and he was highly committed to making their family unit strong. Many of the people that had moved on to the property, not only worked at the juke joint, but also helped Nathaniel tend the fields of the property. They had crops, plenty of hens and eggs, dairy cows, cows for meat, goats and pigs. Their small commune was the talk of Marianna and everyone wanted to live on the property where a person could actually make a decent wage and have the added bonus of free food. Well, not really free because they had to earn it, but the Gage farm was the place to be. Juanita watched as Otis sat slobbering on a chicken leg and staring at his father intensely as he counted money. The two oil lamps that they'd lit burned brightly. The shadows of the flames danced and wiggled against the wooden walls. Remnants of the night's dinner still hung heavily in the air, giving the house a homely smell. Much to Juanita's surprise, even after Nathaniel had plowed the entire eastern five acres, he'd still come inside and cooked fried chicken, collard greens, yams and cornbread. The mashed yams were Otis' favorite and Nathaniel catered to the boy. He often remarked to Juanita that she'd only carried Otis, because that child was his and his alone. She knew that he only said it teasingly, but she didn't take it that way. Nathaniel borderline coddled the boy and she worried that he was going to be the cause of him growing up soft. Juanita looked at the money spread out on the floor in front of Nathaniel. She wasn't sure exactly how much money it was, but it was more money than she'd ever seen in her life.

"How much we done made so far baby?" She asked.

"Well, you might have to count it all up Nita. I's just been putting likes with likes and so forth. I can count to fo' hundid, but that's far as I can git. Why don't you come count it while I tends to Otis?"

Juanita sat down and started with the coins first. There was almost $800 in coins and almost $6,000 in bills. They'd just had Ma Rainey at their juke joint and had made and astonishing $547 profit. $6,800 didn't make them rich by any stretch of the imagination, but they had a nice nest egg just in case they needed it.

Nathaniel caught a flicker of fire from the corner of his eye and it startled him. He handed Otis to Juanita and ran to the front door. His heart dropped as four hooded men on horses, carrying torches raced toward the small cottages at the back of his property.

"Nita, white folk speeding toward the quarters! Come on!" Nathaniel screamed. He jumped from the front porch and ran full speed toward the men. If they started burning the old wooden buildings, it would surely spread and he would have no way of putting it out before it reached the main house or the juke joint. Juanita caught up to Nathaniel as he made it to the quarters.

"How can I help you suh?" Nathaniel asked nervously.

"You can help me by minding your own business boy!" One of the men said.

"This is my business suh. This here's my property!" Nathaniel shouted.

"You sassin' me nigga?! Nigga's don't own nothing, but what we let 'em own coon. You'd do well to remember that boy!"

"Yessuh, I just don't wants no trouble on this here land suh. My daddy gimme this land and I's just tryna do right by it tis all." Nathaniel squirmed. The white men had deflated his sails in front of his woman and his ego was bruised.

"That's better porch monkey. Now, you got a mulatto name Fletcher Graham on this here property and we aims to string him up tonight. You can either have him come on out, or we can burn him out!"

30

Tenants peered through the curtains of their small houses, but one house was dark with no signs of life. Nathaniel walked to the door of that house and knocked.

"Fletcher, if'n you in there you needs to come on out. Ain't no sense in the rest of us getting into no ruckus because you done did wrong. Now come on out here and face these here men," Nathaniel said.

"I ain't coming out unless they say they gone listen to my side! I ain't done nuffin to give them cause to come 'round here!" Fletcher yelled back.

"We just wants to talk to you boy! Come on out and we can settle this! What you did is against the law boy. You can't consort with a white woman in Lee County!" A white man said.

"If'n I done broke the law, why y'all ain't got the sheriff witcha?" Fletcher asked.

"Enough of these goddamned questions nigger! Bring your black ass out of there, or we'll smoke you out!" Another white man said.

"Fletcher come on out of my house now! I don't want this here kinda trouble on my land!" Nathaniel said.

Slowly the door of the small, dark cabin opened and Fletcher Graham emerged sweating. He was shirtless and he looked terrified. Other tenants had started to file out of their respective residents to watch the spectacle happening. Fletcher stepped out of the house and stood before the racists.

"Come on out of there Sarah Ann! Yo' diddy plum worried about you!"

Moments later a young, white woman came running out of the cottage, crying and pulling at her dress. "Thank God you found me. Oh my God, please take me home to my daddy! This here nigger dragged me out here and raped me!" She screamed.

"I did no such thang suh! She…" Fletcher started, but before he could finish his sentence one of the men struck him in the face with the butt of his rifle.

"Be careful nigga! You calling this good, clean, innocent white woman a lie? You saying she chasing after you, nigger?"

Fletcher knew that he was in a no win situation, but, if she was willing to lie on him to save face, he had no qualms about telling the truth.

"I'm saying she lyin' and she know she lyin'. Look boss, I knows y'all gone strang me up, so ain't no sense in me tryna talk my way outta dis. She come to me suh. She say her mammy told her how well niggas is hung and she reckon she wants to try some. I told her it's wrong. I told her I get in a heapa trouble if'n we gets caught. She say, she a protect me from harm if any white man say something. She say her pappy real important and she make sho I's protected. That's the truth boss!"

The white men all looked at one another curiously. There had to be some truth to what the black man was saying, or how else would he know that her father was an important man? Sarah Ann Dimwitty was Orville Dimwitty's pride and joy and it was he who had sent the masked men to retrieve his daughter. Orville nearly owned the small town of

Marianna, Arkansas. He owned the bank, the slaughter house and the old cotton mill at the edge of town. The Dimwitty's had old money, most of which had come from the lucrative slave trade that his grandfather Milton Dimwitty had parlayed into a substantial fortune.

Juanita couldn't believe that Nathaniel wasn't doing more to defend his property. He'd basically given Fletcher to the white mob and everyone present knew it.

"I don't believe a word of that bullshit boy. Now come on over here and let's get this over with!" One of the white men shouted.

As Fletcher neared the posse of men, one of them jumped from his horse and retrieved a rope from his saddle bag. He tied the rope into a noose, put it around Fletcher's neck and led him toward the juke joint.

"Nathaniel, you just gonna let these crackers disrespect yo' property like this?" Juanita asked sternly.

"What you 'spects me to do Nita?"

"Yeah Nita, what do you expect him to do. You'd do well to mind your tongue girl. You keep sassin' and you can swing next after we string this one up!" One of the men barked.

The gaggle of onlookers followed closely behind the angry mob that dragged Fletcher toward his death. Sarah Ann Dimwitty smirked, knowing that her costly lie had been effective, or so she thought. As they neared the barn that had been converted to the juke joint, the leader of the Klans men spoke harshly.

"Let this be a lesson to all of you no account niggers! The good white folks of Lee County won't tolerate you coons breaking no laws. Either you behave and know your place, or there will be consequences! String him up boys!" He shouted.

The man that had been dragging Fletcher threw the rope over the rafter beam above their heads and stiffened it so that only the tips of Fletcher's toes were touching the ground. He kept his eyes trained on Sarah Ann Dimwitty as the noose grew tighter and tighter. His eyes silently pleaded with her to intervene, begging her to tell the truth. She stared at him, not certain whether the moisture that welled in his eyes was from approaching tears, or from the tension of the old hemp rope that slowly wrenched the breath from his throat. The masked man that held the rope tied one end to the saddle of his horse. He walked to the front of his steed and guided her gently forward, further restricting Fletcher's airway. As his feet left the ground and the last of the air escaped the small opening of his throat, Fletcher's legs bucked and thrashed wildly. The putrid odor of urine and human excrement emanated from his rigid body, soiling the material of his pants.

"Well I'll be, this here nigger done plum shit himself!" The men shouted, laughing at Fletcher's torture. The whole time, his eyes remained trained on Sarah Ann Dimwitty, burning holes in the flesh of the tattered white woman who had ultimately cost him his life. His eyes were red and bulging, threatening to launch from their sockets. A sight that years later, during a conversation with a close friend,

Sarah Ann Dimwitty would admit, gave her endless nightmares. She would recall how she'd lied and nearly pissed herself when they'd been found out. She shared this with her friend from behind the walls of the Arkansas State Hospital. She'd literally gone insane from the guilt that she harbored inside, wandering the streets of Marianna Arkansas, insisting that Fletcher Graham was haunting her for what she'd done.

Not only did they hang Fletcher, but they had been instructed by Mr. Dimwitty to make sure that, *the coon was dead*, as he'd put it. The men stepped back and each pumped a round from their Winchester rifles into Fletcher's lifeless corpse as they took turns keeping Missy, the frightened mare, calm. One of the men removed a machete from his saddle bag and chopped the rope that held Fletcher's body taut against the rafters, causing him to come crashing down, slumping lifelessly to the ground. The night had grown extremely still; nothing moved. No crickets chirped and no coyotes bayed. It was as if God had frozen time in memory of a soul taken far too soon by those who had no authority to judge. They rode away into the night, leaving his battered body for Nathaniel and his property dwellers to dispose of.

CHAPTER 7

For days after Fletcher's brutal lynching, Juanita walked around their small house refusing to speak to Nathaniel. He'd gotten used to it and actually welcomed it, because in the days before her self-imposed silence, she'd been on his case heavy about everything from chopping wood, to plowing the fields.

Juanita was in the kitchen cooking when Nathaniel came up, snuggled closely behind her and wrapped his arms around her. He was trying desperately to seize the opportunity to bury the hatchet.

"Sho' smells good up in here baby girl. What you got brewing in here?" He asked jovially. Juanita didn't speak, but rather sucked her teeth and wiggled out of his clutches.

"Why you wanna know Nathaniel? What you gonna do? Tell the white man on me?" She hissed.

"What's that s'posed to mean?"

"You know what it means! This here is your land and you let them white men come here and strang Fletcher up, knowing that, that damn, little po' white trash, white girl was lying!" Juanita said.

"So you rather for me to put our family in danger taking up for that nigga?! He knowed better than to be messin' with that white girl!"

"It ain't about taking up for nobody, I wanted you to stand up for what we got going on around here! Did you know that people are talking about leaving because they say it ain't safe here? Clem and Phyllis done already left with their kin and more might be leaving soon! They say you're a coward. They say if the white man wanna come here and have target practice you ain't gonna say nothing, because you're vexed by him!"

"Them white folk got mo' guns and mo' people ready to shoot than we do. If they wanna leave, let 'em. Fuck 'em all!" Nathaniel barked.

"What about me Nate? That go for me too?"

"What about you? What you mean?"

"What if I wanna leave?" She asked.

"You ain't going nowhere Nita! What makes you think I'ma let you take my boy?"

"That's not my concern. I don't wanna be here no more and you can keep Otis!" She whined.

"How can you just throw him away like that? How can you do this to us? I thought we was gonna get married?"

Juanita's laughter was loud, high pitched and borderline cruel. It echoed, hovering in corners and pinging from the crevices of the rotting wood.

"Marry you? Boy please! You're spineless Nathaniel and I'd be ashamed to carry the last name Gage. I'm going to Detroit!" She shrieked.

Nathaniel slapped Juanita with so much force that she fell to her knees. "Bitch, I'll kill you before I let you leave!" He spat.

Juanita looked up at Nathaniel as she held her cheek. Hellish fury beamed in her eyes as she glared at him. "Nigga, you will hafta kill me if you ever put your hands on me again, you high yella, coward ass, little man! You'll beat me, the woman that you *say* you love, but you let a white man run you? You go to market and take a nickel a dozen for your eggs while the white men is getting fifteen cent! Folks is paying forty three cents a pound for bacon and you letting these crackers give thirty cents a pound for a whole hog, but you beat me for wanting to leave right? Either you're a dummy, or you're plain terrified of these folk. Either way, I'm done. You can be sweet when you wanna be, but I gots dreams and they don't include being no coward's wife!"

"Mind your tongue women, 'fore you really catch a beating!" Nathaniel said. He raised his hand to strike her again, but the front door flew open, nearly off the hinges.

"Lower your hand nigga. You touch that woman again and I'll put a hole in you!" A deep voice bellowed.

In the doorway stood one of the darkest men Nathaniel had ever laid eyes on. Even through the thick material of his expensive suit, Nathaniel could see his bulging muscles. His hair was slicked to one side and his pencil thin mustache was complimented by the deep dimples in his cheeks. Nathaniel recognized him. He was Ma Rainey's bass player Tobias Crutcher, the slick Detroit player with the silky conversation and strong features. Tobias was dark, manly and ruggedly handsome. That only served to heighten Nathaniel's inadequacies, because Tobias was everything that Nathaniel was not.

"This here my woman and my house! You better get out, or..."

"Or what country nigga? Fuck you gonna do?" Tobias asked, as he cocked his shotgun. He looked around the sparse dwellings and smirked incredulously. He turned his attention to Juanita. "You 'bout ready pretty girl?" He asked.

Juanita giggled like a school girl. "Yeah Tobias, lemme just grab a few things and pack this here food for our trip."

"Okay, everybody is in the car waiting for you baby, so make it quick!"

Juanita handed Tobias the raggedy suitcase that she'd packed and inconspicuously placed behind the couch. After Tobias left, she turned to Nathaniel. "I took the money Nate. I left you some, but I'm taking what I feel like I'm due."

"You can't do this to me Juanita; to us baby!" Nathaniel said between tears.

"I can do whatever I want! Tobias and Ma Rainey gonna make me a star! Don't worry Nate. I left you what you're worth. Don't worry boy. You can probably make some money back if you sell this dirt pile!" Juanita disappeared through the door with her freshly cooked meal of neck bones, greens, yams, macaroni and cheese and cornbread. Nathaniel watched as the second woman in his life vanished down the long dirt road. Even in the darkness, the clouds hung low and the moon bounced playfully from cloud to cloud as the tail lights of Ma Rainey's car became mere beads of red infidelity. *Left you what you're worth*, she'd said. Nathaniel walked to the loose floorboard where they'd kept their money. He couldn't think straight and he felt dizzy as he pulled the board from the floor and removed the nearly empty pillow case. He reached inside and his heart dropped. Nathaniel removed his hand and opened his clutched fist. Juanita Mention had left him two crumpled one dollar bills and two dull pennies.

CHAPTER 8

For months after Juanita left, Nathaniel sulked around the house. He would sit on the front porch for hours in the rocking chair that he'd built with his own two hands. The land that he'd been so proud of had all but gone to shit for the lack of a better term. He hadn't tended his fields in quite some time, allowing the thick weeds to nearly choke the life from his crops.

Nathaniel sat with Otis in his lap, rocking in his chair, sipping from a dusty bottle of rye whiskey that he'd found in the remnants of the now defunct juke joint. Somewhere beyond the recesses of his mind, he heard the familiar riffs and licks of the guitar that Tobias had used to seduce Juanita. He hadn't realized that he was crying until he kissed the top of Otis' head. It was then that he felt the moisture that had settled in his baby boy's curly, sandy red hair. He wanted to get himself together. Better yet, he *needed* to get himself together for Otis' sake, but he'd allowed himself to fall for Juanita's lies. In his youthful naivety, he'd allowed himself to believe that she was different. He'd fallen hard, and cursed himself for it. Nathaniel continuously questioned himself. Had she really loved him at all? Had he been wrong for not trying to defend Fletcher? Nathaniel cursed again. That time quite loudly, or so he'd thought. He looked down at Otis.

"Done left me with this damn baby. I don't know shit about being no pappy!" He slurred. At eighteen years old Nathaniel Gage felt less like a man and more like a frightened child.

Nathaniel squinted against the beaming sun, trying to make out the cluster of figures moving in his direction. As the people got closer, he was able to make them out. They were dressed like the cigar store Indians who sat regally in front of Dimwitty's five and dime. Nathaniel went into the house, put Otis in his crib and walked out front to meet his guest.

"May I help you?" Nathaniel asked, trying to sound as sober as possible.

He surveyed the people before him carefully, trying to gauge what they might want on his property. There was an older man dressed in Indian garb, holding the reigns of a sway backed mule. On top of the mule sat an old woman, too old to be the man's wife, with a stoic look about herself. To his right was a tall, red skinned, young Indian wearing a decorated band with a lone feather. He was shirtless and stood almost a full foot taller than Nathaniel. To the rear of the ass standing demurely, with her head bowed, was a young Indian girl who was maybe sixteen or seventeen years old. The other three looked to her as if she was the matriarch of the family. In fact, they looked to her, because she was the only one that spoke perfect English.

"My father would like to know if you have work in exchange for room and board?" She asked.

"Who would like to know?"

"This is my father Running Bear, my brother Lazy Fox, my grandmother Matilda Little Stream and I am Gertrude."

"Very nice to meet you and your family. I 'spects I can find some work for you all to do around here. Can yo' daddy and brother tend to these fields?" He asked.

"Yes sir, they can."

"I don't mean to sound rude or nothing, but your gramma looks kinda old, what can she do to earn her keep?" He asked, staring at the older woman.

"My grandmother is old, yes, but she's a terrific cook and she can help you with the baby that I saw you holding earlier. That is, if you don't have a wife."

"No, I don't have a wife, so that would be nice. What do you do?" Nathaniel asked.

"I do everything. I'll help out everywhere that I'm needed," Gertrude said, and she made good on her promise.

In the few months that her family had been on the Gage farm, they had managed to turn the place around. In addition to clearing the land and replenishing Nathaniel's dwindling crops, they had almost doubled his livestock. Gertrude's brother proved to be a very capable field hand. He was also a very shrewd negotiator, often procuring payment for crops that had yet to be harvested. Her grandmother kept food on the stove, preferring to slaughter and cure the meat herself. Her strength and endurance belied her elderly status and over time Nathaniel came to see her as the mother that he wished he'd had. Over the course of those months Nathaniel and Gertrude became extremely close. They talked about everything and nothing all at once. Nathaniel shared with Gertrude the craziness that was his life. He explained that he was afraid to give his heart to another woman, because the women that he'd had the displeasure of knowing in his life had always used and abused him. Gertrude listened to Nathaniel each day, longing to hold him, to reassure him that love was possible. She told him that she too found it hard to trust and that was the reason that she was still a virgin. She was raised to believe that a woman was meant for her husband's eyes and his eyes only, so she would be a virgin until she met the man that she would spend the rest of her life with. She said that when she got married it would truly be until death did them part. Gertrude's greatest joy on the Gage land was Otis. He was enamored with Gertrude, often crying when she left the room. Nathaniel found it next to impossible to get Otis calm, or put him to sleep when Gertrude left late nights.

It was a particularly brisk fall afternoon when Nathaniel and Gertrude decided to take Otis for a short walk. Their conversation as usual was intense, so much so that Gertrude forgot about their friendship and weaved her arm through Nathaniel's, holding his hand with her free hand. He abruptly snatched away from her with a look of disgust plastered across his face. Gertrude stopped walking and stared at him.

"Nate, sooner or later you're going to come to realize that life is what you make it. I know I'm young and I don't have any experience when it comes to matters of the heart. I also realize that you don't trust women because they've hurt you, but I'm not here to hurt you. Otis needs a mama and you need a wife," she declared, twirling one of her jet black pony tails.

"I don't need shit. Otis is just fine and so is I!"

"You can fight the way you feel about me all you want Nate, but I see the way you look at me. I see how you watch me with the baby and I see the love in your eyes. I know what you want and what you need. You need a good woman who will be your best friend and dedicate the rest of her life to making and keeping you happy. A woman who will fill your life and your heart with sons who will carry your legacy for an eternity." Gertrude didn't wait for a response. She picked Otis up and kissed him on the cheek, put him back down and walked away.

Otis toddled after her with outstretched arms, beckoning to her. "Ma, ma, I go, go!" He squealed.

Gertrude smiled at the boy and then at his father. She was heartbroken that Nathaniel couldn't see everything that she had to offer, but she wouldn't force herself on him. For months after their conversation on the dirt road between the quarters and Miller's creek, Gertrude avoided Nathaniel. She would only come around when Nathaniel was away from the house and if by some strange chance he *was* there, she all but ignored him. Nathaniel found himself longing for her presence. It was the same feeling that he had had when Juanita left, but slightly different. After Juanita, it had taken a while, but Nathaniel's heart had begun to slowly heal, especially after Gertrude and her family had arrived. Somehow with Gertrude avoiding him though, he felt lost. He felt as if she was just on the other side of a pane of glass just beyond his reach. He needed her kind words and the soft touch of her hands.

Nathaniel dressed in his finest suit and went to the garden beneath his kitchen window. He picked a dozen apple blossom flowers and made the short trek to the quarters where Gertrude lived with her family. He knocked lightly and waited, hiding the flowers behind his back. Nathaniel couldn't control the wide smile that spread across his face upon seeing Gertrude answer the door. Otis stood next to her with his thumb in his mouth, holding on tightly to her leg with his head pressed firmly against her outer thigh. He looked up at his father with his huge doe like eyes as if he'd disturbed his time with his Gertrude.

"What are you all dressed up for Nathaniel Gage? You look really handsome," Gertrude said.

"Thank you. You mind if'n I comes in?"

"Sure." She stepped to the side.

"Is your pappy home?"

Gertrude moved to the side and revealed her father sitting in his rocking chair, whittling a small wooden horse, probably as a toy for Otis.

"Missa Runnin' Bear, I's pretty taken with your girl here and if'n you gives us your blessing, I wants her hand in marriage. I's only had a little schoolin', but I'll do right by her if'n you lets me marry her. Now, I know you don't speaks my language, but I reckon Gertrude can tell you what I done said," he said.

Running Bear sat up straight in his chair, bringing the motion to a squeaking halt. "I understand you perfectly well. My daughter is young and impressionable. I'm sure in spending time with her, you've had plenty of time to get inside of her head, but I cannot bless this union. You see, Gertrude has been promised to another. She is to be wed to Red Claw next spring. So again, I cannot bless this union."

The flowers in Nathaniel's hand seemed to wilt before his eyes as the wind left his sails.

"Poppa, I love Nathaniel and I'm going to marry him with, or without your blessing!" Gertrude whined.

"You're just a girl Gertrude. What do you know of love?" Running Bear asked.

Before she could respond, her grandmother entered from a back room, berating her son in their native tongue. They argued and it caused Nathaniel to feel somewhat uncomfortable. He leaned in close to Gertrude and whispered, "What are they saying?"

"My grandmother is reminding him of how much she hated and disapproved of my mother. He says that my mother was a pure bred native and she's telling him that she was pure bred Cherokee, not Choctaw. He says why should tribe matter? My grandmother say exactly. She approves, but my father is adamantly against it. He says that if I marry you, he's going to take my grandmother and my brother back to the reservation," she explained sadly.

"I don't wants to be the cause of you being separated from your family. If it comes to that, then we can just forget it."

"If you promise to be a good man to me, always be honest with me and treat me good, then I'm yours and you and Otis are my family now," Gertrude said.

On the eve before their departure, Gertrude stood outside of her father's small shack and cried on his shoulder. "Poppa, I'm not doing this to defy you, or your wishes. I love Nathaniel and I know that he loves me. In less than an hour I will be a married woman and it would mean the world to me if my father was there." She cried.

"Gertrude, dry your tears. You have taken this child as your own and are about to take a husband. My opinion no longer matters, my sweet chula. I will be there and I will see you take this lusa issish as your husband."

She loved when her father called her chula, it was the Choctaw word for fox and it was his way of calling her smart and cunning. His reference to Nathaniel as lusa issish, or black blood disturbed her greatly, because she knew that her father would never see Nathaniel as a son-in-law and her children would never know their grandfather.

CHAPTER 9

By the following summer Gertrude was pregnant with their first child, but to her, it was their second. She had jumped into the role of Otis' mother and caregiver with all of the vigor that she could muster. She hated the ride into town, because the old rickety cart squeaked terribly and the ride was extremely bumpy. The baby in her tummy didn't like it either, because he'd always bear down on her bladder, making it nearly impossible to not urinate immediately. Gertrude's dark, silky skin glistened in the smoldering July sun, contrasting perfectly against the soft, yellow dress that she wore. She just hoped it would stay that way because she had to pee something fierce.

"Whoa, whoa!!" Nathaniel yelled. The old steed that pulled the wagon bucked slightly, but came to a decided halt in front of the general store. Nathaniel hopped off and helped Gertrude down from the carriage and then Otis. Gertrude waddled into Bergstrom's General Store with her family following close behind. The store was one of a very few select white establishments that sold goods to blacks. They proudly displayed a sign in their front window that read: WE SERVE NEGROES, ONLY COLOR THAT MATTERS HERE IS GREEN.

"Welcome back Mr. Gage. How might we serve you today?!" Mrs. Bergstrom asked in an overly chipper tone.

"Yessum, my wife is 'spectin' any day now, so I wants to get some supplies. Maybe a trinket or two for the new baby."

"Oh wonderful! Do you know if it'll be a boy, or a girl?" She asked.

"I reckon if'n old Miss Ludell know what she talkin' about it's gonna be a boy. She say she can tell it's a boy 'cause Gertrude is carrying low."

"Well then, let me show you some new blankets and rattles that just came in," she said.

Gertrude smiled at Mrs. Bergstrom. She liked the lady, but she wasn't in the mood to have her throwing her new wares in her direction. Gertrude preferred to mill around the store on her own. She loved her homemade preserves, especially on buttery toast. The baby gave her very peculiar eating habits also. She'd taken to dipping her pickles in milk and eating hot sauce on fresh baked cookies.

The bells above the door rang and two teenaged white boys no older than fourteen years old entered. They moved toward Gertrude and stood on either side of her. One of the teens grabbed Gertrude around the waist while the other one attempted to slide his hand up her dress.

"Let's see if injun pussy is the same as nigger pussy!" One of them said.

As if by reflex, Gertrude slapped the boy and pushed the other. "Don't touch me!" She screamed.

Nathaniel turned around quickly, but turned back around just as fast. Otis ran to Gertrude's side to defend her.

"Leave my mama lone!" He shouted.

"You boys get out of my establishment with this foolery!" Mrs. Bergstrom yelled.

"Shut up Jew bitch, or you're next!"

Nathaniel never said a word while the two boys assaulted and molested his wife. Gertrude however, screamed and fought, clawed and scratched at the disrespectful boys. It wasn't until one of them pushed Otis to the ground did Nathaniel finally make a move toward them. He crossed the room swiftly and snatched Otis up by one arm and planted a firm swat of reprimand on his son's back side. He then grabbed a handful of Gertrude's silky hair, lifted her to her feet and slapped her across the face.

"Don't be giving these good white gentlemen no hard time!" He shouted. Nathaniel turned to the two white teens and spoke. "I's sorry suh. Forgive my wife. She jussa dumb old injun. She don't know no better, suh, I's gon' teach her 'bout sassin' good folk. I's make it right though suh. I'mo leave five dollars here with Mrs. Bergstrom and you boys can gets what you wants," Nathaniel said.

"You see that girl? This here is how you address a white man! Your nigger husband has plenty of sense and you would do well to let that good sense rub off on you, or you just might find yourself swangin' from the nearest tree," one of the teens said, rubbing his bruised cheek.

"Apologize to this man Gertrude, right now!" Nathaniel shouted.

The forcefulness in Nathaniel's voice caused her to flinch and wince. He'd never put his hands on her before and as she looked at her husband, she could barely fight back the tears. Maybe he had a reason to be afraid of the boys, but she didn't see it. Gertrude muttered a nearly inaudible *sorry* in their direction, but Nathaniel pushed the issue. "Speak up woman." He said.

"I sorry suh, I's just a dumb ol' injun. I's never reject you again suh. I 'spects even doe slavery is over and I's ain't never been no slave don't give me no cause to reject you, or inconvenience you suh. Lawd knows I don't mean no harm suh!" She said sarcastically. Gertrude turned on her heels, took Otis by his hand and stomped out of the store. Nathaniel walked out moments later with the two boys, laughing like old friends, bowing and scraping, playing step and fetch it. She heard one of the boys say something about Nathaniel being a *good nigger* and the smile that spread across Nathaniel's face made her stomach twirl. Gertrude was fuming, but her father had always instructed her to think before she spoke. In Choctaw culture, a woman was little more than her husband's property, but she was no longer in Choctaw culture. She didn't want to question her husband's actions no matter how much she disagreed with them.

"Why you gotta be all sassy with them men? You know you don't talk like that," Nathaniel spat.

"Those *boys* have no respect, but I guess what they did to me, to our son was okay right? You said it yourself though, I'm just a dumb old injun remember? How could you degrade me like that in front of those people? I'm your wife and I thought you'd always protect me. I will always follow your lead and obey your wishes, but what if they had harmed Otis, or the baby that I'm carrying?"

"You calling me a coward Gertrude?" He asked. Nathaniel Gage had a storm brewing inside of his cowardly soul and it wouldn't take much to push him to the edge.

"No baby, but..." She started, but before she could finish her sentence Nathaniel had slapped her so savagely that she fell from the wagon.

"Get your ass back on up here. You gonna learn not to sass me. Hurry up, I wants to get home 'fore dark," he hissed.

By the time that they welcomed Julius Gage into the world, Nathaniel Gage had slapped Gertrude Gage seven times, kicked her three times, punched her once and poured scalding hot water onto her feet for walking too hard while he was taking a nap.

CHAPTER 10

Otis and Julius sat with their feet in the cool waters of Miller's creek. The cold water was a refreshing and welcomed change to the hard bottom, hand me down shoes that Julius had inherited from Otis.

"I don't see why daddy made me stop going to school. He don't let me do nuffin' while y'all in the fields anyways," Julius said, tossing pebbles into the creek.

"That's just the way he is Julius. He thank if we get too much schoolin' we gon' get uppity."

"Well that's bullshit!" Julius exclaimed.

"Mind your tongue boy. Daddy doing the best he can. He's trying. There ain't much coming in from the crops and he got six mouths to feed. With mama 'bout to pop out another baby that's gon' be seven of us if'n we include mama and daddy, so cut him some slack!"

"Okay daddy's boy. I just hope this one is a girl!" Julius said.

"Why? Girls can't do nothing but play with baby dolls and learn how to cook."

"Because I'm tired of looking at you nappy head heathens all the time," Julius said playfully.

"Heathens huh? I got your heathen!" Otis pushed Julius, laughed and stood up. "We best be gettin' back. Otha Lee and Eugene will be home from school soon. Otis slid his feet into the dusty church shoes beneath him and backed up near a huge oak tree. He took off running full speed and jumped Miller's creek effortlessly. He drew a line in the dirt with his foot and yelled across the creek to Julius. "This is the line to beat. Whoever jumps the farthest wins! If you win, I'll do whatever you want. If I win, you have to milk Esther."

Julius hated Esther. She was his father's favorite dairy cow, perhaps because they were both bull headed and she acted more like a bull than a heifer. Whenever Julius went to milk her, she nipped at him with her big teeth. When he'd go to the pasture to coral the other cows, Esther would always charge at him. Head down, she'd rush towards him as if she had horns. She was an evil cow and Julius was convinced that Esther's greatest pleasure came from watching his frail nine year old frame run for dear life to escape her wrath. Julius picked up his shoes and backed up. He took a few deep breaths and took off running toward the creek. He imagined that he was Jesse Owens preparing for the long jump as he neared the stream. He increased his speed and then he jumped. The world seemed to move in slow motion as he glided across the creek. He could feel the wind whistling between his toes and then he opened his eyes. Julius had started his descent, but he was nowhere near the other side. He flapped his arms wildly reaching for the bank of the creek, but it was too far away.

"Stop panicking Julius, it's just water down there."

"I'm too high in the air, I'ma hurt myself!" Julius cried.

In reality Julius wasn't that high up, but at nine years old it felt as though he was a hundred feet in the air. He felt the coolness of the water splashing up his thigh and water rushing between his toes and then he felt a searing pain in his foot. Julius looked down to see his crimson blood mixing with the semi-cold water of Miller's creek. He watched as a reddish cloud of blood mixed and flowed with the stream. Silently, he wondered if piranhas would eat him, since he was bleeding in the water. Then his mind shifted to one of the Bible stories that his mother always read to him. Particularly, he thought about the story of Moses and how the river ran red with blood. Julius saw his shoes floating downstream, slowly bobbing and flipping as they flowed further from his reach. If he could get to them, maybe they would dry before he made it home, but when he stood up the pain from his foot shot up his leg and came to rest in his hip. He wanted to cry, but he couldn't. He and Otis had always teased Otha Lee and Eugene about crying too much and he knew Otis would never let him forget it. As he lamented over his pain, his shoes floated further until they were nearly out of sight.

"Cowboy up Julius! I see them tears in your eyes!"

"Ain't nobody finna cry!" Julius screamed through clenched teeth.

"You gon' be crying when you go home and daddy see you ain't got them shoes!"

"Fuck them shoes! They was too little anyways," Julius said shrugging. He climbed up onto the bank and surveyed the wound on the bottom of his foot. There was a gaping slash that ran from his arch to the heel of his foot and it bled profusely.

"Man that's bad! It won't stop bleeding."

"No shit Sherlock," Julius snapped sarcastically.

"You got a smart ass mouth, you know that? I'ma see how smart your ass is when you gotta walk all the way home by yourself." Otis started walking toward the large cornfields that bordered his family's property.

"Otis wait! Otis! Okay, okay I'm sorry! Otis I'm sorry!" Julius yelled out frantically.

Otis turned around with a knowing smile on his face. His little brother was all bluster. Julius Gage talked big, but he was still a little boy and Otis knew it. He walked back to his little brother, turned around and knelt down to allow the frail youngster to climb onto his back.

"When we get home man, go straight into the bathroom and wait for me," Otis said.

Julius nodded, and imagined that Otis was a horse carrying him across the dusty plains of Arkansas in search of wayward cowboys. Knowing that his mother was Indian had always filled him with great pride and whenever he played cowboys and Indians, he always opted to play the Indian. Otis trudged through the mucky soil of the cornfield, relieved to see the edge. Otis stopped to catch his breath and motioned toward the house with his head.

"Just a little more to go Julius. Remember what I said." He shifted Julius' weight to give himself the leverage he needed to complete the trip. As they approached the house, Julius' heart dropped. His father was on the front porch in his rocking chair talking to Emmett Mays. Mr. Mays was their nearest neighbor, if he could be called that, because Mr. Mays' property was nearly five miles away. The only things that Emmett Mays and Nathaniel Gage had in common was their love and mutual respect for the bottom of a whiskey bottle. Emmett Mays was older than Nathaniel and never seemed to tire of interjecting his unwanted opinions. Nathaniel, for whatever reason, seemed to look up to him. The Gage boys hated him though, because they'd heard him instructing their father to beat them and their mother during past conversations. Well, he hadn't used those exact words, but in a nutshell that's what he'd meant.

"Women and chillun is just like hawses. You gots to break 'em. You know how hawses a buck 'til you whips 'em into mindin'? Well that's 'zactly what you 'posed to do wit' yo' chilluns and wife. Hell, I walks in the house sometimes after I done fought with the back side of that rye and whoop erbody in da house. I lets 'em know, I da pappy and they gon' 'spects me as such. Shit, I kicks my wife in the ass so much, she need to sew some shoes in her draws!" Emmett had said.

"You thank that's right? You thank women respect that?" Nathaniel asked.

"Fuck respect Nate! The good lawd gave man dominion over all things 'cludin' women and chillun. He say spare the rod spoil the child and since we takes care of our wives like they our chillun, they 'sposed to get the rod too!"

Otis climbed the stairs carrying Julius on his back with the hope that his father and Mr. Mays would be too drunk to take notice of him carrying Julius. His father was staring into the bottle when he made it to the top of the stairs and had it not been for Emmett Mays' incessant pestering, they would have made it inside the house with no incident.

"Why you carrying that big ol' nigga on yo' back?" Emmett asked.

Otis attempted to ignore the question and continue walking, but Mr. Mays wouldn't leave it alone and addressed their father directly. "Nate you ain't taught these nigglets shit 'bout manners? They don't know nuffin 'bout 'spectin' they elders?" He said.

Nathaniel looked from his bottle with eyes that were low and nearly crossed. "Huh?" Nathaniel slurred.

"Huh? Huh my ass, you gon' just let these little mothafuckas dis-a-spect yo' guest? Shiiiiiit my sons know better than that shit, but guess I shoulda knowed and 'spected that though," Emmett sneered.

"Answer Missa Mays goddamnit! Y'all knows I taught you better than that!" Nathaniel said.

"Julius cut his foot crossing the creek, so I's helping him home," Otis said.

"Julius brang yo' little black ass here boy! Did you cut your foot on purpose to get outta working 'round here?" Nathaniel asked.

"No suh, it was a accident!" Julius said.

"Shiiiiiiit accident my ass. Lazy niggas always got a excuse to get outta work!" Emmett Mays accused.

"You need to mind yo' own business. Ain't nobody tryna get outta no work!" Julius snapped.

"Julius! What I done told you 'bout yo' mouth? Otis put his ass down! Julius get yo' goddamn ass in the house and wait on me! You thank you grown, I'ma treat you like you grown."

Julius limped into the house, wincing with every step that he took. When he stepped inside, he saw Miss Ludell at the stove boiling a pot of hot water.

"Yo' mama 'bout to have this baby any minute now honey. Lawd what you done did to yo' foot? Brangin' blood up in this house," Miss Ludell said.

"I cut my foot tryna jump Miller's creek," Julius said smiling. He liked Miss Ludell. She was the only black midwife in Lee County and had delivered nearly every colored boy in their town. He and all of his brothers had been delivered by her.

"Lemme look at that foot baby. Otis, go get me that salve out the bathroom."

Nathaniel staggered into the house around the same time that Otis came out of the bathroom with the ointment.

"What you about to do with that salve boy?" He asked Otis.

"Miss Ludell needs it to put on Julius' foot."

"We ain't wastin' no good salve on this nigga just because his ass did some stupid shit," Nathaniel said incredulously.

"Nathaniel, if you don't let me tend to this boy's foot, then he might lose it. All it's gon' take is for an infection to set in and you gon' be callin' me back outchea to cut it off," Miss Ludell said.

"Ludell, I don't give a shit 'bout his damn foot."

"How in the Lawd's name you 'spects to get work outta the boy if'n his foot gone?" Miss Ludell huffed.

"He shoulda thought 'bout that 'fore he tried to play damn Superman cross Miller's creek. I ain't finna argue with you. Just get on back in there and tend to Gertrude! I'll take care of my boys how I see fit!" Nathaniel barked. He turned his attention to Julius. "Yeah, I think this little bastard was tryna get outta work!"

"No I wasn't!" Julius argued.

"Don't argue with me boy! You gettin' besides yourself!"

"I ain't arguing with you. You lying on me, talking 'bout I'm tryna get outta working."

"I'm lying? I'm lying? You thank you grown nigga. That's what your problem is! A grown nigga ain't got no place in my house!" Nathaniel said looking around frantically, searching for the nearest weapon. The only thing that he could find was a ball ping hammer that lay atop the kitchen table. He gripped it tightly and his chest heaved with pure fury.

"Daddy, mama is in the other room 'bout to have a baby. Please don't do this!" Otis screamed.

"Mama, mama, mama, that's all I hear coming outta yo' nigga mouf boy!" Nathaniel yelled, turning to Otis. "Well for your goddamn information, she ain't ya mammy. Nah, yo' no account mammy ran off to Detroit with some ol' guitar playin' nigga after you was born! Maybe thatta change yo' tune 'bout yelling mama all the time. Now gon' go tend to yo' little brothers and stay outta grown folks' business!"

A look of shock and terror spread across Otis' face as he tried to process what his father had just revealed to him. Nathaniel had dumped it out there and just casually breezed past it like no one had heard what he'd said.

"Not my mama?" Otis questioned in a dazed state. He wasn't talking to anyone in particular, but Nathaniel seized the opportunity to answer.

"You heard what I said nigga, now get on!"

Otis dropped his head and stepped outside. He headed toward the barn where Otha Lee and Eugene were playing.

Back in the house it seemed as though the liquor had taken an even greater effect on Nathaniel. He faced Julius with his fist clutching the hammer so tight that his knuckles had turned white.

"Now sass me again you little, black sonofabitch. Say one mo' goddamn word!" Nathaniel said.

Julius was mortified. Of course his father had whipped him and his brothers on occasion, but he'd never seen him that angry. Julius tried to think of what he could say to calm his father down, but he couldn't think because he was afraid.

Julius' eyes shifted from the hammer in his father's hand to his menacing face. Maybe his father was mad, because his mother kept having boys. Maybe he wanted a daughter to help his mother cook and clean. So maybe, just maybe the prospect of having a girl would abate his anger. Yeah, that's what he would say. Julius opened his mouth to speak, to tell his father he hoped that his mother was having a girl.

"Daddy I..." He started, but before he could finish his sentence, Nathaniel struck him across the head with the round end of the ball ping hammer. Blood leapt from Julius' head as he dropped to his knees and then fell backwards onto his back, staring up into his father's angry eyes. As he slipped into a blunt object induced slumber, the last thing that he remembered was the sound of his mother's screams. He heard Miss Ludell telling his mother to push and then he heard the high pitched wail of a baby's first cry. While Julius lay slipping into darkness in a puddle of his own blood, his mother welcomed Charles Boyd Gage into a family plagued with lies, abuse and dark secrets.

CHAPTER 11

Gertrude had tried her best over the years to convince Nathaniel to go to church with her to no avail. As she walked toward the church with her five boys, the rain from the night before had turned the red clay road into a gummy mess. She looked back to see Nathaniel standing on the porch with his beloved bottle of rye, looking at them as if they were doing something wrong.

"Mama, can I ask you a question?" Otis asked.

"Sure baby, you can ask me whatever you want."

"Well, a while back daddy said that you wasn't really my mama. Is that true?" He asked.

Gertrude stopped and faced Otis. She handed Charlie Boy to Julius and took Otis by the hands.

"Yes, it's true baby. Your mama left when you were just a baby and your daddy was a mess. When I met your daddy, it was just you and him and I loved you from the first time I saw you. You might have not come from my womb, but I love you just like you did. I can't apologize for loving you baby. I won't do it! You're my baby; my oldest joy and

64

you're the best son a mother could hope for. Your brothers love you and so do I," she assured him.

Otis looked into the eyes of the woman who had taught him everything from how to tie his shoes, to how to say his ABC's and felt a mix of emotions. On one hand he loved her and all that she'd done for him, but he was equally as mad. She had lied to him his whole life. When he'd asked why his brother's skin was so dark and his so light, she'd told him because they'd gotten their hue from her and that he'd taken his father's fair skin. Had she deprived him of knowing his mother intentionally? If she hadn't, it sure felt like it in his fourteen year old brain.

"I hear you Miss Gertrude, but I wanna find my own mama," he said flatly. Tears streamed down his cheeks as he attempted to remove himself from her emotionally. Gertrude's face dropped. Since the day he'd learned to talk and form sentences, he'd always called her mama and to hear him call her by her first name pulled a piece of her heart out. She pulled Otis to her and hugged him tightly. She felt him melt, and go limp as he sobbed uncontrollably.

"I love you Otis Gage and I never want you to forget that. If you feel the need to go search for your mama, baby, I understand. Ain't no worse feeling than not knowing who you are, but just know that you can always come home if things don't go the way you plan. I got a few dollars saved up in that old lard can on top of the Frigidaire that you can have to help you on your way," she said sadly.

Otis nodded his thanks. There were no words that could explain the pain that he was feeling and he felt as if he might begin to cry again if he opened his mouth to speak. His heart felt heavy and he felt alone. He turned on his heels and headed toward Miller's creek; the one place that he'd always been able to find a measure of peace.

"Where you going baby? The reverend is expecting us at church here shortly. Charlie being baptized this morning. You forget?" Gertrude asked.

"No ma'am, I ain't forget. Just got a lot on my mind, that's all. I don't rightly feel like sitting in a church house hearing some jack leg preacher tell me how much God loves me. I don't imagine the Lawd even knows I exist 'cause if he did, I reckon I wouldn't feel the way I do right now."

Julius tugged at his mother's dress and motioned for her to bend down. She put her ear near his mouth and listened as Julius whispered in her ear. "Can I talk to him mama? I be on to the church directly," he said, handing Charlie Boy back to her. He watched as his mother and his little brothers disappeared down the dirt road. When they were out of sight, he turned toward Otis.

"Otis wait up!" He shouted. He ran to his brother full speed until he reached him, out of breath and barely able to speak.

"What you gon' do?" Julius asked.

"I don't know. Yo' mama say she gon' give me some money to get me by. I reckon I can work my way to Detroit, you know? Every town I stop in, I can do a little work to get me a little money. I ain't gon' be able to rest 'til I find my real mama."

"Don't leave Otis. Mama loves you and we do too. You know if you leave daddy gon' be real mad," Julius said sadly.

"I love y'all too, but I gotta go. I ain't concerned 'bout daddy being mad. Shit I feel like he don't want me here anyway, so this might make him feel better."

"Yeah, but if you leave, then who you thank he gon' take being mad out on? Otis please don't leave!" Julius pleaded.

Otis put his arm around Julius' shoulder and led him to the creek. "Man listen, when I get to Detroit, I'll let you know where I am. When you get older you can come find me. I love you baby brother, but I gotta go," Otis said. He kissed Julius on the forehead and walked toward the house. "Remember, find me Julius, find me!"

Otis walked back to their house to find Nathaniel passed out in a drunken stupor across the couch. He went to the room that he shared with his little brothers and threw his belongings into a pillow case. He tried to be as quiet as possible as he went into the kitchen to search for the money that Gertrude had promised him, but the change jingled and clanged at the bottom of the can until Nathaniel stirred awake.

"Fuck you thank you doing yella nigga? You stealing from your mammy now?"

"She ain't my mammy, remember? 'Sides she told me that I could have this here money," Otis said.

"You sassin' me boy?"

"No suh, I'd never sass you. You might take the notion to bust my head like you did Julius!" Otis said sarcastically.

"What you got in that pillow case boy and what you need money fo'?"

"These here is my clothes and I'm going to search for my real mama," Otis declared proudly.

Nathaniel's shrill, drunken laughter filled the entire house. "Your real mama? Good luck nigga. It's a big ol' world out there boy. When you find her tell her I said go to hell for what she did to this family."

Otis had some choice words for his father, but he didn't dare say them inside of his home. He kept his mouth closed until he got outside and then turned to face his father.

"Yeah, when you get to Detroit and you find that bitch, you make sure you tell her what I said.

"I know why she left," Otis said softly.

"What?"

"I said, I know why she left. She left because she knew what the rest of us are just finding out."

"And what's that smart man?" Nathaniel asked.

"That you spineless. That you torture your family, because it makes you feel big, make you feel important. You ain't gon' be satisfied 'til you run off everybody that loves your miserable ass!"

"You better mind your tongue nigga, 'fore I cut it out your head," Nathaniel threatened.

"You mark my words old man. One of these days you gon' get yours. You gon' try to bluff the wrong one and you gon' get yours. I'm shame to call you my pappy!"

Upon hearing Otis' harsh words, Nathaniel attempted to run after the boy, but tripped over his own intoxicated feet and found himself sprawled out, face down in the dirt.

"Gone on, get, get on outta here. You ain't no real Gage! Get off my property! I don't care if you leave! You look too much like your rotten mammy anyway!" Nathaniel shouted. He was still screaming at his son long after Otis disappeared. Truth of the matter was; he was more hurt than angry that his son had chosen to find his mother. She'd been the one that destroyed the family with her selfishness. It had been *her* that abandoned *them* and now he was losing his son to the woman that didn't love them enough to stay around and be a real family. Whether because of his ego, or sheer stupidity, Nathaniel Gage didn't seem to understand that he had created those circumstances. He was so hell bent on his family fearing and respecting him that along the way, he'd forgot how to be a husband and a father.

CHAPTER 12

"Julius, Eugene, Otha Lee, Charles, you boys hurry up with your chores. It's a storm brewing out there!" Gertrude screamed.

The four boys yelled a resounding, "yessum" in their mother's direction. Julius looked up into the sky and saw the black, low lying clouds rolling in from the south of their Marianna, Arkansas farm. Light drizzle began to fall and Charles tugged at Julius' tattered shirt tail, drawing his attention.

"Whatchu want little man?" He asked.

"You wanna wace back to the house?"

"I don't know why you always tryna race Julius, Charlie. Yo' little ass ain't gonna win," Eugene teased.

Charles looked at him with a mixture of anger and hurt. Eugene teased him relentlessly and it seemed to the young Charles Gage that his brother for whatever reason, hated his guts. It couldn't have been further from the truth though. Eugene loved his little brother, but he was somewhat jealous of him. Eugene had been the baby of the bunch until

Charles came along. Now it seemed as though the family's attention was focused solely on Charles, so he teased him, much like Otha Lee had done to him and Julius had done to Otha Lee and Otis had done to Julius.

"Don't pay Eugene no mind, Charles. I'll race you if you want little man. I'm not going to let you win though, so you'd better run as fast as possible okay," Julius said, rustling his baby brother's hair.

"Okay, but I've been practicing. I'm getting' fast!" Charles exclaimed.

"Otha Lee, call it."

Otha Lee, backed up a few feet, facing them and lifted his hands. "On your mark, get ready, set, go!" He screamed, dropping his hands.

Charles struck out across the prairie that bordered their property. Before making it to their house they would need to jump a small creek, cross the corn field, and hop the wooden gate that stretched from their property to the widow Sister Whitaker's dilapidated farm house. Julius laughed as his little brother kicked up dust, running as fast as his small legs would carry him. He picked up the small burlap sack that Charles had filled with corn and trotted toward the house. Otha Lee and Eugene both passed Julius, slapping him on the back of the head as they passed him. "You better hurry up bro, you know how the old man is if we're late for dinner," Eugene said.

"Man, I'm not worried about that old, grouchy ass dude," Julius said stubbornly. Just the thought of his father's attitude irritated Julius. He blamed the brothers and their mother for any and everything, including Otis' decision to leave. If the grub worms invaded the collard greens it was their fault, if the coyotes killed a hen it was their fault. Nathaniel Gage had gone so far as to require his sons to drop out of school when they finished the third grade. Two things necessitated that decision, first he believed that by third grade boys knew the basics to make them good workers. Basic reading and arithmetic skills were all that were needed to work on a farm. Second, he didn't want his sons smarter than him. Nathaniel Gage had only gone as far as the fifth grade and in his twisted mind he had two whole grades on his sons. An educated nigger was a dangerous nigger, especially if the educated nigger was in his household.

Julius made his way to the house slowly and before he made it to the front steps, he heard his father's voice.

"Bitch, do I look like I enjoy eating cold food? Bring me another godddamned plate!" Nathaniel shouted.

The sound of shattering glass echoed through the house and reverberated in Julius' eardrums. He walked into the house and saw his mother kneeling, picking up the plate that his father had thrown from the table. Julius placed the two burlap sacks full of corn next to the wood burning stove and kneeled next to his mother.

"I'll help you mama. Eugene, you boys go wash up for dinner," Julius instructed.

"Since when you start barking orders around my fucking house tar baby? You think you grown now boy?" Nathaniel sneered.

Julius ignored his father and touched his mother's hand softly. He didn't understand how his father could treat her so callously. She was the sweetest person that he knew and she catered to his father. Her hand trembled uncontrollably as she attempted to clean up Nathaniel's mess. "Nate, there's only enough left for me and the boys. How about I fix you a sandwich?" Gertrude asked sweetly.

"I've been tilling that field all day and you expect me to eat a sandwich? What kind of woman are you? Nah, I tell you what. You pick which one of your nigglets that ain't eating tonight and I'll take his plate."

"Nate, these boys are still growing. They need to eat. I'll just go without. You can have my plate." Gertrude said.

"You boys get on over here now. Come line up in front of me." Eugene, Otha Lee and Charles lined up in front of Nathaniel, but Julius held his position on the floor next to his mother. She looked at Julius with her soft eyes and silently pleaded for him to join his brothers for fear that his father would enact his ruthless brand of punishment. Julius rose to his feet slowly and joined his brothers. His eyes burned into Nathaniel's flesh, almost daring him to meet his gaze.

"So, which one of you little bastards worked the hardest today? Whoever did the least amount of work ain't eating, so don't all you little fuckers answer at the same time," he barked, but nobody spoke, so he continued, "Either answer me, or all you little black bastards can go to sleep on an empty stomach goddamnit!"

"Man, we all did the same amount of work. You can have my plate," Julius said.

"I decide who did what in this house, and I decide who eats and who doesn't boy!"

"You like playing God Nathaniel? You like having control over us, don't you? You done almost broke mama down to the point where she ain't even got the same twinkle in her eye!" Julius countered, pointing to his mother. He knew that it irritated his father when he called him by his name, but Nathaniel knew something about Julius that irritated him as well. Julius was extremely protective of his younger brothers and his mother.

"Charlie didn't do shit today did you boy? Yeah, that's who won't eat. Go get in the bed little nigga!" Nathaniel spat. Charles dropped his head and shuffled his feet toward the back bedroom that he shared with his brothers.

"Charlie come back in here! You can have my plate!" Julius countered, with his eyes still trained on Nathaniel.

"Are you trying me boy? You think you got what it takes to man this family?"

"I'm more man than you, old man! What kind of man sends his children to bed hungry?" Julius snarled.

All the while Gertrude stood behind her other three sons, petrified. She cradled them close to her and felt the tremble of their terror. Julius had her sensibilities, but also had his father's volatile temper. The two of them arguing was like shaking a mason's jar full of nitroglycerine and it was bound to blow. Nathaniel stood slowly and came within inches of his son's face.

"Let me make this perfectly clear boy. I pay the cost to be the boss around here. I run things and if you, ya mammy and ya little brothers all died tonight, I wouldn't lose a second of sleep; you ungrateful sonofabitch!"

"Is that what you believe old man, that you're a boss? I don't understand why you're so hateful and why you hate us so much, but then again I suppose it's not my place to understand. You already ran Otis off, so I guess we're next huh? I know two things for sure. My little brothers and my mother *will* eat tonight," Julius said. His tone was low and menacing and his dark brooding eyes burned into his father's mulatto skin.

"Don't you eyeball fuck me boy! Oh, they can eat, but for every goddamn spoonful they eat, I'm going to give you lashes with that cat-o-nine tail. You little nigglets get to this table. Your brother is gonna take a beating for y'all sins like Jesus."

Julius stripped out of his shirt, all the while keeping his eyes locked with those of his father. He waited ever so patiently for the pain to come; a pain that he knew all too well. His mother stared in shocked horror at the scars that he bore on his teenaged back. There were dozens of zig zagged keloid welts that had bubbled and healed from years of beatings doled out by his father for the smallest infractions. Julius smiled at his father, more out of pity than anything else. He knew that his father didn't know love. Even with as much as his mother and brothers tried to demonstrate love, Nathaniel Gage never recognized it. He was always heartless, but after Otis left Nathaniel became merciless. Julius felt like a slave as he stretched his frail arms above his head with his palms placed flat on the splintered wooden wall.

"You ready boy?" Nathaniel asked.

Julius never said a word, but simply redirected his gaze from his father to his mother and brothers. Julius clenched his teeth hard and thought about his brothers. They were his reason for living and his reason for bucking at their father. He nearly screamed out when the whip first touched his back, slashing into the already tender meat of his young back. The tip of the cat-o-nine tail fought unsuccessfully to find an untouched place to rest. Again and again the whip whistled through the air, crackling against Julius' tender skin.

"Nathaniel, that's enough!" Gertrude screamed.

"Nah it ain't! This nigga ain't even crying yet. He don't feel it!"

"Nathaniel, baby please, Lord Jesus please, look at his back!" Gertrude fell to her knees, holding Nathaniel's hands. He tried to shake loose, but she begged him again. "Nathaniel please, look at our son's back. Look what you've done to him."

Nathaniel looked at Julius' back and dropped the whip. He didn't drop the whip from remorse, he dropped it from fear. How could a boy take such a savage beating and not cry out? "Ah, gone and go clean the little bastard up 'fore he make me kill him!"

Gertrude put Julius' arm around her neck and led him to the cot where he slept. "Gene, you and Otha Lee go get me some rags, some warm water and the salve. Charlie Boy, you stay with me. Your pappy is probably gonna go and drink and he'll want to start up again when he comes back," Gertrude said.

"Why he hate us so much mama?" Julius asked.

"I don't think he hates us baby. Your daddy done been through a lot in his young life and he don't rightly know how to channel his anger. We just have to learn not to get up under his skin, that's all," she advised.

"I'm going to kill him. You mark my words. I'm going to blow his head off," Julius promised.

"Don't you talk like that Julius Gage! He's your father and the Bible says thou shalt not kill!"

"The Bible also says an eye for an eye mama and Nathaniel is gonna have his day of reckoning. If not by me, then by somebody. He ain't no father of mine," Julius whispered.

Gertrude continued to nurse Julius' wounds until she was finally able to stop the bleeding. She didn't believe in letting children indulge in drinking liquor, but with the amount of pain that she knew that her son was in, she encouraged him to drink some of his father's rye whiskey. It was bitter to the taste and most definitely not something that Julius wanted to get used to, but if it would take the pain away the way that his mother said, then he would try it.

CHAPTER 13

Gertrude had finally gotten Nathaniel to relent and allow her to get a job working for a rich family in town. The Ransom family was very rich, very reserved and very prejudiced against nearly everyone. They paid her a fair wage for her services and always sent their table scraps home with Gertrude, who always tossed them into the hog pen on the edge of the Ransom property. They'd even gone so far as to give her the entrails and bad parts from their pigs when Christmas had come around. She was both offended and saddened by the gesture, because Nathaniel had made it clear that food on the table was Christmas every day, so he wouldn't be buying gifts. She'd hoped that the Ransoms would give her a few extra dollars as a Christmas bonus, so she could at least get the boys decent shoes. Nathaniel was jealous of Gilbert Ransom, because he was young and he didn't carry himself like the country bumpkins of Lee County. He was a very handsome man and whenever Nathaniel saw him, he openly showed his disdain for the man. He stared at him, sucked his teeth and rolled his eyes at Mr. Ransom, who either didn't notice or didn't care.

"You fucking that cracker, ain't you Getrude?" He'd asked.

"No Nathaniel, I'm not. Mr. Ransom is just my boss. I work for him and he pays me. That's it. That's all."

"Uh huh. You gon' get you and Gilbert Ransom killed. Keep fucking with me! You been getting real sassy since you been working for them folks. Don't get no ideas 'bout leaving," he threatened.

She worked extremely hard at keeping both her employer's household and her own intact. It was a job that she neither loved, nor hated, but it was however, a means to an end.

Gertrude was walking home from a long hard day of cleaning toilets and taking verbal abuse from her white employers when it had begun to rain. It was a heavy constant downpour, so she had taken shelter in an abandoned warehouse on the long country dirt road that led to her family's farm. Although she decided that she would wait there until the rain subsided, she knew her husband would be angry, because she would be late getting home to cook dinner. But if she walked all the way home in the rain, she would surely catch her death of cold.

The rain beat a rhythmic pattern of trebles and basses on the roof of the old warehouse. As Gertrude stood in the doorway of the building, looking out at the rain, she thought of how dramatically her life had changed, and not for the better. She had endured many years of torture and beatings at the hands of the man that she called her husband.

Nathaniel Gage was a mean man. He was very hard to deal with and even harder to live with, but they were married, and in her mind once you were married it was until death.

Enough was enough though, and she decided that maybe she should just take her boys and move back to the Reservation. At least there she would have the support of her family. She had disobeyed her father's wishes by marrying Nathaniel, but he had promised her the world, with his light features and syrupy tongue and she had fallen for it hook, line and sinker.

Now as she looked out into the dark sky her world felt as though it was crashing down around her. How could he beat her so mercilessly if he loved her? Nate would beat her for breathing too loud. Gertrude was beaten for any small infraction and it was getting old. Each time he beat her, he would apologize, only to beat her again. She felt like every time he put his hands on her he took a little bit more life from her. A once gorgeous woman with a glowing smile had now become a pretty face with a faded smirk. The memories of how Nate had once treated her lit the corners of her mind like candles. It gave her a mix of emotions. She was angry with her husband for treating her as if she didn't matter, but she was still deeply in love with him. She wanted to leave, but she knew that he and the boys needed her. Besides, his mother had abused and left him. Juanita had left him alone with the baby Otis and sadly, as soon as Otis was old enough to leave, he'd also left Nathaniel. Gertrude didn't want to add to the list of the people that he had considered abandoners.

The rain was beginning to lift and had settled into a light drizzle, so Gertrude picked up her bag and exited the warehouse. Knowing full well that there would be hell to pay when she got home, she shuddered. If she couldn't make Nate understand how the rain had put her behind schedule, he would surely beat her. She glanced at her watch and noticed that she was an hour late. She was usually home by six p.m., but it was a quarter to six and she still had miles to walk. She looked to the heavens and said a small prayer, asking God to protect her and her children from all harm and to bless her husband. She knew why Nate was the way that he was. They owned their farm outright, but in Arkansas you were only as valuable as the color of your skin. Nate had the skin tone of a white man, but his kinky hair removed any doubt as to what his ethnicity was. He was the son of a fair skinned black mother who had been the mistress of her white boss, or so the rumors went. He was a bastard child, who had hatred for all white people and didn't trust any women. To him, women were tools meant to carry children, cook, and clean. No more, no less.

Every harvest Nate had to go to town to sell their crops, and no matter how beautiful the harvest, he was never given fair value. He was shortchanged for the eggs his hens produced and the milk that came from his cows. The unfairness ate at him and made him bitter, because as much as he wanted to, he couldn't say a word to the hillbilly white men in town for fear that they would burn his farm to the ground. Nathaniel Gage was looked upon in town as a "good nigger." He dropped his head when talking to the white man and never made eye contact because to them, that was a sign of aggression. He took the abusive name calling and constant taunts with a mixture of disdain and fear. He wondered which one of the old honkies in town was his father. He knew that they were aware of his origins and it angered him. He would do as most cowards did when faced with men that he either couldn't handle, or wouldn't handle. He would merely go home and take it out on his wife and children. Gertrude made it to her property line just as the sun was setting. She could see her husband sitting on the front porch in the wooden rocking chair that he had crafted by hand. He was looking out over the field with a menacing grimace on his face. Gertrude knew it was well after six and Nate was angry, but it wasn't her fault. Her sons were performing their usual duties. They would milk the cows, collect eggs from the henhouse, and clean the barn before they were allowed inside the house to eat dinner. Before Gertrude could make it to the front porch, Nathaniel abruptly stopped rocking, got up from his chair and walked inside. As soon as she stepped inside the small, two-bedroom farmhouse, he slapped her to her knees.

"Stand up and face me, cheating whore!" He spat. Gertrude's head was spinning, and she couldn't focus her eyes. She looked up at her husband and could only see a blur of a man. She was only able to steal a quick glance before he struck her again, but that time with a closed fist, and everything went black. She didn't know how long she had been out by the time he'd poured water in her face to wake her up.

"Nathaniel, baby, listen! It started to rain so I stopped in the old Tucker family warehouse to wait the rain out! Please, baby I would never cheat on you!" Gertrude pleaded, but the anger had overtaken Nate as he pounded her.

Finally, her body had gone limp. Nathaniel tried to revive her so that he could beat her more, but she wouldn't move. Her lifeless body was twisted into a heap of soulless flesh. The heartless bastard hadn't even given her body time to cool. He simply dropped her on the floor, walked to the tool shed, grabbed a shovel and started digging a grave behind their house, as if digging a grave for a dead pet. By lantern light he dug until the sweat covered his brow in huge beads of salty moisture. Nathaniel was filled with both exhaustion and exhilaration. He had been chided and teased throughout his entire life, and he would be damned if he let his own wife laugh with the white man, then come home and lay in his bed.

Charles happily burst into the house. He was sure that he would see his mother's beautiful face greeting him as she did every night. He was anticipating her soft sweet voice, but when he entered, he stopped in his tracks. Lying crumpled on the floor was his mother's lifeless body. Her eyes were open, staring into the abyss with no sign of life in them. Charles dropped to his knees next to his mother, hoping that she wasn't dead. He called to her softly and touched her face.

Her skin had begun to cool and he knew in his young heart that she was gone. He knew that she was dead, and he knew who was responsible.

As he ran from the house full stride to get to his brothers, he took the rickety steps two at a time and fell face first at the bottom of the stairs. He sprang to his feet and continued his stride, screaming for his oldest brother at the top of his lungs.

"Julius! Julius!" He screamed.

He found his brothers all huddled in the barn like rebellious slaves hatching a plan for escape. Julius looked at his little brother's face and instantly panicked. Charles was a very cool little brother and he never got excited about too much. For him to be that upset meant there had to be something wrong.

"What's wrong, little one?" He asked.

"It's mama! She's layin' on the flo' and she's not movin', Ju!" Charles exclaimed.

All four brothers started to move towards the house in trepidation. Julius reached the house first, and there on the floor just as Charles had said, lay his mother with her face cradled by a nest of long, jet black hair. Blood was leaking from her head and seeped down between the wooden slats of the floor. Julius knew instantly that his father was responsible.

At thirteen, Julius was almost as tall as his father, if not taller. His young anger was apparent, and as his hatred started to build, his grief gave way to an overwhelming rage. He knew in his heart that his beautiful mother was dead. He stood over her body and silently wept. He didn't want his younger brothers to see him fall apart. Since Otis left, Julius had become the "father" to his siblings, because their father had no interest in holding that title.

Julius went to the corner by the couch, grabbed his father's .223 Winchester rifle and headed for the door. He knew exactly how to use the rifle, because his father had made sure of it. According to his father, a man wasn't a man if he couldn't kill his own dinner.

On Julius' heels were his three brothers. Charles had grabbed a box of ammunition from a nearby table, and Otha Lee and Eugene had armed themselves with knives from the kitchen drawer. None of the young boys knew what to expect from the encounter with their father, but one thing was certain; Nathaniel Gage would pay for what he had done to their mother. As they rounded the corner of the house near the shed, they saw their father hard at work digging their mother's grave. Julius had always been respectful of his father because his mother had demanded it and he loved his mother, but his father had taken that away.

Julius pointed the rifle at his father. "What the fuck did you do to Mama!" He screamed.

Nathaniel looked at the young man with a dazed craziness in his eyes. "This here is grown folk's business, boy. You would do well to gon' in the house and tend to your brothers," his father stated calmly.

"Naw, old man, you got some answering to do. Me and these boys see every day how you treat mama. Now she's dead, so you need to tell us something, or you can sort it out with the Lord when you get to the Pearly Gates!" Julius spat.

The Gage patriarch threw his head back and laughed wildly and hysterically. "Boy, I been dead inside a long time. Between you boys and your triflin' ass mammy, I ain't lived in years. Do what you got to do, youngster," he said, hoping to call his son's bluff, but inside he was terrified. There was something about the look in his son's eyes that told him that the boy was as serious as cancer. Julius walked closer to his father and pointed the rifle in his face, nudging him slightly with the barrel of the gun in the forehead.

"Get in that grave, old man!" He barked, poking at his father's head harder with the barrel.

Nathaniel pleaded with his son. "Julius, don't do this, son, please!" The desperation in his voice was evident. Nathaniel was a coward. He was the type of man who loved to pick on women and children, but he would never confront a man. Julius was nobody's child. He looked at his father and started to cry. He didn't really know why he was crying. Maybe it was anger, maybe sadness, maybe confusion, but whatever the case, he knew what had to be done.

"Don't beg, you red bastard!" Julius pulled the trigger once, and his father's head exploded into a mass of blood and brains. It resembled the watermelons that he had used for target practice on so many occasions.

His father stumbled back and fell into the grave that he had so tirelessly and effortlessly dug for their mother.

Charles shrieked in fear, but quickly regained his composure.

Julius turned to his younger brothers, searching their faces for some sense of approval. They were so young and innocent, and now, just as he'd always done, he would take care of his little brothers the best way he knew how.

CHAPTER 14

For weeks after Julius had killed Nathaniel, he did his best to keep his brothers calm. Charlie wasn't as hard to control as Otha Lee and Eugene, who seemed to think since they were now parentless, that it somehow gave them free reign to do as they pleased.

"Eugene, I need you to go down to the hen house and get a half dozen eggs. Otha Lee, I need you to go down and milk Esther," Julius gave orders.

"What you gon' be doing while we doing all the work?" Eugene asked defiantly.

"All what work? I'm finna roll this dough, so I can start these biscuits. You wanna eat? If so, stop arguing with me and do like I ask!"

"What you want me to do Julius?" Charlie Boy asked.

"You can go to the smoke house and get me a slab of that salt jowl baby boy."

Each of his siblings went out into the early morning sun to carry out their prospective tasks, while Julius himself kneaded and rolled the dough to make his mother's homemade biscuits. He hummed old gospel hymns that he'd heard his mother sing on so many occasions. The sound of hooves and reigns pulled Julius from his gospel inspired revelry. He wiped his hands on his dish towel and threw it across his shoulder. Julius walked to the front door and felt his knees grow weak. The sheriff was outside in front of their house accompanied by Mr. Ransom and four other white men on horseback.

"Is your mammy home boy?" The sheriff asked.

Julius thought about lying, but if they had taken the time to come all the way out to their house, then they would most certainly return later if he lied.

"She dead!" He admitted.

"What? Ain't been no reports of no deaths natural, or otherwise boy! How'd she die?"

"My daddy beat her to death!" Julius said.

"Wait a minute, your paw beat your mammy to death boy. Is that what you're telling me?"

"Yessuh." Julius nodded.

"Where your pappy at now boy? If that coon is here, you need to tell him to get out here now!" The sheriff screamed, cocking his rifle. Two of the men with the sheriff jumped from their horses and ran to the rear of the house as if to keep Nathaniel from escaping.

"He ain't here," Julius said.

"Well, where the hell is he boy? Don't you be trying to hide him nigger!"

"Why would I hide the man that killed our mama? He ain't here, like I said before."

"Don't sass me boy. Let's try this here another way. Do you know where your paw is?" The sheriff asked.

Julius didn't give the sheriff an answer. He just pushed past him on the porch, walked to the side of the house and showed the sheriff his mother's grave and the crude tombstone that they'd created. It read; *We will love you 4ever mama*.

"We buried our mother beneath these apple blossom flowers because they were her favorite. He took everything from us and gave us nothing sheriff. He didn't bother to think about what four boys would do with no mother. He beat her so much that she was afraid to smile sir. Can you imagine how that made me feel to see my mother afraid of her own shadow?" Julius asked. He was reflecting on abusive times past, rather than talking to the sheriff. "She still took care of us and went to work with black eyes and everything."

"The boy ain't lying sheriff. She showed up to work on many occasions with a black eye, busted lip or both," Mr. Ransom confirmed.

"Where's your paw son?" The sheriff asked quietly. There was something about the calmness in the boy's voice that made the sheriff nervous. Julius walked to a patch of red clay and withered grass and pointed. "Here he is sheriff," Julius said.

"Your pappy dead too? How'd he die son?"

"I kilt him suh. I ain't want to, but the Bible says, it's s'posed to be an eye for an eye. He took our mama from us, so I sent him back where he came from. That red nigga was hell sheriff, so I sent him back to hell." Julius said.

"Son, that's considered murder in the great state of Arkansas. You gon' be tried and probably hung for this boy!"

"What about my little brothers? Who gon' care for them if I hang?" Julius asked.

"Well, they'll more than likely be placed in an orphanage until they are old enough to care for themselves."

Julius couldn't breathe. He had killed their father out of pure hatred for the death of their mother, but he had never intended to have his family split up. In his young mind, he would be able to handle being both mother and father to his younger brothers. After all, he'd played father to them in his father's emotional absence anyway. Now, he was on his way to the bad end of a rope and the fate of his little brothers was unclear.

The two men that had gone to the back of the house returned moments later with Eugene, Otha Lee and Charlie Boy in tow. Charlie broke free from the man's grip and ran to Julius. He threw his arms around his brother's waist.

"They say you in trouble Ju. They say we ain't gon' never see you no mo'!" Charlie Boy cried.

Julius loosened his little brother's grip and kneeled in front of him. "Dry your eyes baby boy! I'm in trouble, but Lord knows I only did it to protect y'all. You believe in the Lord Charlie Boy?" He asked.

Charlie Boy nodded and wiped his eyes and nose on his sleeveless arm, smearing tears and snot across his dirty face.

"If you believe in Jesus like you say, then pray as much as you can. Don't worry about me, I'ma be fine. Y'all hear me? I'ma be fine!" He stared at Eugene and Otha Lee. "Y'all promise me that y'all gon' always take care of each other," Julius said, but neither brother spoke. "Promise me!" Julius shouted.

In unison, they all promised in a somber tone. Julius turned to the sheriff, "I'm ready suh," he said. He extended his hand to the young boy and pulled him up onto his horse. Julius watched as his little brothers were being put onto the wagon with Mr. Ransom.

Julius and the sheriff rode alongside the wagon until they crossed the bridge at Miller's creek. On the south side of the bridge the wagon veered right at the fork in the road and Julius' heart nearly stopped.

"Julius! Julius! Ju!" Charlie Boy cried. Julius could hear the fear in his youngest brother's voice.

"Where they going sheriff?" Julius asked.

"They are going to St. Joseph's and you're going to that nigger reform school over in Wrightsville."

By nightfall Julius was being ushered through the gates of the Arkansas Negro Boys Industrial School. The name would have implied that it was a segregated institution of education, but nothing could have been further from the truth. It was for the lack of a better term, nothing more than a teenage slave camp. A large population of Negro boys between the ages of twelve and eighteen were housed there. They were made to pick cotton, chop trees, pick up trash on the side of the mostly dirt road of Pulaski county and it all furthered the greatness of Arkansas. The only real education being gained at the boy's home was a higher education in the commission of crimes.

The sheriff kept a firm hand planted on Julius' neck as they entered the institution. The doors creaked ominously as they entered and slammed a resounding clang of finality behind them. A lump of foreboding caught in Julius' throat as he listened to the officer's hard soled shoes thump against the tile floor. The musty smell of depression and hopelessness hung thick in the air and Julius felt hot. He began to sweat uncontrollably and his knees felt weak. The sheriff put his arm out as if signaling Julius to stop and walked ahead of him. He stopped at a desk where a large, burly white officer sat. The sheriff walked past Julius and gave him a nasty look.

"Good luck nigger," he said with a smirk as he left.

"Well, looks like we got ourselves a little killer on our hands. That's a good skill to have here coon. You'll need it!" The officer sneered as he opened the door to a room and shoved Julius inside. The room was cold and drab, with very little light. A sliver of moonlight barely pierced the small, dirty window of Julius' confinement. The officer slammed the door just as Julius opened his mouth to ask how long he would be there. He walked to the far corner of the room and sat on the cold slab of concrete beneath his feet. He brought his knees up to his chest, buried his head between his knees and sobbed softly. His only fear, the fear of being all alone had been realized. Julius had the same nightmare on far too many occasions. He'd wake up in their house to find everyone gone, his mother, his brothers, even his father. He'd run outside and their entire parcel of land would be reduced to a barren wasteland. Buzzards gnawed at the dying carcasses of what used to be their livestock. In the dream he'd make it as far as Miller's creek, but when he'd try and cross, Charlie Boy would always be lying at the foot of the creek bed. His small, frail body would be contorted into a grisly mess of blood and guts and the buzzards would be circling overhead. He would try and get to his baby brother, but his feet were always mired in the thick, red, mucky clay. At the top of the bank Eugene and Otha Lee both laughed uncontrollably, but cried at the same time. As his anger grew, he'd free himself and just as he'd approach Charlie's battered body, he'd be jolted awake by the sound of his mother's voice. "Julius!" She'd yell, except that time it wasn't his mother's voice. Julius had fallen asleep in the small room and what he'd believed to be his mother's soft voice was actually that of Rebecca Ransom. Julius groggily opened his eyes and tried to focus on the adults standing in the doorway. There, stood Gilbert and Rebecca Ransom and a man that Julius had never met. His features were stern, but compassionate and his demeanor was regal. His clothes were immaculately pressed and Julius couldn't help, but notice how shiny his loafers were.

"Guard! Your treatment of this child is unacceptable. I'll need an office with chairs and a table!" He said sarcastically. They were led into a room that was quite the opposite of the room that he had spent the previous night.

"Julius honey, do you remember me and my husband Gilbert?" Rebecca asked.

"Yessum, Mr. and Mrs. Ransom, who my mama used to work for."

"That's right son," Gilbert said, putting his hand on Julius' shoulder. "Your mother was a good, humble, God fearing woman and yesterday when I came out to the house and heard you tell of the horrible thing that your daddy did, my heart ached. I prayed to sweet Jesus for justice concerning your dear mother. We paid her a decent wage, but I feel like we could have done more to help her secure a future for you boys," he said regretfully.

Julius didn't quite understand why Mr. Ransom was telling him those things, but he had no choice but to listen.

"Mr. Ransom believes that your mother came to him in his sleep last night," Rebecca said.

"It's not what I believe Becca, it's what I know! I saw her face just as clear as day. She was crying and asking me to help you. The scary part about it is that she was crying tears of blood. She picked you up, as big as you are and put you in my arms like a newborn baby. You were so small, so innocent and just as quickly your face changed to Xavier's," Mr. Ransom said as tears stained his cheeks.

"Excuse me, suh who is Xavier?"

"Forgive Gilbert, Julius. Xavier was our son. We lost him to yellow fever when he was just a baby. He would have been around your age right now. The part that Mr. Ransom didn't get to was that while he was holding you, your mother was holding Xavier's hand and as he looked down at you, your mother and Xavier both smiled and walked into a bright light."

Julius looked at the adults in amazement. He'd thought that he and he alone was the only person who had dreams so vivid.

"We think that the Lord almighty sent your sweet mama to me and we want to honor her wishes by helping you out of this mess."

"My name is Mr. Watson's son. I'm an attorney and I've been retained by the Ransom family to represent you in the event that this goes to trial."

"What about my brothers?" Julius asked.

"Let's cross this bridge first. Your little brothers are safe for now. My main concern is to get you out of here Julius. This is not a good place to be. There have been more boys murdered here than those that have been rehabilitated. These officers don't care about rehabilitating young Negro boys. So, we're going to get you out. If we can show that your pappy was beating your mama regularly and if we can appeal to the sensibilities of the women in that courtroom, we may be able to have you walk away free," Mr. Watson said.

"What happens if we can't do those things?" Julius asked.

"Well, there are a lot of grown men in this town who would love to see your young neck in a noose," Mr. Watson said.

"Wait, Julius, I think it's important to point out that first of all we are very wealthy and secondly, there are a lot of poor whites here who would do just about anything for the right price," Gilbert Ransom said.

CHAPTER 15

Charlie Boy stood between Eugene and Otha Lee with his head held low, afraid to make eye contact with the white woman who spoke. He tried to listen, but she was speaking so slowly and her voice sounded like cats fighting in a pillow case.

"I expect you older boys to look after your little brother. If we all do our share, we can make this transition much easier. Breakfast is served promptly at eight o'clock am, classes start at nine o'clock am, church service starts promptly at ten o'clock am. If you're late for breakfast, you will not eat. If you're late for class will you will not eat lunch and if you're late for services you will be granted lunch, but you will be denied supper. If you are caught stealing food, you will be punished and the sheriff will be notified of your thievery. Do you have any questions?" She asked.

"Yessum, how long we gotta be here?" Otha Lee asked.

"Well, you'll stay here until a nice Christian family adopts you, or until you reach eighteen years of age."

"Some family gon' adopt all three of us? Why can't we just go home?" Otha Lee asked.

"It's highly unlikely that a family will adopt all three of you boys. Most families want a child that they can train."

"Train? I ain't no dog! Ain't nobody training me to do shit!" Eugene sneered.

Before Eugene knew it, he saw a flash and felt the harsh sting of the nun's yardstick. Next he was being dragged to a sink on the other side of the room and made to bite a bar of soap. "Open your mouth. Bite it! Now chew it!" She said.

He chewed the soap until his mouth was a frothy mess. "Rinse your mouth out. Let's be clear. Sassing will not be tolerated here at St. Joseph's," she said.

Otha Lee and Charlie Boy were stunned at Eugene's behavior. Not because of what he had said, but rather what he had not said. For whatever reason, even though he was next to the youngest, he loved to bark orders like he was Julius' age. He was a self-proclaimed badass and the fact that the nun had silenced him amused them both.

Sister Mary Agnes was by all accounts considered a young nun. She'd married at a tender fifteen years old at the start of the First World War. Her husband had eagerly enlisted in the Army, even amidst her protest. He'd felt it was his patriotic duty and Mary Agnes had cautioned him that his duty was building a family with her. After all, what kind of man left his young wife all alone at such turbulent times? Not long after his deployment, she'd received a visit from two military policemen offering an opened letter from her husband and their deepest condolences. Private McCaffrey had died a national hero, according to them and the country had been fortunate to have had him as a soldier. She was sure that they had given that same hero speech to every other grieving widow that they'd encountered, but it did nothing to console her broken heart. Soon after that Mary Agnes McCaffrey joined the convent. She would take the Lord Almighty as her husband, her one and only, because he would never leave her. She had a different way of thinking and most people frowned upon her views. Unlike most southern whites, she didn't see Negroes as animals. She believed that God had created all men in his image and skin color was just a shell. Especially the children who were so innocent and trusting. So, it stood to reason that when the position opened up at St. Joseph's, she petitioned for the job. It would give her the opportunity to fight the good fight and bring their young souls to Jesus.

Sister Mary Agnes escorted the boys to one of the four extremely large rooms that the orphanage had to offer. Metal bed frames with thin mattresses lined both sides of the massive room with one row of beds in the center. "You'll sleep here, here and here." She pointed to three beds that were side by side. She bade the boys good night and left them to settle themselves in.

"Man this is bullshit!" Eugene sniveled.

"Shut your ass up before that lady makes you eat some mo' soap!" Otha Lee laughed.

"That shit ain't funny! I started to punch her ass!"

"You ain't start to do shit." Otha Lee said.

"Julius say we ain't sposed to hit girls!" Charlie Boy said.

"Is Julius here little nigga? No, so shut up!" Eugene snapped.

"Man you ain't gotta talk to him like that. Come on Charlie Boy, climb on up in the bed," Otha Lee said.

Charlie Boy climbed into the bed and fluffed his pillow. Large crocodile tears welled in his tiny eyes that didn't go unnoticed by his older brother. Otha Lee knelt next to Charlie Boy's bed and kissed him on the forehead.

"Don't pay Gene no never mind Charlie Boy." He said, shooting Eugene a mean glance as he stood up. Otha Lee's glance carried a meaning that Eugene must have known far too well, because he promptly sat on the side of Charlie Boy's bed and rustled his hair. He pulled the covers up to the little boy's chin and kissed him on the forehead.

"I'm sorry little man, I just wanna go home. I shouldn't have snapped at you. I love you buddy," Eugene said.

"Goddamn, you spooks sound like a bunch of fairies! Shut the fuck up and go to sleep!"

"Ain't no fairies over here nigga, fuck you!" Eugene barked.

The room was filled with an eerie hush and before Eugene knew what hit him, a set of hands were wrapped around his throat. He looked up to see the biggest kid he'd ever seen breathing through flared nostrils as his grip got

101

tighter and tighter around his neck. He had to stand at least six feet tall and just as wide. There was no muscle, only fat upon fat, upon compacted mounds of fat.

Fight, fight, fight, fight! The other boys in the room chanted. Otha Lee tried to break the death grip that the boy had on his brother's throat, but the kid was too strong. Charlie Boy sprang from the bed, scaled the giant and clamped his frail legs around the boy's waist. He had one arm locked tight around the boy's neck and with his free hand, he produced a small broken icepick, which he put underneath the boy's chin.

"What's your name?" Charlie Boy asked.

"My, my, my name is Scrumpy."

"Hi Scrumpy, I'm Charlie Boy. This is Otha Lee and that's my brother Eugene that you choking," Charlie Boy said.

"I'm only choking him because he cussed me out."

"Yeah, I know he talk too much, but if you don't let him go I'ma kill you!" Charlie Boy spat.

Slowly, Scrumpy released his grip on Eugene's neck.

"See, now we can be friends. Eugene this is Scrumpy," Charlie Boy said.

"Y'all niggas crazy!" Scrumpy cried out.

"That's right. We Gages and anybody fuck with us, they gon' pay the price!" Eugene said between coughs.

Charlie Boy handed the icepick to Otha Lee and hugged Eugene. He crawled into his bed and smiled at him. "That's right Gene, we Gages and we all we got. Julius said we gotta take care of each other." With that said, he drifted off to sleep.

CHAPTER 16

Julius still had yet to talk to anyone concerning going to court. He was sent back to the same room where he'd spent the previous night and told to wait.

As nightfall approached Julius barely had his dinner of mush and stale bread when he heard the clang of keys unlocking the door. The sheriff that had brought him there stood in the doorway. He smelled like Nathaniel, with whiskey oozing from his pores. He yanked Julius to his feet and rushed him out into the darkness.

"Do you know where St. Joseph's is boy?" The sheriff asked.

"No suh."

"It's about ten miles outside of town. I'm gonna take your black ass to the edge of town and you can make your way there. Can you read nigger?" He asked.

"Yessuh, I can read."

"Here." The sheriff handed Julius a small envelope. "Climb on in the back of that wagon and cover up. When I say last stop, I want you to get out and run toward the moon. You think you can do that?" The sheriff asked.

"Yessuh, I can do that. You think I can get my brothers when I get to St. Joseph's?"

"That ain't my concern. The Ransom family paid me to get you outta town and that's what I'm doing. You seem like a pretty smart boy, so I'm sure you can figure out a way to get your brothers out. Now get back there and cover up."

*****

Julius didn't know how long they had been riding by the time he finally heard the sheriff yell last stop, but it wasn't a moment too soon. He had to piss something fierce and he was anxious to get to his little brothers. He leapt from the wagon and looked into the sky.

"Here boy, you'll need this!" The sheriff said, handing Julius a small oil burning lamp. "Remember, follow the moon." He disappeared down the long dirt road. Julius wasn't exactly sure how far ten miles was, but he needed to make it there before morning. He darted off quickly, running toward the wood line. He ran as fast as he could until his lungs felt like they were on fire. Julius sat down near a large oak tree to rest and reached into his pocket to read the letter that the sheriff had given him. Julius sat the lamp down and lay on his stomach and unfolded the letter.

Julius,

We decided to not take a chance with the courts. The sheriff informed us that you had yet to be processed so there is no record of you being arrested. You are not in the system son, so disappearing should be fairly easy. We know that you'll more than likely go after your brothers, so we've included a small token to help you on your way. Be careful and God bless you.

PS: This is our little secret.

Always, RR

Enclosed with the letter were ten twenty dollar bills. Julius had never held two hundred dollars in his hands before, but it felt good and he was grateful. He rewrapped the money in the letter and stuffed it in his shoe near his toes. Julius continued his journey, walking briskly, running at times, but keeping a steady pace. He was sure to keep the moon in his sights as he traveled. Sooner than he'd expected, he happened upon a road with a sign indicating that St. Joseph's orphanage was less than a mile away. He felt as though he'd gotten a second wind, but he'd still need to stay away from the road. If he was seen wandering the roads at such a late hour *and* if it was discovered that he had two hundred dollars in cash on him, he'd be murdered for the money alone. In the distance through the woods, he could see the top of the steeple of St. Joseph's. As he made it to the edge of the wood line that bordered the orphanage, the magnificence of the structure held Julius in awe. He stepped into a small cemetery on the edge of the property between the woods and the first building. He sat atop a tombstone and removed his shoes. He rubbed his aching feet and checked the inside of his shoe. The money was still there, as if it could have somehow escaped. He blew out the flame of the lamp and crept toward the main building. The thick clouds overhead played hide and seek with the full moon, only partially shadowing the large courtyard that surrounded the orphanage. Julius didn't believe that anyone in the children's home would be awake at that hour, but he didn't want to take any chances. He was still underage, so if he was caught, the orphanage could very well make him a ward of the state. Julius stopped at a small shed in the center of the field and nearly fainted when a light inside of the orphanage clicked on.

He dove to the ground and rolled over onto his back, staring at the passing clouds overhead until he caught his breath. He rolled over onto his stomach. His heart was beating so loudly that he swore the patrons of the orphanage could hear his approach. Sure the lights were still on in one of the offices, but the silhouette that he saw was shaded. Julius sprang to his feet and ran as fast as he could toward the building, making sure to keep his eyes planted on the room with the light. The entire complex was eerily quiet as Julius drew near. His first thought was to go through an open window, but he just as quickly dismissed the idea. The time that it would take to find something to stand on was precious and it was time that he couldn't afford to lose. The sun would rise in a few hours and he wanted to have as much distance between them and the orphanage as possible. No, he would try his luck with the doors. If they were locked, he'd just have to mix in with the children of the orphanage after they'd gone outside to play. Why should the doors be locked? After all, the boys and girls in the orphanage would in all actuality be happy to have somewhere to go, a warm bed to sleep in and three hot meals a day. The chance of them wandering off, or making a run for it was miniscule. Julius turned the lever of the door and it sprang open. Even with Julius being as quiet as he could be, the stillness of the building caused an uncomfortable echo to reverberate throughout the hallowed halls. One after another, Julius opened doors, revealing empty office after empty office. Some of the offices had been converted to dusty storage rooms and others held rickety desks, with pictures of children with the families that had been kind enough to adopt them. Smiling black children in the midst of white families, eager to show that they had *taken in* one of the less than fortunate Negro children of Lee County. When he reached the end of the hall, he squinted against the darkness at the signs on the wall ahead. One sign read, *Colored Boys*, the other read *Colored Girls*. He made a left and crept in the direction that the sign for colored boys had pointed. The soles of his shoes clicked and clacked against the celadon colored tiled floor. He stopped to remove his shoes and then continued his journey, making sure to stay close to the walls as if he might blend into them and go undetected. He came to a large set of double doors and inhaled deeply, trying to calm the voice screaming questions into his head. *What if you open the door and there are adults inside? What if you open the door and some of those kids are awake? You think they'll give you up? What if they scream and a grown up comes running out? What if, if was a fifth? Yeah, I'd be drunk as hell.* He thought. Julius opened the door and eased it closed behind him. Charlie Boy was the only sibling that he had that would more than likely be awake. He was always the first in bed and would often wake up before the roosters had a chance to crow back on their farm.

"Charlie Boy! Charlie, Eugene, Otha!" He whispered loudly.

"Ain't no goddamn Charlie in here nigga! If you looking for them new little niggas that they brought in here, they next door in the green room. Go through them there doors back yonder. They in the middle row," a croaky voice said.

"Thank you man."

"Whatever muhfucka. Just hurry up 'fore you piss me off goddamnit, you fuckin' up my sleep."

Julius didn't exchange words with the boy. Any other time he would've had to fight Julius for his obvious disrespect, but Julius was grateful for the information. He pushed through the double push doors and moved soundlessly down the center aisle of the chartreuse colored room until he reached his brothers. He reached Otha Lee's bed first. Julius kneeled next to his bed and roused him softly.

"O, wake up man! O, get up we gotta go!" Julius said.

Otha Lee woke up and stared at Julius for what seemed like an eternity. "Julius, is that you?"

"Yeah, man, it's me, get up. Wake up Eugene and I'll get Charlie Boy up. Come on now, we gotta get outta here!" Julius said.

Otha Lee had believed himself to be dreaming, but it wasn't a dream and when it dawned on him that his older brother had come to rescue them, he bounced from his mattress with a start. Julius ran his hand across Charlie Boy's head and his eyes immediately popped open.

"Julius! I knew you were coming. I just knew it!" He said as he jumped up and threw his arms around Julius' neck tightly.

"Shhhh, we gotta be quiet little man, okay?" Julius said to Charlie Boy.

"Can we take my friend Scrumpy?"

"Nah, I got enough money for us to eat off of. I ain't got enough for no 'nother nigga Charlie Boy," Julius said.

Eugene slapped Julius in the back of the head playfully and hugged him tight. "Man I was just finna come up with a plan to get us out of here, but I guess I fell asleep by accident," Eugene said.

"You wasn't finna do shit, but slob on that pillow like you were doing," Otha Lee teased.

"Man, we don't have time for you two jokers and y'all bullshit. Do you wanna stay in here forever, or do you wanna go home?"

"We wanna go home, but if we go home won't they just come get us again?" Otha Lee asked.

"Yeah, they will, but if we make a new home somewhere else, we won't have to worry about that," Julius explained.

"What about all of our stuff?" Eugene asked.

"What? Some raggedy ass clothes, a few fishing poles and some hand me down toys?" Julius sneered.

"No, I mean the land and our house and stuff."

"Man, fuck that house! That's Nathaniel's house, not ours! We'll get a bigger house than that when we make it to where we're going," Julius said.

"Where we gonna go?"

"I'm thinking Detroit, or somewhere up there," Julius said.

"Detroit? What's in Detroit?" Otha Lee asked.

"Our brother is in Detroit. We're going to find Otis!" Julius said.

CHAPTER 17

Julius looked at his little brothers with worry and concern plastered across his face. Maybe he'd bitten off more than he could chew. They looked tired and hungry and to top it off, Eugene had almost been bitten by a rattle snake as they made their way through the thick brush of the Arkansas swamps. If they could make it to the rail yard, they would have plenty of time to rest. There was no way that they could afford to buy four tickets to Detroit. Even if they could afford it, Julius doubted very seriously that they would allow four underage boys to purchase train tickets without their parents present. Then Julius remembered that he had the two hundred dollars from the Ransoms. They emerged from the woods at the south mouth of the rail road tracks.

As they walked the tracks, Eugene's complaints started to grate Julius' nerves. "How long we gotta walk? I'm hungry, when we gonna eat? My feet hurt, can we rest a while? These mosquitoes are eatin' me up. I be glad when we get there. How much longer Julius?" He'd whined over the course of their journey, until Julius finally snapped.

"Eugene shut the fuck up! Goddamn you sound like you're Charlie Boy's age. He ain't saying shit, but your super tough ass is whining like a baby. We'll get there when we get there. If walking and talking with your brothers is too much for you to handle, then turn your black ass around and go back to that dirty ass orphanage. I'm sick of your mouth. We're all hungry, dirty and tired, so don't feel like you're the only one. I got some money in my shoe and when we get to the train station I'll get us something to eat, but for now shut up! You understand?" Julius barked.

"I guess he told you nigga!" Otha Lee laughed.

Julius shot Otha Lee a glare as if to tell him to shut up also, but before Otha Lee could contest, he heard Charlie Boy scream. "There go the train station right there!"

Even in the early morning hours the one building train station was bustling with business. Julius felt the train tracks beneath his feet begin to vibrate and then he heard the faint whistle of the approaching train.

"Come on y'all. We don't have much time!" Julius grabbed Charlie Boy by the hand and ran toward the station. As the train approached, Julius scanned the crowd for his victim. Someone that he could perhaps use to purchase tickets for him and his brothers. "Y'all stay here with Charlie Boy, I'ma go inside and see something right quick," he said.

He needed to find a bathroom, or somewhere private where he could remove some of the money from his shoe. The sign above the restrooms said *Whites Only,* but there was no sign for the blacks. "Excuse me sir, is there a colored toilet here?" Julius asked an old grizzled conductor.

"Niggers use the outhouse 'round yonder boy," he answered in a gruff tone.

Julius simply nodded and headed in the direction that the old man had pointed in. He knocked lightly and entered the outhouse, trying desperately to hold his breath, but to no avail. The malodorous stench of fecal matter, urine and vomit tickled his empty stomach and made him wretch. Julius kicked off his shoe quickly and rustled through the bills. He counted out forty dollars and put the rest back in his shoe. He shoved the money deep into his pocket, straightened his clothes and exited the outhouse, welcoming the fresh Arkansas morning air. That's when Julius saw her. She was conceivably the most beautiful woman that he had ever laid eyes on, next to his sweet mother of course. She was of reddish brown hue, with smoldering smoky eyes. She couldn't have been much older than Julius, maybe seventeen or eighteen and she carried herself with a grace that he'd never witnessed. He wanted to look away. He needed to look away, before she caught him staring at her with his mouth wide open. She stood alone, staring at the old black man shining shoes in front of the station. For reasons unknown to Julius, his pulse quickened and he had begun to sweat. He had to either shit, or get off of the pot though, because people had started to board the train.

"Excuse me ma'am, but can I talk to you for a minute?" Julius asked.

"I don't know sugar, can you?"

"I really need your help ma'am," he said.

"Well ma'am is my mother. I don't believe I'm old enough to be called ma'am. Besides, the way you were looking at me suggests that you don't quite see me as a ma'am either. What can I help you with sugar?" She asked.

Her voice was smooth like brer rabbit syrup over hot buttermilk biscuits. Her words flowed effortlessly and Julius was at a loss for words. "I-I-I." He stammered.

"Spit it out cutie, I ain't got all day."

"Can you buy me and my brother's tickets to Detroit? I got my own money," he said.

"I suppose I could, but why aren't your mother and father here to buy ya'lls passage to Detroit?"

Julius dropped his head and mumbled something inaudible, even to himself.

"Speak up sugar. What was that?"

"They dead!" Julius barked.

"Oh my! I'm sorry to hear that."

Before Julius could say another word, his brothers joined him on the landing of the train station. With pure innocence Charlie Boy walked up and took the girl's hand in his own. "You pretty!" He said.

"Well thank you little one. You're a cutie pie yourself." She pinched Charlie Boy on the cheek.

"I'm Julius, that there is Otha Lee, that's Eugene and the little one is Charlie Boy. I guess it would be easier to remember us all by our last name. We're the Gage boys," Julius said.

"Well, I'm Annette and I'm pleased to meet you Gage boys. Now let's get those tickets before we all miss our train."

Annette disappeared with the forty dollars that Julius had given her and reemerged from the interior of the station moments later with four tickets. She handed Julius the tickets, along with his thirteen dollars change.

"Why don't you keep that for your trouble?" Julius suggested.

"No sweetheart. You boys will probably need that when you get to wherever you're going. Detroit is a big, expensive city. You put that away. I don't want your money."

"Where you going?" Charlie Boy asked.

Annette knelt in front of Charlie Boy and kissed him on the cheek. "I'm going home to Chicago. I was down here visiting my grandparents, but guess what?"

"What?" Charlie Boy gushed.

"Chicago and Detroit aren't that far from each other, so I just may get an opportunity to see you Gages again," Annette said.

"I hope so. You pretty!" Charlie Boy reiterated.

"Oh my goodness, you're just too cute. I'm on the same train, so we'll sit together. Would you like that, Charlie Boy?" Annette asked.

"Yessum!" He said gleefully.

"Allllllllllll aboard!" The conductor screamed.

Steam poured from the smoke stack and the whistle hissed its rhythmic toot as the passengers lined up to board the train. The white patrons boarded the majority of the train, while the blacks were relegated to the rear caboose of the locomotive. Annette spoke with such vigor about the importance of education. She made Julius promise that no matter their situation when they made it to Detroit, he'd make sure that not only would he enroll himself in school, but he would enroll his brothers as well.

"My daddy said that a man knew everything that school could teach him by third grade, so I don't think we need no schooling!" Julius said.

"The fact that you just said need no schooling lets me know that there are still things that you need to know. I hope this doesn't offend you Julius, but your father was a fool! There is nothing on God's green earth more important than family and a good education."

"I know he was a fool and I'm ashamed to say that he was my father, but my main concern when I get to Detroit is to find my big brother and make some money for me and my brothers," he said.

"The world is a big place Julius Gage and by the time you see the first three blocks of Detroit, you'll realize that you really don't know as much as you think you do. There are no eggs to gather and no cows to milk. There are no fields to tend and if you don't have a hustle, you can best believe that those city slick niggas in Detroit are going to eat you and your brothers alive."

"Ain't nobody fucking with me, or my brothers! I'll kill a nigga first!" Julius hissed.

"I like that spirit and you'll need it. Don't get mad. Just keep that same fire baby boy!"

"I ain't mad about shit! I just don't like nobody talking shit they don't know!" He snapped.

Annette reached across, rubbed Julius' knee and smiled brightly at him. "Apologies for overstepping my boundaries honey. Can I at least offer a little help?"

Julius could only nod. Annette had stirred something deep inside of him that he'd never felt before. She scrawled something onto a piece of paper and handed it to him. "This is my uncle. He's a good man. He's into some crooked shit, but he's a good man just the same. When you go and see him tell him Nettie sent you."

"What I'm s'posed to say?" Julius asked, staring at the address written on the paper.

"I just told you, tell him Nettie sent you and that you're looking for work. He'll take care of you."

CHAPTER 18

Michigan Central Station was a metropolis compared to the modest train station in Arkansas. The black folk in the Detroit station seemed to carry themselves with an aura of pride and self-assuredness that Julius had never witnessed amongst the blacks in rural Arkansas. They walked with their heads held high and didn't appear to bow down to the white man. Julius looked over he and his brother's tattered rags and felt a pang of shame. The black people hustling and bustling through the train station were stylish and chic. They all wore suits, with wing tipped shoes, topped off with fedoras.

"Hey mane, you cats look countrier than a muhfucka jack! I mean you niggas look like y'all fresh off a plantation. Where you boys from?"

"We're from Arkansas. What about you?" Julius asked.

"I'm from here in Detroit mane. Just got back from St. Louis making a little scratch. What brings you boys to Detroit youngsta?"

Julius didn't really understand the man's lingo, but he didn't want to appear lame to the older boy.

"We're looking for our brother mane, but what's with all the questions?" Julius asked. His muscles tensed up and he assumed a rigid and defensive posture.

"Say, be easy cat daddy. I'm just tryna be friendly. My name is Chester, Chester Wheeler. Cool down baby!"

"Well, I'm Julius and these are my brothers Eugene, Otha Lee and Charlie Boy. Sorry for being uptight mane, it's just been a long trip," Julius said.

"I can dig it. So where you cats headed?"

Julius handed Chester a small sliver of paper and waited for a reaction.

5216 Ivanhoe Street

Detroit Michigan 48204, West Side (ask for Roman Guthrie)

"Yeah man, yeah, I know this cat! He's heavy on the west side baby!" Chester shouted.

"Cool, you think you could drop us off at his place?"

"I don't know about all of that bruh. This nigga Roman ain't to be fucked with and if I come around there with some little snot nosed kids that nigga will probably kill me man," Chester scoffed.

"Man, he ain't gonna kill you. Just show us the house and drop us off if you're that scared." Eugene sneered.

"Damn, I didn't even think these other little muhfuckas could talk. Since you know so much about Roman, that means that your little smart mouth ass got some bread then right?" Chester countered.

"Ain't nobody tryna make no fuckin' sandwiches Chester! We just need to get to that address!" Otha Lee chimed in.

Chester's hearty laughter echoed from wall to wall, causing the busy station goers to stop and stare.

"Nah mane, some bread. You know moolah, greenbacks, frog skins, cheese, or money cat daddy." Chester laughed.

Julius might have been from the sticks, but he was nobody's fool. Why should he tell this kid what kind of money he had? What would stop him from robbing him and his brothers and leaving them for dead?

"I got thirteen dollars left from what my granny gave us to help find Mr. Guthrie, but that's it." Julius said pitifully.

"Uh huh, well I ain't no goddamn taxi mane, but since you little country niggas is cool, I'll drop you off!"

The sun had begun to set and a light drizzle had started to fall as the sky transformed into an array of fiery oranges and majestic purples. Chester's Cadillac Deville floated through the city streets effortlessly. The city lights played tricks on Julius' eyes as they caused the asphalt to sparkle from the rain like diamonds glimmering against bright lights.

"So, how you cats know Roman?" Chester asked as he lit a stick of reefer.

"Family friend," Julius muttered, trying to hold his breath.

"Uh huh. Well dig these blues baby, when you cats get settled in, I'll take y'all to get some presentable threads mane. Y'all can't be in the motor city dressing like no sharecroppers. Niggas on the west side stay casket sharp mane, so we gots to get you niggas cleaned up bruh. That's Roman's crib right there," Chester said, as he pulled up to the curb, pointing.

"Thanks mane, I appreciate it," Julius thanked him.

"Yeah you owe me one farmer."

"Yeah, I hear you." Julius smiled broadly.

"I wanna hear you say it."

"Hear me say what Chester?" Julius asked.

"I wanna hear you say, I owe you one Chester."

"I owe you one Chester," Julius said.

"No doubt."

"Aye, one more thing Chester."

"Lay it on me my man."

"Do you know a cat named Otis, Otis Gage?" Julius asked.

"Nah slim, I can't say that I do mane. By the way, if the nigga Roman is happy to see you little niggas, tell him that Chester turned y'all on to his address. If the nigga seems pissed that ya'll found him, then don't mention my name, get it?"

"Got it mane. Be easy." Julius said. They watched Roman drive off as night fell over a new city pregnant with possibilities.

*****

Roman Guthrie was an imposing figure with an even more imposing disposition.

Julius had almost swallowed his tongue after he knocked on the door and heard a resounding, "Who the fuck is it?" Coming from the other side.

"J-J-Julius Gage."

The door swung open and a huge, medium, brown skinned man stood on the other side of the threshold, breathing hard, staring menacingly down at Julius and his brothers.

"What the fuck you kids want man? Matter of fact, whatever the fuck you selling, I don't want none. Now get the fuck away from my door!" Roman snapped.

"We ain't selling shit!" Eugene snapped back.

"Looka here little nigga, it's obvious you don't know who the fuck you're talking to. Just to give you an idea muhfucka, I don't care if you're eight or eighty eight, I will beat the shit out of you. Little nigga, I will fillet your little ass and grill you like a steak, then pick my teeth with your bones goddamn it!" Roman growled.

"He didn't mean any harm sir. Nettie told us to look you up and said that you might be able to help us," Julius said.

Roman Guthrie, for as much of a beast as he appeared to be, softened a considerable amount at the mention of his niece's name.

"Why didn't you say my Nettie sent you bruh? Come on in man."

The four boys walked into Roman Guthrie's house astonished at the contents. From the outside, yes, the house was a veritable castle compared to the humble digs that they had come from, but the inside was a smorgasbord of high end velvets, woods and paisley patterns. Women walked around in fishnet stockings and stilettos; nothing more. Young Charlie Boy's eyes darted from woman to woman, each one of them different shades of the Negro color chart. There were chocolate nipples, rosy nipples, tan nipples, caramel nipples, all jutting forward, beckoning to the young Gage boys.

"You boys come on back here to the parlor where we can talk in private," Roman said, motioning toward a back room. "So what kind of help you boys need? Shit, if my Nettie Belle sent you boys to me, then she must see something special in you and that's good enough for me! What you need?"

"We came up here from Arkansas to find our brother Otis. Until we find him we gonna need somewhere to stay. We can buy our own food and stuff. We just need somewhere to lay our heads," Julius said.

"Looka here man, if you need some bread to float you until you get on your feet, I can do that. Shit if you need a job I can even do that, but I can't afford to have no kids hanging around here. Shit, all I need is some damned truancy officers knocking on my door. It's too much going on around here for me to have some nosey white folk beating on my door. I'm sorry. I can't do that son."

"I understand. We'll be alright. We always are. Can we at least stay the night though?" Julius asked.

"Muthfucka, are you deaf or retarded? I just told you I can't afford to have no fuckin' kids hangin' around my spot. Best that I can do is have my bitch Rosetta fix you little niggas some sandwiches, then y'all gots to get the fuck on!" Roman snarled.

"Man, we don't need your fucking charity! We'll find our own food nigga!" Eugene spat.

Roman smiled, since he understood the boy's hostility, but he was Roman Guthrie and if word ever got out that he had been disrespected by a kid, he would never live it down. He crossed the room swiftly and yanked Eugene from the ground with one hand and slapped him with the other. "I told you to mind your tongue boy. Your little ass needs to learn to respect your elders, nigga."

"Just because he sassed you don't give you no cause to slap my little brother around man. We gonna just leave before some shit gets started that we'll all regret," Julius said, picking Eugene up off the floor.

"I ain't gonna forget how you little fuckers came and disrespected my house, trust me," Roman said.

"Yeah, and I ain't gonna forget that you put your hands on me either. I'm gonna make you pay for that shit one day nigga!" Eugene cried.

"I hear you little nigga. If I had a dollar for every time a son-of-a-bitch said he was gonna get me I could retire and stop selling smack. Now get the fuck outta my pad before I forget my Nettie sent you muthafuckas!" Roman sneered.

CHAPTER 19

Julius cradled Charlie Boy close to him. He could feel his baby brother shivering, not from the chill, but rather from fear. At such an early age Charlie Boy knew far more than he was given credit for. Out of the brothers, Julius was perhaps the only one that understood the extent of Charlie's knowledge. Perhaps as much as Otha Lee seemed to understand Eugene's penchant for saying the wrong thing at the wrong time. Julius looked at the two middle boys, sitting with their backs against the brick wall. Their heads were touching like Siamese twins joined at the scalp. Hours earlier as they'd left Roman Guthrie's place, Otha Lee had caught up to Julius, who walked ahead of his three siblings briskly.

"Wait up man. Why you walking so fast?" Otha Lee asked.

"Tryna get the fuck away from 'round here. That nigga Eugene is just like Nathaniel man; always opening his big ass mouth. He's gonna fuck around and get us killed one day. Just watch!"

"Aw man, he don't mean no harm Julius. That's his defense mechanism. If you ever notice, the nigga only talk shit when he's nervous," Otha Lee said.

"Yeah? Well he needs to keep his nervous ass mouth shut before he gets somebody hurt. I didn't sign up for this shit!"

"Actually you did bro! Look, we didn't ask to be out here in the middle of the night, in a city where we don't know no damn body! We're following our big brother though, looking for another brother that obviously don't give a fuck about us, or that selfish ass nigga wouldn't have left," Otha Lee said. He was heated that Julius cared so much about finding Otis, but he was always on Eugene's case. He continued speaking as he threw his arm around Julius' shoulder. "You killed daddy, hell *we* killed for each other. That nigga Eugene just talks big tryna impress you man, that's all."

"If that nigga wants to impress me, he needs to learn how to speak when spoken to. As far as Otis goes, that's all the family that we have left. He left the same reason that we did, because of Nathaniel," Julius said.

"Nah, that bastard left because he was selfish. He left us there to pick up the pieces."

"Let me ask you a question and be honest. What if mama had left us with Nathaniel? Would you have stayed there with that son-of-a-bitch, or would you have gone to look for her?" Julius asked.

"That's not even a real question, because our mama was sweet. Shit she took care of that red nigga and he wasn't even hers!"

"That's exactly why we need to find him. If mama loved him enough to protect him, then that means we love him that much too. Family is family O!"

Now they all did their best to rest in the trash ridden alley way of East Detroit. Julius placed Charlie Boy's small frame across the laps of Otha Lee and Eugene before running his hand through the boy's hair. He walked to the end of the alley and made his way to the front of the two story brick structure where they had taken refuge. From the looks of it, they were nestled behind Galici's Deli. The second floor of the bakery looked abandoned from what Julius could see. Pieces of ply wood were attached to the upper windows with rusty nails. Julius trotted back to the alley and made his way up the fire escape just past where his brothers rested. There was no door on the second story, only a piece of ply wood leaned haphazardly against the opening where the door should have been. Julius slid into the gap between the wood and the door jamb. It was the rear entrance to a long corridor with four apartments on each side of the hall. He tried each doorknob and all of them were locked, except apartment number two. It sat across the hall from a set of stairs that probably led to the deli below.

Julius walked inside and whispered. "Hello, hello is anybody in here?" No answer. From room to room he repeated his question until he was sure that the space was uninhabited. Julius made his way back to the doorway that he had come through and called to his brothers. "Otha Lee, Eugene, Charlie Boy!" He shouted.

They woke up, stretched and looked around groggily. "Up here y'all!" He said.

They stood looking around in bewilderment, trying to gather their bearings. One by one the younger Gage boys climbed the stairs, nearly unable to see through the blurriness of their little, sleep deprived eyes. Once inside apartment two, Julius addressed his brothers.

"Listen, we gonna use this place to rest. I'll take the first watch. When y'all wake up I'll go and get us something to eat and see what the fuck this neighborhood has to offer," Julius instructed.

CHAPTER 20

Jimmy Galici had a regular routine. Every morning at 5 am sharp, he opened his bakery. Most people thought he opened too early, but he did it to get ready for the 7 am rush *and* his morning business meetings. Well, they weren't actually business meetings, but rather social gatherings of some of his closest associates. After the breads were put into the oven, the dough for donuts were mixed, the cannolis were in the fryer and the coffee was brewed, his daughter Gina usually showed up. She ran the bakery along with her husband Albert and her best friend Sophia. His friends would usually file into the deli around the same time. They were a mixture of merriment and murder from the old country; a group of men that Jimmy Galici had grown to love and trust. Vincent Finazzo was Jimmy's oldest and dearest friend. They'd come to the United States from Palermo. Vincent, or Crazy Vinny as he was called, was a bullish man. Although short in stature, he was thick necked and heavily muscled. Jimmy Galici was also short, but he had nowhere near the musculature that his counterpart had. The two of them had come up in the rackets together; oftentimes playing good guy, bad guy to the business owners in various neighborhoods. Jimmy Galici would play the bad guy, waving a pistol around, demanding a massive amount of money as tribute to his presence. Just when he'd cock his pistol to exact his retribution for noncompliance, Crazy Vinny would burst in, disarm him and run him away. Crazy Vinny would then offer to protect the unsuspecting business owners from Galici and others like him for a nominal monthly fee. Most times they went for it just because his fee seemed to pale in comparison to the money that Galici demanded.

There was Robert Tassiano, Dominic Alleveto aka Joey Craps, Salvatore Bagnasco aka Sammy Bags, Erasimo Timpa aka Black Sam and Carlo DeLuna aka Tuffy. Each man had their hand in different illegal rackets around Detroit, but none were as profitable as Sammy Bags' heroine operation, or Joey Craps' gambling operation. They'd tapped into the money train of the blacks on the west side of Detroit and between gambling and dope, the Negroes kept them with an endless supply of cash. Robert Tassiano had joked with Sammy Bags that he didn't understand how the moolee's could come up with so much money to gamble and get high, when they lived in the most depressing part of the city. Sammy Bags hadn't taken it as a joke, but he felt obligated to let his friend in on a little secret. The blacks, he said, spent money gambling in the hopes of striking it rich and living the American dream. Once the realization hit them that the cards were stacked in favor of the house, they inevitably got high to escape the reality that they had squandered away the few pennies they had managed to save.

Today was bittersweet for Jimmy Galici and his friends though, because Tuffy would be turning himself in to the authorities. He'd been adamant that he didn't want a fancy party, or anyone making a big fuss about his departure. Instead he wanted some of Gina's famous homemade cannolis, endless cups of expresso and uninterrupted hands of poker. He'd convinced Black Sam to cook up a batch of sausage and peppers on a bed of linguine and Jimmy Galici would supply fresh bread. Tuffy's incarceration was going to be a devastating blow to the organization, because he was the enforcer of the outfit. Even with his diminutive stature, the very mention of the name Tuffy struck fear in the hearts of men. With a gun he was precise, with a knife he was surgical, but with an icepick he was legendary. It just so happened that he had ice picked the wrong man. He'd gone to collect a gambling debt owed to Joey Craps, but the man had been resistant. Even when faced with certain danger, the man had continued to belittle Tuffy, calling him a grease ball, wop, dago guinea and a slew of other racially charged slurs. Tuffy had tried to let it go, because he understood that dead men didn't pay debts, so if he killed him, in all likelihood he would never be paid. The man, Brian O'Malley just happened to be the cousin of Detroit's Mayor, Albert Cobo. After O'Malley's death, Cobo made it clear that someone would burn for his cousin's murder. Unfortunately, Tuffy's name had crossed law enforcements' desks in connection with the murder one too many times, so Cobo had set his eyes on Tuffy. Even though they couldn't tie him to the murder, Carlo DeLuna, aka Tuffy, was most definitely on their radar. On Cobo's orders, Tuffy had been charged with so many frivolous charges that by the time the judge was finished adding them up and imposing sentences to be served consecutively, he would be gone nearly two years. By noon cigar smoke and laughter filled the back room of Galici's Deli as they smoked stogies and reminisced about old times. In Jimmy Galici's years, he had lived a life that most men only dreamed about. He'd made more money than most people would ever see, but his greatest joy was his grandson Ernesto. At fifteen years old he was wise beyond his years and Jimmy could see him one day taking over the outfit. He was highly intelligent and good with numbers, moreover he was a compassionate kid. He got along with everyone; Italians, blacks, Irish, it made no difference to him. As long as he was shown respect, he always showed it in return and those were qualities of a good leader.

"Hey Papa."

"Ernestooooooo, how's my little paison aye?" Jimmy asked cheerfully.

"I'm great Papa! So, are there any girls?"

"What do you mean girls? Look at this kid, only fifteen years old and already he's girl crazy! How about you concentrate on books and business." Jimmy laughed.

"No, I meant the new tenants upstairs. Are there any girls that moved in, or just the one kid that I saw?"

"Nobody has lived up there since your sweet grandmother died Ernesto."

"I saw a black kid about my age going in through the back with a grocery bag a few minutes ago."

"Forget about it, you're seeing things Ernie," Jimmy scoffed.

"No, seriously Papa, I think the kid is living up there!"

"Show me Ernie, because I ain't gave no one permission to be squatting in my place!" Jimmy screamed.

He and Ernesto walked out into the street and looked up toward the boarded up windows. By all indications the property was still abandoned. "See Ernie, no movement," Jimmy pointed out.

"Papa, how would you see movement through brick and wood? Follow me," Ernie said.

Jimmy Galici had a half mind to turn on his heels and walk back inside of his bakery, but Ernesto had never lied to him. Well, not to his knowledge. His grandson had been too adamant about what he'd seen. He followed him up the fire escape and through the gap in the plywood, feeling like a child as he tiptoed quietly through the hall. A faint light glowed from beyond the door of apartment two.

"See Papa, I told you," Ernesto whispered.

Jimmy Galici considered boldly kicking in the door, but he had never been a rude man. Dishonest yes, manipulative yes, but never rude. Besides, why should he destroy his own property only to spend his money to repair it? Instead, he knocked quietly and heard a light rustling, then the sound of small feet scurrying away from the door.

"I know you're in there, because I can hear you moving. So open the goddamn door, or we can let the cops sort it out!" Jimmy shouted. He heard the soft click of the lock on the doorknob and the clumsy clunk of the two deadbolt locks that separated the old man from his young squatters. Julius stood in plain sight of Jimmy Galici, staring at him, eye to eye with an unwavering gaze.

"You think you can just break into my place and not suffer the consequences?" Jimmy asked.

"We didn't break in man. It was open."

One by one Julius' siblings came out of hiding.

"Jesus Christ, you have your whole family here? Where's your mother?" Jimmy asked.

"My daddy kilt her."

"So, where's your father?" Jimmy asked, trying to get some viable answers.

"I kilt him, 'cause he kilt my momma."

Jimmy Galici looked into the boys' eyes. They were devoid of emotion, but his quivering voice belied his demeanor. "So, you boys are all alone? Who's taking care of you?" Jimmy asked.

"I take care of us and no we're not alone. We got each other!"

"I'm Ernesto, but everyone calls me Ernie. This is my grandpa Jimmy Galici." Ernesto introduced them.

"Nice to meet you. I'm Julius, this little one hiding behind me is Charlie Boy, this one," Julius said putting his hand on Eugene's shoulder, "is Eugene and that there is Otha Lee hiding in the corner."

"Otha Lee, Eugene, Charlie Boy and Julius. Those names sound southern son. Where are you boys from? How old are you son? You can't be much older than Ernie," Jimmy Galici said.

"Man, you sho' ask a bunch of fucking questions!" Eugene barked.

But, before Jimmy Galici could respond, Julius back handed Eugene in the mouth and sent him spiraling to the floor. "Mind your manners boy! This here is a grown up and we're on his property. Long as he show us respect, we gonna do the same!" Julius snapped.

"You hit me for this old cracker man? You wrong Julius, you dead wrong! This honky don't care about you, *or* me!"

"I ain't gonna tell you again Eugene, shut the fuck up!!" Julius spat.

Jimmy Galici walked past Julius and extended his hand to Eugene, who shirked his offer and stood on his own.

"Eugene right? Well, Eugene, you're wrong all the way around. First off, I'm not a honky, or a cracker as you put it. I'm Italian and believe it, or not, life isn't peaches and cream for us either. Now, I'm not saying that we've had it as bad as the blacks, but Italians and Irishmen are looked upon as only one step above the blacks. And believe it or not, I do care. How could I call myself a good man if I didn't help kids in need? We might be different skin tones, but we're all the same underneath. Now where are you from and how old are you?" Jimmy Galici asked, once again extending his open hand to Eugene, who reluctantly took it.

"We from Arkansas. I'm thirteen, Otha Lee fourteen, Charlie Boy six and Julius finna be sixteen," Eugene said meekly.

"You boys hungry?"

"I am, but I don't eat peas!" Charlie Boy said, moving to the front of Julius at the mention of food.

Jimmy Galici picked the small boy up and tickled him gently. "Who doesn't like peas? Why don't you like them?" He asked.

"Because they look like boogas!"

"Well, my daughter Gina makes the best sweet pea casserole I've ever had and it doesn't taste like boogers!" Jimmy Galici laughed, then added, "Why don't we go sit down, have a nice meal and discuss your plans for my property?"

Jimmy took the boys down to the bakery through the door at the bottom of the staircase. The old wooden door creaked loudly from the sound of the unused hinges. As the six of them entered, every eye in the bakery was trained on them.

"Hey Pop. Who's that, that you have with ya?" Gina asked.

"This is Julius, Eugene, Otha Lee and my new found friend Charlie Boy!" Jimmy said.

"What a bunch of handsome boys. I'm Gina, Ernie's mother. There's plenty of food in the back. When you're done, if you have room, how about some cannolis and ice cream, huh?"

Wide smiles spread across all of the boys faces; even Ernesto's, because not only did he love ice cream, but his mother's canollis were the best.

"Julius, after dinner I want to talk to you about a few things. Maybe we can find a way to put some money in your pockets," Jimmy Galici said.

"Okay Mr. Galici. I'm all ears."

Chapter 21

In the short time that Julius and his brothers had been living in apartment two above the bakery, he and Ernesto had become fast friends. Julius spent his days running errands for Jimmy Galici throughout the streets of Detroit. He had kept his promise to Nettie about his brothers and had Gina enroll Otha Lee and Eugene in Sydney Miller High School on the lower east side of Detroit. Money had allowed Ernesto to go to a fine Catholic school, but the Gage boys hadn't fared as well. They were less than welcome when Gina had taken them to St. Rita Catholic School. The lower east side of Detroit, or Paradise Island as it was called, was where the blacks were educated, so Otha Lee and Eugene made the daily trek to school. Charlie Boy, however, had it best of them all. Gina had chosen to home school the boy rather than send him to school alone and without the comforts of his older brothers. Julius couldn't have been happier with the arrangement, because according to Gina, Charlie Boy was a bright student who was eager to learn. While his brothers learned, so did he, except his education was steeped in criminal activity. He ran errands for Mr. Galici true, but those errands had the potential to land him in the nearest reformatory. Where else could he make $30 a week and have a nice place to stay? So, he was content with living out his academic dreams vicariously through his younger brothers and his friend Ernesto. He generally met Ernesto at the bus stop and then walked half way to the lower east side to meet Eugene and Otha Lee. After his brothers were safely inside of their apartment, Julius would continue his errands with Ernesto in tow. They'd talk for hours about just about everything that their young minds could think of. Week after week their talks intensified, until Ernesto shared with Julius the extent of his grandfather's business.

"Julius, do you know what the outfit is?" He'd asked.

"You mean like clothes?"

"Like clothes he says. No, not clothes. It's like a family where all of the people work together toward a common goal. Kind of like a gang."

"Wasn't no gangs in Arkansas unless you count the Klan as a gang." Julius sniggered.

"This is serious business Julius. As it stands right now a black can't join the outfit, but when I take over I'm going to change all of that. I'll make you my right hand man! We'll run Detroit, St. Louis and Omaha all from the bakery like my grandfather does," Ernesto said.

"Uh huh and what makes you think your Italian buddies are gonna go for that shit?"

"I told you. It's about family! We're brothers right? So, how can they deny you if I'm in charge?" Ernesto asked.

"Yeah, that sounds cool and all that, but look around Ernie man. Niggas have no place in nothing outside of their own kind."

"I'm telling you Julius, things are about to change. Mark my words. Before you know it blacks will be moving throughout this city, owning property. Shit, we might even have a black Mayor one day!"

"Does your grandfather know?" Julius asked with a sly smirk.

"Does my grandfather know what?"

"Does he know that you're getting high? You know, snorting the white girl. Powdering your nose with the booger sugar?" Julius laughed, but continued seriously. "I mean, come on Ernesto, a black man is considered the bottom of the barrel, but in reality we're treated worse than that. Shit, we're the black sticky shit on the underside of the barrel. We slaved for this country and still get treated like shit, and in case you forgot, Detroit is still in America. Truth be told, I thought me and my brothers escaped that Jim Crow bullshit by coming up here, but it ain't no different. You should see some of the looks I get when people see me riding through town with Mr. Tassiano. All I can do is shake my head, because all of these honkies are just alike," Julius said.

"So you think I'm one of those honkies Julius?"

"Shit, naw man. News flash Ernie, you's an I-talian and according to your grandpa, white folk only see y'all and Irishmen as just above niggas, so we in the same boat," he mocked Jimmy.

Ernesto didn't know what to say. Of course he'd always listened to his grandfather and he'd made it clear on more than one occasion that all men were to be treated with dignity and respect. Ernesto was optimistic about the future. If he had his way, he'd be the first to usher in a new era of family business by making Julius Gage the first black made man in the history of the outfit.

A little drizzle had begun to fall over the dark streets as Julius and Ernesto made their way toward the bakery. Both of them had disregarded Jimmy Galici's instruction of staying away from the alleys when they were running errands. Partly because they hated walking around the main streets in plain sight and partly because as Ernesto had said, his grandfather owned Detroit. He felt untouchable and that invincibility had found its way into Julius' ego. The overhead street light in the alley flickered and the rain fell heavier. Julius shoved his hands deep into the pockets of his tattered slacks and tried to shrink away from the rain. He looked toward the edge of the alley in front of him and thought that he saw something move in the shadows.

"Ernie man, maybe we should turn around and hit the street instead of these shortcuts bro," Julius said.

"Forget about it. We're only two streets away from the bakery."

"Yeah, but I thought I saw something move up ahead man. I still have Mr. Galici's delivery money in my pocket."

"You're probably just seeing stuff man. Besides, even if you did see something, or somebody, they know better than to fuck with me or you. My grandpa doesn't play that shit. Come on."

They walked faster than before, trying desperately to not only get out of the alley, but off the streets period. Being outside at night was dangerous, especially for Julius because, although he and his brothers had found a measure of acceptance with their extended family, the other residents in the neighborhood were less than receptive. As they neared the street, two figures appeared from the shadows, guns drawn, blocking the alley. The two boys had to be close to their age, maybe a few years older, but definitely not grown men. "Well, look at this shit will ya Jacob."

"Yeah, I see it Selwin. A wop walking his little nigger pet."

"We don't want any trouble fellas. Just let us pass and we'll forget that you pulled guns on us," Ernesto bargained with them.

"Oh, we're sorry. Did we scare you with the guns? Noooooo, these aren't meant to scare you. These are meant to spill your guinea blood if that nigger doesn't give up the cash."

"Do you know who the fuck I am? You're starting to piss me off! Now fucking move or suffer the consequences," Ernesto said.

"This little fucker is talking like he's the one with the gun Jacob."

Julius looked both of them up and down. They resembled one another like they might have been kin, but the skinnier of the two seemed to be in charge.

"Hold on fellas. Ain't no need to be pulling no guns," Julius said.

"Shut up nigger! When I want your opinion I'll give it to you."

Julius saw the glint of the chrome pistol against the light as the slender boy took aim, first at Julius and then at Ernesto.

"You know; you wops think you own this fucking city. Well, your time is coming and you're going to get what you deserve."

"Fuck you, you half dick Hymie motherfucker! You fucking Jew kikes need to know your role before shit gets ugly!" Ernesto screamed.

"Ugly? Oh, it gets no uglier than this. Just so you know, we were going to just rob you, but since you have such a huge fucking guinea mouth, then I might as well deliver this message from Abe Bernstien for your wop grandpa!" Jacob leveled his pistol toward Ernesto's chest.

"Yeah, and what is that?"

"Tell him Abe said..." There were no words that followed, only the numbing crackle of his pistol firing. Julius watched in dazed horror as his friend's body slumped to the rain slickened pavement. Ernesto's blood mixed with the dirty rain water and came to rest in the gutter line just a few feet in front of them. Julius looked at the boys, then to his friend and back to the boys again.

"Something on your mind boy?" Jacob spat.

"Nah, you got it. You made your point man. Let me get him some help!"

"Made my point? My point ain't made until you're lying in the gutter next to your boyfriend!" Jacob spat, as he leveled his gun once again.

Julius closed his eyes and said a silent prayer. *Lord, not like this. Not like a dog in an alley amongst the rats and roaches.*

"We can't kill him Jacob. Who's gonna tell Galici so that it gets back to Bernstien? This is the only way for us to make our bones and get the bounty. We'll save this monkey for another day. Let's go!" Selwin said.

Julius opened his eyes to see the pair of boys racing away from him down the alley. He kneeled next to Ernesto and heard his shallow breath clinging to the last little bit of life that he had left. "Ernie, Ernie, can you hear me?" Julius asked.

Silence.

"Ernesto!"

Silence.

"Ernie, please bro! You can't die man. You said you'd make me a made man!" Julius pleaded.

There was silence and then a throaty groan from somewhere deep within his recesses, giving voice to his will to live.

"Hooooooome," he muttered softly.

Julius struggled against Ernesto's dead weight, dragging him to his feet as he limped his way two blocks to Galici's Bakery. He labored to take his friend home, leaving a distorted trail of blood that had been diluted by the persistent beat of raindrops. As Julius got closer to the bakery, his sense of dread grew stronger. What if they somehow believed that he was responsible? What if they got angry because it was their beloved Ernesto and not him? What would become of him and his brothers? Truth of the matter was, Julius was angry. Ernesto had been the only friend that he had made that was close to his age. How dare they kill his friend and not so much as leave him with a scratch. Not to mention they had left him with the entire $400 in policy money that he held for Mr. Galici. With Julius' anger came a newfound vigor, a second wind of sorts, so when he burst into Galici's Bakery, he appeared far braver than he actually was. Now, by all accounts, Julius Gage was terrified. He crashed through the door and collapsed on the floor with Ernesto.

"Oh my God!" Gina screamed. The deafening, ear piercing shriek that followed was maddening. A deliberate bout of pandemonium ensued as patrons gathered around, trying to make sense of what it was that they were witnessing. "Daddy, daddy, come quick!" Gina screamed.

"What's all the commotion about and what's everyone looking at?" Jimmy Galici asked as he came from the back room of the bakery.

"It's Ernie and Julius daddy!"

Julius caught his breath and sat up. He tried his best to shield Ernesto's body from the growing number of spectators.

"Julius, what happened? Wait, don't answer that. Everybody out *NOW*!" Jimmy Galici's voice boomed.

One by one, people vacated the small bakery, but they only went as far as the front stoop, still peering in through the large plate glass window. All that remained inside though were Jimmy's closest friends and Ernesto's parents. Jimmy Galici turned to Julius. "Okay son, spill it and don't leave out any details."

Julius recounted for Mr. Galici how Ernesto had accompanied him on his policy runs. He explained to him how Ernesto had insisted that they take the alleyways even after Julius had warned against it and how Ernesto had wanted to make it home in time for the new season of the Lone Ranger.

"This was supposed to be a message for you!" Julius said hesitantly.

"A message for me? A message for me from who?"

"The skinny kid Jacob said from someone named Abe Bernstein!"

"Bernstein? That Jew bastard is responsible for this? Would you know these kids if you saw them again Julius?" Jimmy Galici asked.

"Yessuh, that was our second time seeing them, so I'll definitely recognize them."

"Second time? Where was the first?" Galici asked.

"We saw them during our run to Dilbeck's Cleaners."

Jimmy Galici didn't try to conceal his tears as he helped young Julius to his feet.

"I'm sorry that you had to witness that and I know that you two were very close."

"He was like my brother Mr. Galici. It's not fair. He said we'd be brothers forever. He said that when he took over, he'd make me the first black man to ever be a made man," Julius told him between sobs.

Jimmy Galici put his arm around Julius and pulled him close. He turned to his friends and nodded. "I loss a grandson today, but by God's grace I've gained four more. Julius, I may not be able to keep Ernesto's promise of making you a made man, but I will do my best to get you as close as I possibly can!" Jimmy said, then added, "I want the people responsible for this dead! I've got $20,000 for anyone who can get Bernstein and $10,000 a head for the two kids that he had do his dirty work!"

CHAPTER 22

For weeks after Ernesto's death Gina had barely left her room. Her grief was so strong that she was hardly eating, and she wouldn't talk to Albert, or her father. She'd essentially barricaded herself in her room, only leaving to take the occasional shower, or relieve herself. It wasn't until the third week that progress was made with a simple gesture from the most unlikely source. Gina lay across her bed sobbing softly as she looked through Ernesto's baby pictures. She wiped her tear streaked face in an attempt to hide her pain as a light tap on her door pulled her from her reminiscing.

"Who is it?" She called out.

"It's us Miss Gina," Julius replied.

"Come in boys."

The four Gage boys walked into Gina's room and stood near the door. Well, all of them, except Charlie Boy. He walked over to her bed, climbed up next to her and took her face in his hands. "Mama Gina, I'm sorry Ernie is gone," he said.

"I know baby. It's hard being without him, but I'm trying not to question God's will. You boys are so sweet. Ernie was lucky to have you all as friends. I used to worry about him, because he didn't have many friends, but since you boys came into the picture, he was the happiest I had ever seen him in a long while."

"Miss Gina can I ask you a question?" Julius asked.

"Sure honey."

"Do you want those boys to pay for what they did to Ernesto?" He asked.

Gina sat and thought for a long while. She wasn't exactly sure why Julius was asking her that particular question, but she answered honestly. "You know Julius; I don't really know. As a good Catholic I would have to say no, but as a mother I would have to say hell yes. I want the assholes that did this to my baby! I want their heads on a silver platter Julius!"

"Say no more." Julius said. He crossed the room and kissed Gina on her cheek softly.

*****

Julius searched for weeks to find the boys who were responsible for Ernie's death. It was on a particularly cold and dreary Tuesday four days before Christmas when Julius saw them. He'd taken Eugene and Otha Lee to Woolworth's to buy Charlie Boy, Gina and Mr. Galici's Christmas presents. The trio didn't have very much money, but they wanted to show their appreciation for all that they had done for them. As they passed the front of Woolworth's in route to the back door where blacks entered, Julius spotted Jacob and Selwin. They were at the lunch counter of the department store having lunch, flaunting money, probably money that they had made for Ernesto's murder. They were nicely dressed and the girls inside of the soda shop were fawning all over them. Julius grabbed Eugene and Otha Lee and slid into the alley near the entrance.

"Those boys in there flashing all that money are the boys that killed Ernesto," Julius explained.

"We need to go tell Mr. Galici where they are!" Eugene offered.

"We don't need to tell Mr. Galici shit! We need to handle this shit, so he knows that we can earn our keep," Julius said.

"Man, those cats are bigger than us. I'm with Eugene on this. We need to go and tell!" Otha Lee said.

"Fuck that! Y'all little niggas wasn't there. Ernesto didn't die in y'all arms. He died in mine. I'm not letting this shit go. We owe it to Miss Gina. She makes sure we eat, bathe, and dress nice, right?" Julius asked.

"Yeah," both boys agreed.

"Okay then. This is for her. Eugene, I want you to go inside and say some fucked up shit about Jew girls. Since they are spending money, they'll try to be big men and defend them. When they come at you run and let them chase you. Me and Otha Lee will be waiting."

"What if more than those two chase me?" Eugene asked skeptically.

"They'll be the only two. The other two boys in there are younger, so they won't give chase and the grown man behind the counter won't leave his store to chase after a kid. Just trust me and fucking do it before they leave."

Reluctantly, Eugene made his way to the front door of the soda shop while his brothers looked on from the alley. He looked back at them one last time before he disappeared inside.

"Come on Otha Lee. Look for anything that we can use for weapons," Julius ordered. They both scrounged around the alley until they found make shift weapons. Julius found a piece of pipe and Otha Lee found what appeared to be an old handle from a mop bucket. Meanwhile, Eugene stepped into the soda shop and took a seat at the counter. He turned his back to the owner and stared at the two Jewish boys. They continued their celebration until one of the girls noticed Eugene staring. She whispered to the girl next to her, who in turn whispered to the girl sitting beside her, until finally it garnered the attention of Jacob and Selwin.

"Can I help you with something monkey boy?" Jacob asked.

"Nope, I'm just tryna figure out what these dumb Jew bitches see in you wannabe's!" He said, moving toward the front door.

"What the fuck did you say boy?" Selwin asked.

"I said, you honkies are a couple of wannabe gangsters who probably fuck each other in the ass while you're daydreaming about these dizzy bitches!" Eugene teased.

"I'm gonna rip your heart out and feed it to you!"

"Like you did Ernesto, you piece of shit!!!" Eugene yelled as he bolted toward the door.

Like clockwork the two boys chased him into the alley where they were met in the dark blistering cold by the Gage brother's makeshift weapons. Julius' pipe connected with a dull thwack across the knees of Jacob Bloomberg, sending him sprawling onto the asphalt palms first. Simultaneously, Otha Lee let his tubular piece of old mop bucket connect with Selwin Bloomberg's runny, red nose. He dropped to his knees, holding his bloody nose, trying to see who had assaulted him through blurred vision.

"This is the beginning of the rest of what's left of your miserable lives Jew boys!" Julius spat.

"What the fuck do you want? Do you know who the fuck we are?" Selwin screamed, bloody spittle dripping with every word.

"You coons will be dead before daybreak for what you've done!" Jacob added.

"You don't remember me do you Jew boy?" Julius asked, walking up and standing over Jacob.

Jacob attempted to reach into his waistband to remove his pistol with his skinned up hands, but Julius saw it coming. Before Jacob knew what hit him, Julius let the pipe crash down with such force that it crushed Jacob's entire hand, spewing blood from the fingertips. "Ughhhh, what the fuck?!" Jacob moaned.

"Do I have your attention now?" Julius barked, then added, "Eugene take that gun!"

Eugene stood frozen for a moment, unable to move, surprised and mortified by his brother's show of brutality. Finally, Eugene picked up the pistol, but his hand wouldn't stop shaking. "What do you want me to do with it?" Eugene asked.

"Aim it at chubby over there holding his nose and if he moves, pull the trigger. Matter of fact, why don't we all just slide a little further into the alley?"

"You heard him fat boy move!" Otha Lee hissed.

The five young men moved deeper into the dark alley until there was only the moon above to give light. There were no windows and no doors. It was only them and the nocturnal creatures that went bump in the night, sandwiched between two seemingly endless towers of brick.

In the darkness, holding the pistol, Eugene felt powerful, like the world was his for the taking. He stroked it gently and stared at it lovingly.

"Otha Lee, go find me something sharp, *real* sharp. Eugene! Snap out of it. Here take this money and go get me some of them thick, black trash bags folks use to pick up leaves with and get some ribbon," Julius ordered with a devious smirk. He handed Eugene two crumpled up one dollar bills and took the gun that he was holding.

"Now that my little brothers are out of the way I'ma ask y'all again. Do you two remember me? Come on now, don't both of y'all answer at once. Who am I goddamnit?!"

"I don't knooooow, mister please, let us go. I really have to use the bathroom!" Selwin whimpered.

155

"Oh, I'm mister now? I guess there really is power at the end of a gun huh? Well fuck you! Piss on yourself," Julius taunted him.

"Listen, let's make a deal. Let us go and I'm sure my boss will look favorably upon you. Maybe put a few dollars in your pocket," Jacob said condescendingly.

"Wait, I know you don't think this is about money? No, nooooo, no, no, no, this is about Ernesto, remember him?"

"Who the fuck is Ernesto?" Jacob asked.

"See, that's why I'm killing you first, because you're stupid and disrespectful. Ernesto was Jimmy Galici's grandson!" Julius said.

Terror and recognition registered on both of the young Jewish boys' faces.

"Yeah, that's right. Jimmy Galici. Remember all of that shit you two talked in that alley? You bastards should have killed me when you had the chance," Julius hissed.

Otha Lee walked toward Julius, slowly carrying a piece of rusty metal. It looked like it had perhaps been used to board the window of an abandoned building. It rippled and warbled as Otha Lee carried it and a wide smile of satisfaction spread across Julius' face.

"I guess we can get this party started now," Julius said. He slapped the kid known as Jacob across the bridge of his nose and blood leapt from the open wound. He lay splayed out, afraid to move for fear that the black boy might strike him again. Julius did strike him again. He struck Jacob until he was unconscious. Julius took the metal from Otha Lee and with all of his might, brought the sharp shard of metal down across Jacob's neck, severing it from the rest of his body. A yelp of shock and dread escaped Selwin's lips as his bladder gave way and warm, yellow urine soaked his slacks.

"P-p-p-please mister. I swear I didn't want to kill that kid. Remember? I'm the one that told Jacob to let you go. You don't have to kill me, I'm sorry, p-p-p-please I don't want to die," Selwin pleaded, rocking back and forth.

"It's too late to beg now potna," Julius said moving toward the boy.

Selwin began to scream, "Help, someone help me, please! Anybody help! Please help!" He screamed.

"Shut the fuck up!" Otha Lee demanded, but Selwin continued to scream, until Julius walked up and put a bullet in the center of his forehead. Bone fragments and brain matter flew from the back of his skull, sliding across the slick asphalt behind him as his body slumped over.

"Otha Lee, cut his mothafuckin' head off." Julius ordered.

Eugene entered the alley trotting toward the four teens. "What ha---?" He started, but swallowed his words upon seeing the macabre scene before him. "We gotta hurry up Julius, people starting to leave the stores," Eugene said.

"Look at this shit Julius. This muhfucka's eyes still open looking all scared," Otha Lee said, holding Selwin's severed head up to his own, mimicking the terrified look on the boy's face.

"Uh huh, put them heads in two separate garbage bags and tie some ribbon around them," Julius said.

He dragged both of the boy's bodies to the side of a cluster of nearby trash cans while Otha Lee and Eugene made quick work of their gift wrap job. As they all made the trek back to Galici's Bakery each boy was lost in his own thoughts. Julius silently rehearsed what he would say to present their gift to Jimmy Galici, while Otha Lee and Eugene, had a different thought running through their minds. Julius killed way too easily and it scared them. When he'd killed their father, he'd been emotionless and now it was the exact same thing with the murder of these two boys. Julius didn't mind killing and his brothers could see it written all over his face.

......

Julius and his brothers stood across the street beneath the street lights until they saw the last paying patron leave Galici's Bakery. They crossed the street hurriedly and slipped in through the front door. "Where have you boys been Julius? Charlie and I were worried sick," Gina scolded them softly.

"We really wanted to get you and Mr. Galici something special for Christmas, so it took a while," Julius said.

"That was awful nice of you boys Julius, but you didn't have to spend your money on us," Jimmy Galici said.

"Oh, it didn't cost us any money!" Eugene said proudly.

"No money? What is it?" Gina said.

Julius moved toward Gina and hugged her tightly, then turned toward Jimmy Galici. "Ernie meant as much to me as my own brothers do and he deserved to live as long as anybody else. Mama Gina, you said you wanted their heads on a silver platter, but I thought gift wrapping them would be better since it *is* Christmas and all!" Julius said. He snatched the first bag from Eugene, ripped it open and let Jacob's severed head fall to the floor. Jimmy Galici jumped back to escape the splatter of blood. The blood drained from Gina's face completely as Julius dumped the contents of the second bag onto the floor. Selwin's head rolled and came to rest at the base of a table, staring up at Gina. Julius grabbed Jacob's head by the hair and grabbed Selwin's head by sticking his index finger into the bullet hole in his forehead. He lifted them and held them out in front of him. "These are the bastards that killed your son, your grandson and my brother! I guess it's safe to say that they can cancel Christmas!" Julius said. His laughter bellowed throughout the empty diner.

Years later Jimmy Galici would tell some of his closest associates that the day Julius Gage avenged his grandson's death was the happiest day of his life, but he thought he might die of fear, because he had never met a boy with so much bottled up hatred. He said looking into Julius Gage's eyes was like staring at the devil himself.

CHAPTER 23

At nearly seventeen years old Charles Boyd Gage had grown into an impressive figure. He was the talk of his high school, not only because his older brothers dropped him off every morning in a brand new black Lincoln Continental, but because there were rumors that he'd been adopted by the Galici outfit. That statement was partially true because he was Mama Gina's son in every sense of the word, but Jimmy Galici and his brothers made sure that he went nowhere near crime. He dressed the part though, preferring to don either black, or charcoal grey on most days. While the world was transitioning from pinstriped suits and fedora hats to jeans, tee shirts and penny loafers, the Gage boys were fully immersed in the fashion of the Italian mobsters. As Jimmy Galici had told them on more than one occasion, "Your attire should be your calling card boys. A suit and tie says that you come for business and a watch says that you don't have time for bullshit, because you have somewhere to be. A nice pair of shoes can be the deciding factor between a warning and a busted head. When the police see you sharply dressed they know that you're connected, capisce?"

All four of them had taken the advice wholeheartedly and they lived by that code.

Charlie Boy stood outside of the school waiting for Julius to pull up, watching a group of girls as they passed in their poodle skirts and bobby socks. "Heyyyyyy Charlie Boy!" They all sang as they passed.

"Hello ladies, how y'all doing?"

"I'd be even better if you asked me to the dance next Friday," one of the girls said.

"Yeah, that would be nice, if I was going."

"Awwww, you're not going to the dance Charlie Boy?"

"Nah, previous engagement sweetheart, sorry," he said.

"Well, if you change your mind, give me a call." She stopped, pulled out an ink pen and wrote her phone number on Charlie Boy's hand. He watched them as they sashayed away giggling to one another. A group of boys, who probably considered themselves rebels, stood nearby watching Charlie Boy as if they had a problem with him. "Aye nigga don't let me catch you talking to my old lady again," one kid said.

Charlie Boy looked around and then back at the kid, "Who you talking to playa?"

"He talking to you ol' black ass nigga!" Another kid offered.

The group of boys made their way toward Charlie Boy and formed a circle around him. "I know you ain't deaf nigga. You need to stay the fuck away from Andrea, or you're gonna hafta deal with all of us!"

"Damn all y'all fucking the same bitch? I thought she was your whore? Now you're telling me I gotta deal with all you niggas? What? He fuck on Monday, you fuck on Tuesday, the little fat nigga fuck on Wednesday? How does it work?" Charlie Boy asked.

One of the boys shoved Charlie Boy hard across the circle where he was met with another hard push back in the direction he'd come from.

"Charlie Boy, how long you gonna play with your little friends, man? We got business to attend to," Eugene said, pointing a double barrel shotgun at one of the boys.

"Aw man, I was just about to take my turn Eugene man. Check it out!" Charlie Boy said, as he punched the talkative kid in the throat. The bully dropped to his knees holding his throat, trying desperately to hold back his tears. Otha Lee sat on the hood of the car with a pistol in his hand and a wide smile spread across his face, while Julius sat behind the wheel of the Continental staring at the bullies menacingly. Otha Lee opened the suicide doors of the Lincoln and let Charlie Boy and Eugene climb inside. He slid into the passenger's seat and slammed the door. "Damn nigga you ain't gotta slam my shit like that. This ain't no Chevy nigga. This is a Lincoln," Julius scoffed.

"Man, ain't nobody gonna fuck up your little Lincoln. Sometimes I think you love this damn car more than you love us nigga." Otha Lee laughed.

"Yeah man. This nigga acts like this car is his bitch or something!" Eugene chimed in, laughing.

"Go ahead chuckle it up. What you got to say Charlie Boy?" Julius asked.

"Not shit bruh. I actually agree with you. These cats be jumping in the car slamming shit like cave men," Charlie boy said.

Julius didn't respond, but the smirk on his face said it all. He and Charlie Boy had a special type of relationship. Eugene and Otha Lee swore that he showed favoritism toward their younger brother, but it was deeper than that. He was the oldest and Charlie Boy was the youngest. There was something magical about knowing that he had been their mother's first child and that Charlie Boy had been the last. Charlie Boy looked up to Julius and Julius in turn felt very protective over his baby brother. Julius looked in the rearview mirror and stared lovingly at his little brother. Charlie Boy was a good kid; more than any brother could ever hope for and he was proud to know him. "Fuck you looking at man? Looking at me like I just won the Olympics and shit," Charlie Boy said.

"Whatever little nigga. Seriously, I need all you cats to put on your game faces. We are on our way to a meeting with Mr. Galici and his squad so we need to be on point," Julius said sternly.

"A meeting? What kind of meeting?" Eugene asked.

"I don't know, but whatever it is, he says that it's urgent and private." Julius shrugged.

"The bakery is the other way bro," Otha Lee said.

Julius continued to drive. He was used to Otha Lee's incessant passenger seat driving, so he found it best to ignore him. He drove until they reached their destination. It was a two story brick house in the Birmingham suburb of Detroit and was more of a mansion than a house. Julius began to sweat with anticipation. Mr. Galici had never summoned them outside of the bakery, so Julius was somewhat worried. The only saving grace that gave Julius some sort of comfort was the fact that Mr. Galici had sounded very chipper and in an upbeat mood.

"Man, these muhfuckas are paid bro. This is what I'm talking about. I would have never guessed that Detroit had money like this!" Eugene said excitedly.

"You thought the whole city was broke like us?" Charlie Boy joked.

"Nigga, I ain't broke! I got a fist full of cash!" Eugene snorted.

"Yeah, a fist full of cash is still broke compared to how these muhfuckas living."

"Alright, alright, calm ya nerves. Don't never get excited about the next nigga pockets, unless you're getting part of the pot ya dig? We're about to go in here and tend to this business and I don't need you niggas looking like tourists and shit," Julius snapped.

*****

"Julius, I'm sure that you're wondering why I called you boys here today," Jimmy Galici said.

"Yeah Mr. G, it crossed my mind."

"You and your brothers have been loyal soldiers in our organization and we're forever grateful. Over the years you boys have grown into amazing young men and I for one am very proud. Please have a seat," he instructed.

They all sat around a long table surrounded by at least thirteen men. Julius' favorite amongst them all was Carlo DeLuna akaTuffy. For whatever reason, he had taken a liking to Julius also and he often stopped by the bakery to pick the young black boy up just to ride and talk.

"Now, Julius, my grandson Ernie was very fond of you and over the years we've all come to realize why. From early on he sensed your loyalty and commitment to this family, so much so that he promised to make you a made man when he took over. I can't honor that promise, but what I can do is make you untouchable in Detroit, Chicago, St. Louis and Milwaukee. I've been watching you all and I've had some special gifts hand crafted for you boys," Jimmy Galici said as a maid placed boxes in front of Julius, Otha Lee and Eugene. The look of disappointment written across Charlie Boy's face wasn't lost on Jimmy Galici as he tried to figure out why there was no box placed in front of him. Eugene was the first to open his box. In it was a gold plated 12 gauge sawed off shotgun with a pistol grip. His name was engraved on it in onyx threading and the grips were fitted with gold indentations molded to Eugene's hands. Upon seeing Eugene's extravagant gift, Otha Lee ripped the wrapping from his box. The box itself was made of mahogany wood with raised golden lettering that read: *OLG these will be the twin pillars of your being on which your fortune will be built. With them you will have your pie one slice at a time!* Otha Lee opened the box to reveal four knives. Two of them were switchblades and two of them were throwing blades. They lay across a ruby red sheet of satin that hugged them and held them in place. The blades shimmered brightly on the throwing knives, contrasting perfectly with their red marble handles. The switchblade bodies were black marble and when Otha Lee removed them from their housing and popped the blades, he was astonished to see polished pewter blades. Julius was last to open his present. His was also in a box, but it was an embroidered box of polished ivory with onyx highlights. On the front was a gold tag that had Julius Gage emblazoned on it. Before opening the box, he read the card attached.

Julius,

I never knew your mother or father, but from what you've shared with me I'm sure your mother is very proud of you. I'm proud to have you in my circle and count you among my friends. Today the real work begins.

J.G.

Julius closed the card and opened the box. Inside were two chrome .45 caliber pistols with pearl handles. The barrels had intricately etched details that seemed to chronicle his life. In one scene a small boy kneeled over a woman's

body. In another scene it showed the boy with his feet
wading in the waters of a bubbling brook. Julius felt tears of
sentimentality building in his eyes and he sniffed violently to
thwart the approaching tears.

"Thank you Mr. G on behalf of me and my brothers,"
Julius said.

"No need for thanks Julius. These are tools of the
trade, *your* trade."

"I don't understand."

"You will son. You will," Jimmy Galici said.

Tuffy stood and addressed Julius and his brothers
directly. "Boys, it's no secret what my role is in this
organization. I'm an enforcer and I'm extremely good at
what I do. Eugene do you know what an enforcer is?" Tuffy
asked.

"Yessuh, you get paid to fuck people up."

"Yeah, something like that, but it's deeper than just
fucking people up as you put it. I inspire fear and respect. I
also take care of problems. That's where you boys come in.
We are already feared and we already have respect, but some
of our friends still have problems that need to be taken care
of. I'm not getting any younger, so I want to pass the
problem solving portion of the business on to you," Tuffy
explained. He reached in a bag and retrieved a manila folder
and three thick white envelopes. Tuffy tossed the white
envelopes to Eugene, Otha Lee and Julius. "There's $10,000
in each of these envelopes and it's all yours, but you have to
earn it." He said.

"What we gotta do?" Eugene asked suspiciously.

Inside the manila envelope were three pictures with index cards attached. Tuffy picked up the first photo and held it up for the boys to see. "This is Father Joel McKellen and this piece of shit likes little boys," Tuffy explained. He also told them how the very prominent Catholic Church that he belonged to kept him protected. He also explained how one of those boys had been Sammy Bags' grandson and Sammy wanted the unsuspecting priest dead.

The next picture that Tuffy held up was of Anthony Pagliani. He was an abuser of women and children. He beat his wife and children mostly when he lost at gambling, when the wind blew, when the sun rose, or because he woke up.

The last face and name was Roman Guthrie. A face that Eugene swore to himself that he'd never forget. His eyes lit up, because he hadn't forgotten the man's disrespect years earlier and he was eager to repay him.

"I got this one right here! This is the one I want. He's mine!" Eugene blurted out in anxiousness.

"Really? How many soldiers does he have guarding him? Where does he hang out? What's his favorite food? What's his weakness? Does he have kids? Is he connected? When is the last time he had some pussy? Shit, does he even like pussy?" Tuffy wondered.

"How the fuck am I supposed to know?" Eugene snorted.

"Because it's your job to know! It's more complex than looking at a picture and doing the hit. An assassin has to be quiet, nearly stealth. Sometimes you can destroy a man with more than a bullet and I'm going to teach you."

Julius stood, reached across the table and grabbed Anthony Pagliani's picture, "I want the woman beater!" Julius said.

"Do you want him because he reminds you of your asshole father?" Tuffy asked.

"Yep."

"Wrong reason son. The only reason should be, because it's a job. When you're on the job you check your emotions at the door. A good killer knows that there is no room for emotions. Got kids? Doesn't matter, fuck 'em! Family that loves them? Doesn't matter, fuck 'em! Mother just died? Doesn't matter, fuck 'em! You have to become emotionally unattached from the subject. Your only concern is fulfilling the contract. On these index cards are the names, addresses and information that you'll need to complete your tasks. I don't want street murderers. I want dedicated and committed hitmen. There are many weapons to use, but your mind is your most lethal weapon. Next most lethal is your hands and feet. I'm going to go to my grave teaching you boys the discipline necessary to become what this organization needs," Tuffy said. He coughed violently, reached into his jacket pocket, pulled out a handkerchief and coughed a large clod of blood into it.

"Tuffy will train you boys on the finer aspects of assassination and I will teach you boys proper gangster etiquette. I'm going to treat you guys to some of the finest suits Italy has to offer. I have a tailor downtown named Guiseppe Salvatore from the old country. His suits fit so well, you'll think that you're naked. Otha Lee, Eugene and

169

Julius' faces all lit up with excitement, but Charlie Boy's features remained somber.

"Charles, you'll ride with me. I want to talk to you," Jimmy Galici said.

*****

The ride downtown was long and nightfall had blanketed the city. Charlie Boy stared out of the window quietly brooding over what he perceived to be a slight by the old mobsters. Mr. Galici put his hand on Charlie's shoulder to pull him from his daydream.

"I can read your mind son, just know that there is a method to my madness."

Charlie Boy never turned to face Mr. Galici, "You can read my mind huh? What am I thinking?" He asked.

"You feel disrespected and left out. You feel like Julius and the fellas were shown favoritism over you, right?"

"Yeah, something like that," Charlie Boy admitted, as he watched the city lights zip by in a blurred haze.

"Truth of the matter is; you have more education than your brothers. Plus, you're the smartest of them all. I don't want to ruin you Charles. You're bound for greatness if you want it."

"I want to be great with my brothers. I ain't built to be no school boy lame. I hate school and I only go so I don't disappoint Mama Gina. Why is the life good enough for my brothers, but not for me?" Charlie Boy asked.

"That's not it. Gina loves you Charlie Boy and if she finds out that you're in the life, she'd probably never speak to me again."

"Why? You were going to let Ernie join with no hesitation," Charlie Boy reasoned.

"You're right, but you're very special to Gina. I'm not saying that Ernesto isn't special. I'm just saying that Gina sees something special in you, and she has high hopes for you Charlie."

"All of that is fine and dandy Mr. G and Lord knows I'm thankful for everything, so don't take this like I'm ungrateful. Any two ways about it, if I'm off playin' Joe College and something happens to one of my brothers, I'd never forgive myself. Loyalty before royalty, you know?" Charlie Boy said.

"I can respect that son, and ultimately it's your choice."

"Good, so if it's my choice, then I choose my brothers. If they kill, I kill," Charlie Boy finally made eye contact with the old man. Jimmy Galici eased his Thunderbird up to the curb and parked near Salvatore's Haberdashery. As Charlie Boy met up with his brothers to tell them that he was joining them, Jimmy Galici met with Tuffy to give him the same news. The Gage boys stood talking, all of them that is, except Eugene. His attention had been drawn to a lone figure sitting near the entrance of the tailor's shop.

"Damn, that nigga looks familiar man," Eugene said.

"Who?"

"That yella nigga sitting by the front door begging. That muhfucka look just like daddy man," Eugene said nervously.

"Well, we know it ain't him because that bitch ass nigga ain't nothing but dust and bones now," Julius huffed.

"Nah, for real man. Look at him," Eugene said.

Julius looked at the man closely, very closely. "Y'all come on," Julius said as he approached the man. "Say, look out playa. What you doing out here?" He asked.

"Aw man, just tryna come up on a little bread to come up on my medicine man. You got a little spare change?" The man asked.

"You tell me what I want and I'll give you a little change, cool?" Julius asked.

"Cool, baby cool. Ask whatever you want my man."

"What type of medicine you on?" Julius asked.

The man began to squirm, shifting in the make shift seat that he'd created on the concrete. "Can I stand up man? You cats are making me nervous baby," he said, stumbling to his feet. He shuffled from side to side, patting his pockets as if looking for something. Julius' heart raced. The young man's resemblance to their father was astonishing to say the least. The man reached into his pocket, pulled out a crumpled cigarette and lit it. He inhaled deeply and blew thick white smoke into the air.

"Shit man. I just needs me a little taste of boy man," he said.

"A taste of boy? Nigga you on heroin?" Eugene asked.

"Heyyyyy, cool out baby. This other cat is the one s'posed to be assin' the questions jack!" He said.

"You're right. Forgive my little brother. What did you say your name was?" Julius asked.

"I didn't say what my name was, but if you must know everybody calls me OG," he stated proudly.

"You look really familiar man. Like somebody we know," Otha Lee said.

"Yeah baby, so I've been told. I guess I got me one of them kinda faces."

"What's your real name slim?" Julius asked.

"You assin' questions like you the police man. Let me get a few dollars to take this edge off playa."

"You gonna get your money man. Just answer my question. Now, what's your name man?" Julius asked.

"Gottttttdamn man, my name Otis man, Otis Gage. That's why they call me OG. Come on now baby. I'm hurting man," Otis begged.

Julius and his brothers all stared at one another. They had searched for him the entire time that they'd been in Detroit with no luck. Maybe calling him Otis hadn't been the wisest, because half the black men in Detroit were southern and a name like Otis wasn't uncommon.

"You from Arkansas slick? You got four little brothers back home?" Julius asked.

"Yeahhhhhh man, I left a long time ago though. Our daddy is a mean bastard man. I left and never looked back," Otis said, with a faraway look in his eyes. He took a long drag from his bent cigarette.

"What happened to your little brothers?" Julius asked.

"I don't know man. We lost contact. Shit they had they mama there to take care of them man. My little brothers, hmmpf, damn. I bet them little niggas prolly got they own farms and shit by now!" He said reflectively.

Julius pulled a piece of paper from his pocket and scribbled his phone number on it. He also removed a $20 bill from his pocket. "What if I told you I'm your brother Julius? This here is Otha Lee, Eugene and Charlie Boy," Julius told him.

Otis searched his eyes for the joke, but how else would this man, this stranger, know his brothers' names. Otis moved in closer to get a better look. Julius cringed from the sheer funk of his presence. It was a smell that stung the inside of his nose, but he was his brother.

"Julius can you wrap it up? We need to get inside," Jimmy Galici said, as he walked up to the young men.

"Well, I be gotdamn. It is you man! You look just like Mama Gertrude man. All y'all do!" Otis said.

"Look O, man we gotta get inside, but call me man. Here's my number and a few dollars. Call me man. Damn, I'm glad we found you slick!" Julius said. He ushered his younger brothers into the haberdashery. Stopping at the door before going in, he gave his big brother one last look before disappearing inside to enter the world of assassinations and tailor made suits.

CHAPTER 24

Tuffy had started the Gage boys on a daily regimen that he hoped would give them the discipline that they needed to become effective and efficient enforcers for the organization. They were awakened every morning at 5 am and made to run at least five miles on an empty stomach. At 9 am they were taken to the gun range on Tuffy's property and trained in the art of precision shooting. At noon they were allowed to take a half hour lunch, but by 12:30 pm they were back to work. Next they were required to do hand to hand combat in yet another one of the buildings on Tuffy's estate. Their last daily task was to study blue prints of buildings, safes and security systems. On Saturdays they were required to learn bomb making, both big and small. Tuffy had broken the boys into two teams, Julius and Charlie Boy and Eugene and Otha Lee. Tuffy wanted to play on each boys' individual strengths, but Otha Lee and Eugene seemed to feed off of one another. They took to the entire lesson wholeheartedly, while Julius and Charlie Boy seemed to be more concerned with guns. Eugene, more so than anyone, was Tuffy's favorite. He was an exceptional pupil and his attention to detail was impeccable. The weather was brisk and while the other brothers were busy with a bomb building exercise Tuffy seized the opportunity to speak with Eugene.

"Take a walk with me Eugene?" Tuffy asked.

"Yeah, what's up Tuffy?"

"You've really shown me a lot over the past couple of months and I just want to tell you I'm proud of you," he praised him.

"Thanks man. I really like this shit. I mean I've finally found something that I'm good at."

"You're damn good, I'll say that. Now all you have to do is earn that $10,000 that you've been pinching off of. Keep in mind, the faster you fulfill one contract, the faster you can get on to the next one."

"Yeah, I know. I'm going to get the cocksucker tomorrow," Eugene sneered.

"Have your brothers devised any plans of their own?"

"I don't know, but I've been stalking this muhfucka for weeks and I know just how to get him," Eugene said.

"Yeah? And how is that?"

"Just watch the news tomorrow. That's all I'ma tell you," Eugene said.

*****

Roman Guthrie walked out of his house into the frigid Detroit morning in route to the Little Rock Missionary Baptist Church. His routine hadn't changed much over the years. He did dirt throughout the week and attended church on Sundays. Somehow Roman Guthrie thought that by going to church on Sundays, it wiped all of his sins away. After church he always went to the same soul food restaurant on the west side. That soul food restaurant was owned by an elderly couple that happened to hate Roman Guthrie's guts. He'd polluted their neighborhood with drugs for years and their only son Melvin had overdosed on the poison that he pushed. They were more than willing to listen to Eugene and supply him with details about Roman Guthrie's actions, especially his comings and goings. Eugene was honest with them about the fact that they shared a common hatred for the man. If there was one thing that Tuffy had taught him that stuck in his head was, *a dead man was a silent man, keep your business to yourself and you'd keep the police out of your business*. Those words resounded loudly in Eugene's young head and for that reason his intent to murder Roman Guthrie was never revealed to the elderly couple.

Eugene watched as Roman walked into Little Rock Missionary Baptist Church accompanied only by his most trusted whore. She was a spritely thing, rather on the ugly side, but Eugene guessed she must have been extremely loyal. She was a nonfactor as far as Eugene Gage was concerned. He sat in the church parking lot for hours waiting, anticipating the moment when he could eliminate his prey, but he needed him alone. Roman Guthrie was a creature of habit and getting him alone would be easier than Eugene thought. You see, Roman would undoubtedly always walk across the street to the parking lot where he kept his

Buick Skylark parked. He'd leave his trollop waiting on the curb in front of the church like the short trek would somehow damage her delicate whore feet. That's when Eugene would make his move. He felt his adrenaline racing as the parishioners began to file out of the church. Tiny beads of sweat defied the freezing cold and ran down his face, freezing onto his chocolate cheeks as he exited the car. He kneeled next to his tire, pretending to loosen the lug nuts on his tire. Roman Guthrie approached his car and looked at Eugene suspiciously.

"Say, look out jack. You got a four-way lug wrench? This thing doesn't fit," Eugene lied.

"I might have one in my trunk. Hold on a second."

"I hope so sir, 'cause it's too cold to be stranded out here," Eugene said. He rubbed his gloved hands together quickly. Then he blew into his hands, giving the appearance of being much colder than he actually was. As Roman Guthrie leaned into his trunk to search for the four way wrench, Eugene removed the pistol from the inside pocket of his tweed trench coat. He shoved the gun deep into Roman Guthrie's ribs and hissed at the unsuspecting man. "Get your bitch ass in that trunk nigga!"

"What? Motherfucka if you know like I know, you better get that gun off me!"

"I ain't repeating myself again. Now get in that muhfuckin' trunk." Eugene sniffed.

Slowly Roman climbed into the trunk and stared menacingly up at Eugene. He searched the young boy's eyes for some sort of recognition, but he couldn't place the face.

178

"I guess right about now you're trying to place me huh? Trying to figure out where you know me from right?" Eugene asked.

"Man, I ain't never seen your little dumb ass befo' in my life! I got half a mind to climb out of this trunk, cut your motherfuckin' head off and glue it to my goddamn boot, so you can watch me kick yo' little young ass, nigga!"

Eugene sniggered at the man and spit in his face. "Shut your bitch ass up! That shit was poetic though playa. I'll give you that much, but unfortunately you won't get that chance. I will however, give you the benefit of letting you know who the fuck I am. Remember some years back when four boys came to your house who had been sent there by your niece?" Eugene asked.

He could tell that Roman was thinking. Eugene could almost see the tiny wheels turning inside of his head beneath his processed hair. "Let me save you the trouble of trying to guess. I was the one that told you that I wouldn't forget that you put your hands on me and do you remember what you said?" Eugene asked. Roman Guthrie shook his head frantically with terror written on his face as the recollection of the young man entered his mind.

"You said and I repeat: *I hear you little nigga. If I had a dollar for every time a son-of-a-bitch said he was gonna get me I could retire and stop selling smack. Now get the fuck outta my pad before I forget my Nettie sent you muthafuckas!* That's what you said, and seeing as I like the way you put your words together, I'm going to permanently retire your ass," Eugene said. He smiled his most sinister

179

smile as he emptied the clip of his 9mm luger into Roman Guthrie's body.

CHAPTER 25

Julius walked into Munchie's Bistro and looked around the crowded restaurant. Waitresses weaved their way through the throng of hungry patrons, dropping off homemade pastrami sandwiches and watered down coffee. Short order cooks screamed their orders and rang their bells, eager for the waitresses to return and deliver more of their unhealthy concoctions. Munchie's Bistro was more of a greasy spoon than anything else and Julius knew it well. He spotted his intended target sitting near the back door, enjoying his lunch of grilled cheese and onion soup. Julius took the empty seat across from Anthony Pagliani and raised his hand to get the waitress' attention.

"I'm sorry pal, but this seat is reserved." Anthony said.

"For who?"

"For my wife. What's it to you?" Anthony asked.

Julius didn't respond, but he did reach into the breast pocket of his black leather coat and removed a picture of a battered woman with half of her face bandaged. Her eye was black and blue and her nose appeared to be broken. Julius looked at the picture, then at Anthony and placed the picture face down on the table. He signaled to the waitress again, who promptly shuffled over to the table, "May I help you?"

"Yes you may. Let me have a slice of blackberry cobbler and a cup of coffee. You want a piece of pie Anthony?" Julius asked.

"How do you know my name?"

"I guess that's a no on his pie, but you can refill his coffee. So that's a slice of pie and two coffees and make that to go please." Julius handed the woman a $10 bill.

"How do you know my name?" Anthony asked again, raising his voice that time.

"Don't go causing a scene now. Keep calm and all of this will be over soon. I'm a good friend of your wife's," Julius informed him, flipping the picture over.

Anger flashed in Anthony's eyes. How did that man know his wife? The thing about controlling and abusive men was that they hated to think of someone else touching their women.

"Now that I have your attention, I need you to look outside. You see that black Lincoln sitting across the street? Your kids are in that car and if this conversation doesn't go well, the man inside that car is going to rape and sodomize them, do you understand?" Julius asked.

Slowly, Anthony Pagliani nodded.

"Good, now I know you got paid today, so leave the waitress a hefty tip and meet me in the breezeway next door. I'll leave first and you follow," Julius instructed. He stood and buttoned his jacket while keeping his eyes trained on Anthony.

"Leaving so soon?" The waitress asked.

"Yeah, it looks like there might be a storm brewing." Julius took his pie and coffee and stepped out into the cold. A light flurry had begun to fall, blanketing the street in front of the bistro. Julius stepped into the breezeway and removed his pistol. He shoved both of his hands deep into his pockets, careful to keep his finger on the trigger. Moments later, Anthony appeared in the breezeway with a short red headed man in tow. The ginger haired stranger pulled out a switch blade and leered at Julius, but they had made one fatal mistake. They had stepped into the breezeway and closed the door behind them, making their escape virtually impossible. Julius pulled out his pistol. "Have you ever heard the old saying, never bring a knife to a gun fight?" He quipped.

"Hey brother, I was just trying to help my friend. I don't want no trouble!" He pleaded.

Julius reached into his pocket and pulled out his silencer. He screwed it on while he addressed his victims. "Well trouble found you podna. That's why motherfucka's get killed, because they be in shit that don't concern them," Julius taunted him as he let a round go in the red head's chest. The short man slumped onto the floor gasping for air. "You walk," Julius said, motioning to the back of the breezeway. As they passed the red headed man, Julius let another round go in the top of his head, sending shards of brain fragments and blood blowing from his chin.

"You never told me how you know my Angie?" Anthony said over his shoulder.

"Mm mm mm, sweet little Angie. You know, I was going to hurt you the very first time I found out that you had hurt her. I was going to kill you, but she begged me not to. Well, I think that's what she was begging for. I can't really remember, because my dick was buried inside of her," Julius lied.

Just as he'd hoped, Julius watched as Anthony came to a halt and turned to face him. "I don't care about that gun moolee! Watch your black mouth about my sweet Angie!" Anthony barked.

"Every time I made love to her I made her forget about your bullshit for a little while!"

Julius saw that his lies were getting under Anthony's skin, so he pressed on with his taunts.

"Whenever she sucked my dick, she always hummed and told me how much she loved it, and how much bigger mine was than yours. She said that she was tired of laying with you and wanted to run away together, but you fucked up our plans," Julius said.

Slowly the tears began to roll down Anthony Pagliani's face. "You're lying. She wouldn't do that to me! She wouldn't cheat on me!" He cried.

"What you crying for? Were you crying when you were whooping her ass? That's why I don't care about your tears, because as soon as she's well enough we're leaving. And guess what? I'm going to snap your children's necks and throw them in Lake Michigan on our way to a new life!" Julius said.

Anthony opened his mouth to protest, but Julius shot him in the throat. Blood gushed from the wound as Anthony reached for something, anything to break his fall. He stumbled to the stairs and collapsed, staring at Julius in horror. Julius leaned down and whispered in Anthony Pagliani's ear, "It's a shame that you have to die knowing that your wife, your prized possession is gonna be gettin' dicked down by a nigga. The same nigga that killed you!" Julius said.

Anthony shook his head violently as if in protest, but he couldn't speak. His eyes bucked widely as Julius lifted his pistol once again, that time aiming for Anthony's eye socket. He pulled the trigger and watched as blood oozed out onto the cold floor beneath him.

Tuffy would undoubtedly scold him for toying with the man's emotions, but Julius refused to let the man die peacefully, no matter how violent. He wanted Anthony Pagliani to die feeling the pain and degradation that he had caused his wife to feel on so many occasions. He picked up the slice of blackberry pie and cup of coffee before heading out into the cold element of the Detroit winter. If he drove fast enough, he'd make it to Otis' house before the pie got soggy and the coffee got cold.

*****

Julius climbed inside of his Lincoln and sped toward Otis' flop house. He'd sent Anthony to hell believing that he would murder his children, but in reality with him out of the picture, Anthony Pagliani's children might just have a fighting chance at a normal life. Julius parked across the street where his brother had been living and sat for a minute. The last thing that he needed was to be caught inside of a shooting gallery with loaded pistols on him. He would make it as quick as possible, but he had to make sure that he was okay. Maybe he'd drop off a few dollars and chat for a few ticks while Otis ate his cobbler and drank his coffee. Julius' Stacy Adams wing tip shoes slipped and slid in the snow until he gained his footage. He looked around out of habit to make sure nobody had witnessed his *uncool*. He approached the door, but didn't bother knocking. He simply walked inside and stood in the foyer for the homeowner to greet him. Maxine Moody was an ex Madame who'd seen both her share of ass whippings and hard dicks, but she hadn't allowed that to harden her demeanor. She was still as sweet as a stalk of pure sugar cane and Julius had come to respect her for what she represented. She'd used the small fortune she was able to amass to purchase the six-bedroom house in Paradise Valley. It was her way of doing what she believed to be her part at keeping the streets clean. The drug dealers were allowed to come in and hock their products without the worry of police presence and the heroin addicts were allowed to not only purchase their drugs, but they had somewhere safe to shoot up. Maxine made sure that they had clean rigs to use and a hot home cooked meal if they wanted it. Many

186

people looked down on her for her efforts, but in the dope community she was a saint. There were drug dealers who protected her, simply because of her character and her house of ill repute was funded by money from the grateful dealers.

"Hey honey! Oh my goodness, it's so good to see your handsome chocolate face!" Maxine said to Julius.

"Hey Miss Maxine. How you feeling today?"

"Fair to middling baby, fair to middling. Something sho' smells good. What you got in that bag?" She asked.

"I stopped and grabbed Otis a slice of cobbler and a cup of coffee. Try to get something in his stomach you know?"

"Yeah, I made some salmon patties and smothered potatoes this morning and he ate a little, but not much. He been in the back laying down since 'bout nine this morning," she told him.

"Well, he needs to get up. I wanna take him and get him a nice suit, maybe some shoes and then go out to dinner with the fellas, you know? Make a day of it."

"You know where he is baby. Excuse me now honey. Looks like we have a small crisis here." She scurried off toward the living room. Moments later Julius heard her scream at one of the addicts. It was something about cleaning up the puke in the hall beneath the stairs.

"I'm sick, Mama Max. I'm hurting," the fiend whined.

"Of course you sick baby and as much as I sympathize with you, you know the rules. We all clean up behind ourselves if we gon' keep this place up."

Julius smiled to himself, because even in her most tried moments, she was still able to maintain a sort of maternal heir about herself. She was kind and caring towards all; dope fiend and dealer alike. He made his way toward the room that Otis shared with another man by the name of Dumpy. He lived up to the nickname too, because he was fat, frumpy and smelled like garbage truck juice. He sweated profusely and he breathed extremely heavy like he was always out of breath. Dumpy walked toward Julius in the hall and he tried desperately to hold his breath as he approached.

"Dumpy, my brother in there bruh?" Julius asked.

Dumpy stood in the hall as if he hadn't just left the room and had to think of whether Otis was even there. He stood there in his dingy white tee shirt and faded boxer shorts that had worn thin near the crotch, scratching his musty ass. "Ummm, he been sleep most of the day Julius man, but he in there though," Dumpy said.

Julius sneered at the man. He wasn't fond of Dumpy at all. Not only because of his odor, but because Otis had confided in Julius that Dumpy often bullied him. Even though Otis was older than Julius, Julius felt compelled to take care of his big brother. The only reason that Julius hadn't given Dumpy a hotshot (bad dope) was out of respect for Miss Maxine and Otis had made him promise not to say anything.

"Hey Julius man, you thank I can borrow $10 'til I gets my check on the first brother?" Dumpy asked.

"I ain't your brother and nigga you still owe me $10 anyway. So, no nigga you can't get shit from me until you pay what you owe," Julius said, as he walked into Otis' room. Dumpy's malodorous stench still hung thick in the air. It seemed even worse in the small room like the funk just bounced back and forth from wall to wall, playing tag with Julius' nostrils. Julius sat the cobbler and coffee on a nearby milk crate and kneeled next to the mattress where his brother slept.

"Otis, wake up man. I got you something sweet." But Otis didn't respond. "Damn boy you sleep hard as hell man, get up I wanna take you shopping and go out with our brothers later on man." No response.

"Otis?"

No response.

Julius' heart dropped. This couldn't be happening. "Otis come on man!" He shouted.

No response.

"Awwwwwwww, Otis, awwwwww, come on man, no no no. Otis get yo' ass up!" Julius panicked as he shook his brother violently. No response.

"God damnit bruh, you left me once. Come on man, please don't leave me again!" Julius cried.

He turned Otis over and that's when he saw it. The needle was still sticking from his battered arm and his eyes were cold and dead. Purple bruises were all over his arm where he had searched for a healthy vein only to find a collapsed string of nothingness. There was a thick ring of white froth around Otis' mouth and Julius knew instantly that his brother was gone.

"God damnit Otis." He wanted to cry, but the tears wouldn't flow. He felt hollow and cold inside, almost unfeeling as if this was something that he *must* accept. Julius stood and exited the room. He walked down the hallway in a daze headed for the front door. He needed fresh air. Honestly, he needed to be anywhere but there. Otis' life after Arkansas had been one disappointment after another. He had found his mother who out of *motherly love*, had turned Otis on to his first hit. She had gone so far as to tie him up and inject him with the poison that she swore would bring him fame and fortune. According to Otis, the last time he'd seen Juanita, she was on her way out of town on tour with Ray Charles. He said, no matter what anyone said, he would die with two truths. The first was that he knew his mother loved him deep down in her soul and two that she'd gotten him hooked on dope to keep him quiet about their relationship. She didn't want people to know that she had a child because that would ruin her jet setting image. He lived with the sadness of knowing that he'd come from a broken past that was too fractured to be repaired.

CHAPTER 26

"What's up baby brother? What's on your mind?" Otha Lee asked standing over Charlie Boy.

"Man, y'all niggas out there getting money being useful, earning your keep while I'm being treated like a fucking baby. I told Mr. G that I was getting into the business and he agreed, but he has yet to give me my own job," Charlie Boy complained. He was pissed to the highest levels of pissivity and Otha Lee knew it.

"He'll get around to it Charlie Boy. You just have to be patient!" He tried to pacify his youngest brother.

"I bet if I go work for them Jews across town he'd sit up and take notice, shit!"

"That's some disrespectful and disloyal ass shit right there man. Mama Gina would probably disown your ass if you did that shit," Otha Lee warned.

"Yeah, I know. I'm just talking, but I'm ready man. I'm ready to show everyone what I can do."

"How about you go with me? I still gotta get that priest, so you can help me if you want," Otha Lee suggested.

191

Charlie Boy was still a boy and he had his entire life ahead of him, but if Otha Lee could use him to accomplish his goal, then he would use him.

"Nigga, you want me to help you then you're gonna have to break bread!" Charlie Boy huffed.

"You know I'll take care of you little brother," Otha Lee said lighting a stick of reefer. He took a couple of stiff drags and offered it to Charlie Boy.

"I don't want that shit. We're about to do wrong and the last thing I need is to not be on point," he said.

Otha Lee climbed into the driver side of his new Chevelle and unlocked the door for his brother. The car still smelled of leather and steel, an unbeatable combination in Otha Lee's eyes.

"I hope you got a plan for the priest bruh and we ain't just running out here willy nilly. That's the kind of shit that lands niggas up in Jackson!" Charlie Boy was referring to the state prison in Jackson, Michigan; a place that he'd sworn to himself he'd never see.

"Stop worrying man. I got this!"

"And when you get finished talking muhfucka, I still say you better have a plan," Charlie Boy reiterated.

Otha Lee ignored his brother's harsh words. After all, how hard could killing be? He'd payed close attention to the lessons that Tuffy had been teaching them, but Tuffy was old and he didn't know it all. As far as Otha Lee was concerned, all of that planning shit was for the birds. Nah, he would wing it, put a bullet in the old man and be back home before dinner.

*****

Father Joel McKellen stood on the steps of his church saying his goodbyes to the parishioners as they departed. Otha Lee and Charlie Boy sat in the Chevelle parked across the street from the church, waiting for the crowd to dissipate before they made their move. All the time they waited Otha Lee kept smoking. It was almost as if he was trying to numb himself from the atrocious act that he was about to commit. "Damn, man. I'm hiiiiiiiigh as a motherfucka. Bruh, come on let's do this shit!" He said, as he cocked his pistol.

"Hold on bruh. Who are those wops he's standing with?" Charlie Boy asked.

"I don't know and I don't care. Shit, they can get it too!"

Otha Lee leapt from the car and headed across the street with his gun drawn. Otha Lee was high, drunk on power, and not really thinking clearly. Charlie Boy could see it. His gait was forced like he was floating and not really sure of his footing. Charlie burst from the car just in time to see the first man pull a small caliber pistol from his waistband.

"O, get back to the car bruh. You been made!" Charlie Boy screamed. Otha Lee turned toward Charlie Boy. As he did, the man released a shot, catching Otha Lee in his shoulder. Charlie Boy returned fire, catching the shooter with two shots. He picked up the gun that Otha Lee had dropped and ran toward the trio still shooting. He struck both of the shooters, leaving the distraught priest standing alone, wide eyed and nervous. Below his robe and between his feet

193

was a puddle of golden yellow piss. "My son, let us pray so that God may forgive you for the sins you've committed here today!" He said nervously.

"Oh yeah? So, what does he say about you butt fucking little boys, you piece of shit?" Charlie hissed.

"I will face God's judgement in due time my son."

"I ain't ya son, and you're facing judgement today! Sammy Bags' grandson says hello," Charlie Boy hissed. He put the barrel of both pistols against the priest's heart and pulled the trigger. Crimson red blood drenched his white robe as he collapsed into a contorted heap of lifelessness. His dead eyes stared at the statue of Mary holding a newborn baby Jesus that sat near the bottom of the stairs. There had been one very important rule of killing that Charlie Boy didn't know. While Tuffy was teaching it, Charlie Boy had been learning the finer aspects of reading and arithmetic. The rule stated that one should never leave a witness, but as Charlie Boy retreated across the street to grab his big brother, he didn't see Marcel Franco peeking at him through narrowed eyes. Certain things were off limits in the Italian community and priests were one of them. Marcel Franco belonged to the Chicago outfit and Father McKellen had just married his brother and new sister-in-law. Now his youngest brother lay dead next to the priests and he'd been left alive. He would have his revenge as soon as he was able to put a face with the name of the moolee who had pulled the trigger.

*****

"What the fuck were you thinking O? You could've gotten Charlie Boy killed man!" Julius screamed, as the doctor patched his wounds.

"Man, scratch that shit Julius. I had it man. I didn't need that nigga!" Otha Lee barked.

"Ungrateful ass nigga, if it wasn't for Charlie Boy your ass would be dead right now!" Julius snapped.

"Whatever nigga! We ain't kids no more, so all that hollering and shit, you can save that for your little prize Charlie Boy! I had the shit under control!"

"Is that why you're sitting up bleeding like a stuck hog?" Julius asked sarcastically.

"It wouldn't have happened if that little nigga hadn't called my name."

"Yeah, I bet."

"Why the fuck you in here anyway? Go out there with Charlie Boy. You love that nigga more than you love me and Gene anyway!"

"I'll go as soon as I get what I came for!" Julius said, rifling through the pockets of Otha Lee's coat pocket. He found the envelope that Tuffy had given them and did a quick count. He'd only spent $20, but Julius scoffed at Otha Lee's stupidity. What was the purpose of walking around with that much cash on you? If the police had pulled him over, they would have taken his money and locked him up, or worse.

The shouting continued for what seemed like hours until Julius emerged from the room and slammed the door behind him. "That motherfucka likes to blame everyone but himself for the fucked up shit that he does! Do you know what this ungrateful son-of-a-bitch had the fucking audacity to say to me?" He asked, then added, "He says I love Charlie Boy more than I love you and him!" He said, facing Eugene.

Eugene didn't respond. He turned his back to Julius and headed toward the door of his brother's room.

"I don't think you realize what you do sometimes Julius. You put more stock into Charlie Boy and other people than you do the people that have been with you since day one. Mama gone, Otis gone, Ernie gone, but me and Otha Lee and Charlie still here and we have to fight for your love and it ain't right."

Julius all but ignored Eugene, but he did however toss the envelope full of money to Charlie Boy in plain sight. "Here you go bruh. This money belongs to you since you did the hit," Julius said.

"Hold up! You giving this nigga Otha Lee's money now? What Mr. G gotta say about that?" Eugene asked.

"I make the decisions for this family and since Otha Lee didn't do the job, he doesn't deserve the money!" Julius barked.

"See that's the shit he's talking about! You coddle this little nigga man!"

"The fact that you're even arguing this point says that you're favoring O, man. Understand me when I tell you this little brother. This shit is not up for debate, and this ain't no motherfuckin' democracy. It's a dictatorship and I'm the dictator!" Julius shouted.

"Yeah, well, you keep dictating and you're gonna fuck around and find yourself all alone in your little kingdom!" Eugene stormed into the makeshift hospital room and slammed the door.

CHAPTER 27

The tension between the Gage brothers was thick and anyone who'd known them before Otha Lee was shot would definitely see the difference. Even at Otis' funeral their small family was now broken into two factions. Jimmy Galici, Gina, Black Sam and Sammy Bags stood behind Julius and Charlie Boy while Eugene and Otha Lee seemed to be backed by Tuffy, Robert Tassiano and Joey Craps. They paid their respects to their brother and kept it civil, but there was an obvious riff in the Gage clan's dynamic.

This young man, this lost soul was a child of God and he was taken far too soon! He should've been having fun with his brothers, but the Lord said no man knows the time and hour when he leaveth the eartha! He said if you repent and call on the name Jesus that not only would your sins be washed away, but you'd be welcomed into the kingdom of heaven! But see, this scourge of drugs and violence here on these Detroit streets has gone on far too long. The Italians use the blacks to do their dirty work and the blacks use the blacksa! Why not let the Lord use you?" The preacher eulogized.

"Man, what the fuck that gotta do with my brother? Julius, you say shit about everything else, but you gonna just let this shade tree nigga disrespect our family?" Eugene barked.

There were no words. Of course Julius knew that Eugene was right for a change, but why make a scene? It was their older brother's home going service and he wouldn't disrespect Otis' memory by acting a fool. Eugene's anger wasn't lost on anyone in attendance and they all braced for what they envisioned as an inevitable showdown, but it never came. Instead, as they lowered Otis' coffin into the ground, Julius stepped forward, dropped a dozen black orchids into the ground on top of Otis' casket and turned to leave.

"Where you going Julius?" Charlie Boy asked.

He looked at his little brother and saw that same little chocolate boy that he'd fallen in love with in the recesses of that farm house in Arkansas. "I can't do this man, I'll meet y'all at Tuffy's later. I just need a little time bruh," Julius whispered.

As he walked, he tucked the thick wool scarf into the breast of his tweed over coat. The winter chill was still whipping and threatened to freeze his tears to his face as he crossed the frozen cemetery. He couldn't understand how their lives had been so full of strife at such an early age, especially since the saying said that God took care of fools and babies. His mother was gone, Ernie was gone, Otis was

199

gone as Eugene had so abruptly pointed out and Julius bore the full weight of those losses on his shoulders. Even his piece of shit father, Nathaniel Gage had managed to steal a moment inside of his head. He silently wondered if God would forgive him for murdering his own father. After all, the bible said that a man should honor thy mother and father. He wasn't a scholar, but he was sure that murdering was not synonymous with honoring. He unlocked the door to his car and felt a heavy hand on his shoulder. He and Black Sam had never been particularly close, but Julius respected the old man. He was extremely quiet and equally as private, so for him to step to Julius there had be something important to say.

"My condolences to you and your brothers Julius," Black Sam said in his raspy voice.

Julius looked into his sunken, unfeeling eyes and wondered if he was sincere in his sympathy. Whatever the case, Julius wasn't in the mood to talk. He wiped the tears and snot from his face with the backside of his glove and muttered a *thank you*, against the wind.

"Yeah, listen, we haven't always seen eye to eye, but I respect what you've done with your brothers. You've fought to hold your family together and that's admirable, but everything isn't peaches in paradise Julius," Sam said.

"What does that mean?"

"It means that sometimes hyenas wait until the lion is alone before they attack," Sam explained cryptically.

Julius wasn't in the mood for his riddles. Not that day of all days.

"Alls I'm saying is that there are those that are silently happy that you and your brothers are feuding. They see your feud as a weakness in the fabric Julius. The separation is like a soft spot in the armor. Do you understand?" Black Sam asked.

Before Julius could answer Robert Tassiano walked up on the duo and joined the conversation. "What you's guys down here talking about?" Robert asked cheerfully.

"Nothing, I was just giving the kid my condolences, that's all," Sam lied.

"That was a long conversation for some condolences my friend."

"Yeah, well I don't talk so fast now that I'm an old man," Sam sneered, then added, "Julius call me later. We'll talk more." He walked toward his limousine.

Robert Tassiano and Julius locked eyes. He'd never cared for the man, because he tried to place himself above everyone that he came into contact with. He tried on more than one occasion to intimidate Julius, but he couldn't be intimidated. He had for whatever reason taken a liking to Otha Lee and Eugene and could care less about Julius, or Charlie Boy, which was fine by Julius, because he didn't like Robert Tassiano either. As Julius drove, Black Sam's words kept playing over and over in his head. *Everything isn't peaches in paradise*, he'd said. *Sometimes hyenas wait until the lion is alone before they attack.* Julius couldn't shake the feeling of dread that rattled in his guts. Darkness was just beginning to fall as he pulled into the parking lot of Reba's Joint. It was a small blues club that catered to an older crowd, but that was what Julius liked. In his current mood, the last thing that he wanted to deal with was the testosterone driven youngsters who frequented the sock hops that he and his younger brothers usually went to. The usually packed club was barely filled, which further made Julius feel as though Reba's was the place to be. He walked inside and was greeted with the sound of guitar licks and a throaty blues singer whaling behind the microphone. He was asking the patrons, *had they ever loved a woman so much that it was a sin. He wanted to know if they had ever loved a woman that they couldn't leave alone.* Julius took a booth in the back of the club and waited for Reba to come to his table and take his order. She was perhaps one of the most beautiful women that he had ever had the privilege of knowing. Reba was 5'3, pure fire, smart and didn't take anyone's shit. Her skin had earned her the nickname "Yellabone" and was as smooth as milk. Her oval face was framed in a jet black afro and her smoky eyes hid behind the lenses of rose tinted glasses. Her waist line was narrow, her hips were wide and her butt bounced like she had two midgets in her back pockets fighting to escape. Reba's lips were sensuous and worked to pronounce every syllable of every word in her soft falsetto tone.

"Hey chocolate baby, what can I get you tonight?" She asked.

"What's the special tonight?"

"Tonight it's beef tips and gravy over a bed of rice and your choice of vegetables," she said.

"Yeah, I'll take that with green beans and cabbage."

"You want cornbread?" She asked.

"Yeah and I want a shot of bourbon. Better yet make it two," he answered.

Reba took a seat across from Julius and stared into his eyes. "You look sad baby, what's wrong?" She asked.

"I buried my oldest brother today. Shit just seems unreal you know? Seems like just yesterday we were kids playing on our farm in Arkansas and now he's gone."

"Aww, I'm sorry to hear that. I knew something had to be wrong, because you never drink when you come in here," she said.

"Yeah, I know. I like to have a clear head."

"Well, let me get your order in and I'll come back and keep you company, if that's okay," she said.

"Uh huh," Julius muttered. He didn't really care whether she came back or not. He liked Reba, but there were some things weighing on his young mind that he had never experienced. Of course he'd seen death's ugly face close up, but that wasn't the problem. He felt empty inside, like something was missing. Instead of two shots, Reba had left the entire bottle of bourbon on his table and he sloppily poured drink after drink, until he felt numb. Tears rolled down his cheeks and came to rest at the bottom of his glass. Julius found himself drinking shot after shot of bourbon laced tears, trying somehow to drown his sorrows. He looked at his uneaten beef tips and felt his stomach turn.

"Reeeeba, Reeeeeeba how old, I mean how luch, hi much my owe yo lilla pretty ass baby?" Julius slurred drunkenly.

"This one's on me baby. You need me to call you a cab?"

Julius didn't answer. He simply fished the keys from his coat pocket and staggered out into the blistering cold.

*****

Charlie Boy sat in the dining room of Tuffy's estate listening to Eugene and Otha Lee reminisce about Otis, and found joy and excitement in their stories about the old days. Of course he'd been there, but he couldn't remember much. "Man I wish I could remember Otis the way y'all do." Charlie Boy said reflectively.

"Nigga, why are you even here?!" Otha Lee sneered.

"What you mean?"

"He means, why are you here instead of with Julius muhfucka?" Eugene barked.

"Cool out baby. Why y'all treating me like this?"

"Dig these blues baby boy, your savior Julius ain't here to protect your ass now, so don't get outta line punk!" Eugene said, as he passed a bottle of thunderbird to Otha Lee.

Tuffy and Robert Tassiano both sat nearby and Charlie Boy looked to them to intervene, but neither of them said a word. They merely sat, watching with knowing smirks of satisfaction plastered on their faces. Charlie Boy stood and walked to face his two brothers. "Man, I know y'all niggas is hurting, but that don't give y'all no cause to talk to me like I

204

ain't family!" Charlie Boy said, trying desperately to hold back the tears.

"You Julius' family little nigga. You ain't shit to me!" Otha Lee spat.

"Is it about the money? You can have that fucking money mane. We family, we blood and that should count more than some goddamn bread bruh!" He could no longer hold his tears and Charlie Boy sobbed openly.

"Fuck that money nigga. It ain't about the money. It's about the fact that you two muhfuckas act like me and Gene don't exist, so since we don't exist, y'all don't exist!" Otha Lee said. He was feeling the effects of the wine.

"So, what you saying?" Charlie Boy asked.

"I think he's saying it's time for you to leave, young man." Robert Tassiano said, as he took Charlie Boy by the arm and led him to the front door. He attempted to hand Charlie Boy a $20 bill. "This is for the cab boy." He offered, but Charlie wasn't having it. His sadness for the way that his brothers had treated him gave way to anger at the intrusion of those strangers in family business. "I don't need your fucking charity Robert. When Julius hears about this shit he's gonna make it hard to breathe around this muhfucka, trust me," Charlie Boy warned.

"Just try and survive this blizzard black boy. That's what you do!" Robert Tassiano said as he slammed the door in his face. Charlie Boy could hear the four of them laughing at his humiliation as he descended the stairs. Charlie Boy hugged himself to escape the brutal Detroit wind that whipped, whistled and howled eerily like the cries of children beckoning for better days. He trudged along the city streets thinking of simple days long gone. He thought of his beautiful mother and could almost feel the warmth of the wood burning stove that she'd created heaven on. He could see her standing near that stove in her favorite yellow dress with the daisies on it, shaping salmon patties as she made him practice shapes and numbers. Everyone was so close back then. Well everyone that is, except their father. Charlie Boy's warm and toasty thoughts turned to cold fury as he thought of Nathaniel Gage. He'd managed in the short time as a father on earth to instill violence and malevolence in his children and Charlie Boy found himself cursing his father aloud. "Evil muhfucka, I'm glad you're dead!" He said with his head lifted toward the heavens, like a person as evil as he, might actually make it to heaven.

"Now is that any way to speak of the dead?" A voice said.

The voice startled Charlie Boy and caused him to look around warily. "What?"

"I'm right here, there's no need to look around. I said is that any way to speak of the dead?" Marcel Franco asked, emerging from the shadows between two houses.

"What business is it of yours?"

Marcel laughed and just as quickly became serious again. "I'm just saying. How is it going to look with you speaking ill of the dead, knowing that you'll see them face to face real fucking soon?" Marcel asked as he brandished his pistol.

Charlie Boy considered running, but before he could fully commit two more men appeared from beyond the shadows. There was a dark sedan parked nearby with the headlights on, illuminating a large portion of the block. "Don't run, I see it in your eyes. If you run, we'll pump twenty bullets into you before you take your third step. Now, remember that priest you killed? Well he was a family friend," Marcel said.

"I ain't kilt no priest!" Charlie Boy huffed.

"Okay, whatever you say. I guess we got you wrong huh? I just want to know who ordered the hit."

"I don't know what you're talking about man, and I got somewhere to be!" Charlie Boy argued.

"Let's cut the bullshit! It took me a lot of money to find out who, what, where and guess what? Your fucking name came up as the shooter! Now get in the fucking car Charlie Boy Gage!" Marcel said. He cocked his pistol and put it in Charlie Boy's face. "We can either do this like civilized gentlemen, or I can make sure your brothers have to give you a closed casket burial!"

"Okay man, okay!" Charlie Boy said, lifting his hands in surrender.

*****

Julius sat in his Lincoln doing his best to sober up, but it was all for naught. He thought back to Otis' funeral and his conversation with Black Sam. Jumping out of his car, he staggered to the payphone in front of Reba's Joint. He tried to get Black Sam on the phone, but it just rang continuously. He went back to his car and pulled out into the Detroit night. As he drove the back streets, he avoided the police until he reached Black Sam's modest home in the suburbs. The house was dark, except for a lone light in an upstairs bedroom. Julius knocked on the door lightly, but there was no answer. He knocked a little louder, but still, there was no answer. *Maybe they're out,* he thought. To appease his own curiosity, Julius went to the garage to see if Black Sam's car was there. Using the back side of his gloved hand, he wiped the frost from the pane of glass and peeked inside. Black Sam's Mercury Park Lane was still parked in its usual place and Julius' pulse quickened. There was nothing that Sam loved more than his Park Lane, not even his wife Agatha. He was crazy about her, so if it was parked, Black Sam was there. Stealthily, Julius made his way to the back door and tried the knob. It was locked. He coughed and broke the small pane of glass just above the doorknob. Once inside, he climbed the stairs two at a time until he reached the top and burst through the door where the light was shining. Black Sam was sitting in a recliner in the corner with a bullet hole in the center of his forehead. There was dried blood around his mouth and his eyes gazed at Julius, unnervingly beckoning to him from beyond to save himself from a fate that he had already met. Julius saw where the blood had come from. His tongue had been cut from his mouth and placed in his right hand. A note had been attached to his chest by way of an icepick that had been buried up to the handle.

Never tell the left hand what the right hand is doing! Codice Del Silenzio! It read.

On the bed behind them lay Black Sam's sweet wife Agatha. She was lying in a position that suggested a peaceful slumber, but the pillow covering her face with the bullet hole in it belied that illusion. The shock had completely sobered Julius up and if the note pinned to Sam was in reference to the conversation that they'd had at the funeral, he needed desperately to get to his brothers. If Robert Tassiano was involved, Julius wasn't sure how many, if any of the Italians could be trusted. However, there was one person that he could always trust, and once again Julius found himself in his car speeding off in search of answers. If there was chatter in the streets it would undoubtedly filter down to Mama Gina.

CHAPTER 28

Jimmy Galici answered the door to Gina's when Julius rang the doorbell and Julius nearly back peddled. Of course Jimmy Galici had never given Julius a reason to distrust him, but someone was trying to keep Black Sam quiet and the Italians were notorious for *taking care* of their own.

"Julius come in out of the cold. We need to talk," Jimmy Galici told him.

"Yeah, you got that right."

Julius shuffled past Jimmy and removed his overcoat and scarf before placing them on the coat rack. As he entered the living room, he was surprised to see Otha Lee and Eugene sitting on the couch with worried looks on their faces. Gina sat near his brothers, but her head was buried in her lap and she sobbed loudly.

"Where's Charlie Boy?" Julius asked, but no one answered. He repeated his question, but that time a little more forcefully. "Where the fuck is my baby brother?"

"They got him," Eugene muttered.

"They who? Who is they Gene? And what you mean they got him?"

"The Chicago Italians," Eugene said, like Julius should have known.

Out of all of the Gage boys, Charlie Boy was the most innocent. He was the brother with the most logical approach to any given situation. Why would the Chicago outfit want Charlie Boy?

"Julius calm down. Why don't we all go down to the basement so we can talk?" Jimmy Galici suggested.

Irritation was an understatement for Julius and the fact that nobody was giving him any information only further enraged him. Julius dropped his head and moved toward the basement, but Gina grabbed his hand and stopped him, "Julius, please bring my baby home to me!" She said through tear filled eyes. Her hair had begun to grey around the edges and the corner of her eyes showed cracks from too many nights spent crying, but she was just as beautiful as the first day he'd saw her in the deli. He smiled weakly, nodded and ascended the basement steps. Jimmy Galici, Otha Lee and Eugene all looked intently at something in front of them and once again Julius felt that familiar sinking in the pit of his stomach. What if they were looking at Charlie Boy's mutilated body? He stepped off the bottom step and burst through their semicircular barricade to see what held their attention. In the center of the floor bound to two chairs with duct tape sat Robert Tassiano and Tuffy. Their mouths were also taped and they looked worried and scared. Jimmy Galici snatched the tape from their mouths violently. "Now, we'll start this conversation again now that Julius has arrived. Where the fuck is Charlie Boy?" Jimmy asked, punching Tuffy viciously.

"Maybe they don't want to talk because they're afraid you'll find out that they killed Black Sam and Miss Agatha!" Julius said, thrusting the bloody note into Jimmy Galici's hand. As he studied the note in disbelief Jimmy Galici could barely contain his rage. "You piece of shit!! Bobby you murdered Sammy and Agatha?"

"Don't Bobby me! And that old fucker had it coming! This has always been our thing and he was violating the code. I did us all a favor, because if he was willing to talk to this moolee, it was only a matter of time before he started singing like a bird to the police!"

"You killed Black Sam?" Tuffy shrieked. With that revelation, the flood gates of information flowed from Tuffy's lips. He told Jimmy Galici of Robert Tassiano's growing hatred of him and the Gage boys. Tuffy explained how Tassiano had struck a deal with the Chicago outfit to flood the black neighborhoods of Detroit with smack. Even when Tuffy had told him that he'd be stepping on Sammy Bags' toes he'd replied, "So fucking what? There's about to be a shift in power!" According to Tuffy, Tassiano had gotten in too deep with the Chicago mob, owing them more than he could possibly pay back. When they contacted him, asking about the shooter of the priest and who ordered the hit, Tassiano had been all too eager to give up Charlie Boy in exchange for a little relief in his debt.

"Jimmy, I swear I didn't know until earlier today at the funeral what his plans were for Charlie Boy and Black Sam!" Tuffy pleaded.

"Yeah, maybe so, but you said nothing! That makes you just as guilty as this piece of shit!" Jimmy snarled.

"Where is my brother Robert?" Julius asked calmly.

"Go fuck yourself!"

Julius reached into his waistband and removed his .45 caliber pistol. He cocked it and put the open end of the barrel against Robert Tassiano's family jewels. "I'll ask you once more! Where the fuck is my little brother?"

"Why don't you ask Otha Lee and Eugene where he is?" Robert Tassiano grinned.

Julius eyed his brothers curiously. There was no way that they had participated in hurting Charlie Boy. They had their jealousy issues, but he knew that they loved their little brother just as much as he did. "What the fuck is he talking about Eugene? Otha Lee?"

"Speak up Otha Lee, Eugene! Tell your brother how you sold your soul and hung your little brother out to dry for a few dollars and a house!" Tassiano teased.

"Shoot him Julius! Kill this son-of-a-bitch!" Eugene shouted.

"Yeah, Julius kill me and you'll never find your precious little brother!"

Otha Lee stumbled back to the stairs, sat down, cradled his head in his hands and started rocking back and forth. Julius walked to his little brother and put his hand on his back. "O, man tell me what's going on. Is there any truth to what this motherfucka is saying?" Julius asked. Slowly Otha Lee shook his head yes.

"Julius I'm sorry." He whispered.

"What happened?"

"You gotta understand, we didn't mean for any of this to go down this way."

"What happened?"

"Just try and understand…"

"Man kill the plea bargain bullshit and spill it!" Julius said feverishly, turning his gun to Otha Lee. Between Otha lee and Eugene, they laid it all out on the table. They had been helping Robert Tassiano move his drugs through the ghetto for a nice cut of the profit. Soon as they'd made the money, it went straight to Tuffy as a down payment toward his estate. Tuffy and Tassiano had planned to murder Galici, Black Sam, Sammy Bags, Joey Craps and anybody else that was loyal to the old regime would be eliminated. Otha Lee and Eugene had pledged their loyalty to the pair. Charlie Boy, according to his brothers, had been a casualty and they'd just learned of his kidnapping when Mama Gina called. Marcel Franco had forced Charlie Boy to call Gina so she could witness them beating him as they demanded for Sammy Bags and Jimmy Galici to come forward.

"We didn't know that this shit was gonna happen Julius!" Eugene said.

He had a little too much bravado in his voice for Julius' particular taste and it irked his nerves. So much so that he found it hard to control his emotions. "What the fuck did you stupid motherfucka's think was gonna happen? If you sleep with snakes you die in your sleep from poison dumb nigga!" Julius said.

He grabbed Otha Lee by the back of his neck with one hand and stood him up. With his other hand he forced his pistol into his mouth, but kept his eyes trained on Eugene. "If anything happens to Charlie Boy...If he gets a hang nail, if he gets a stomach ache. I mean, even if he so much as gets an eye lash in his eye while they have him, I am going to kill both of you niggas slowly and painfully!" He said, jamming his pistol further down Otha Lee's throat.

"Jubius, pwease bwo, pwease!" Otha Lee said with a mouth full of pistol.

"Please what? Huh? Please what nigga?"

Julius felt the firm hand of Jimmy Galici on his wrist. "You boys are blood Julius. Let it go. We'll get him back son. I promise, we'll bring him home."

"I'm just trying to do right by us the best way that I know how and these two dummies are fighting me every step of the way! I just want my little brother back!" Julius snapped, with tears rolling down his cheeks. He still had his eyes trained on Eugene when he pulled the pistol from Otha Lee's mouth and pointed it at Robert Tassiano's head.

"Kill me boy! I've made my peace with my sweet savior! Your soul will burn for this, you fucking moolee. You must be a pain freak, because before it's all said and done, Jimmy will break your heart a million times punk!" Robert Tassiano spat.

"I cuddle up to my demons every night. I snuggle deep in the devil's armpit and that motherfucka is funky with

215

despair and hatred. Yeah, you're right, I *am* a pain freak and I stare death in the face every motherfuckin' night because of this life that I chose. What's the Bible sayin'? You reap what you sow? See the difference between me and you is, I know who the fuck I am and I make no apologies for it! You creep around this bitch talkin' too much. I let this pistol do my talkin'. Let's do each other a favor. You lie to your friends, I lie to my friends, but let's not lie to each other though, motherfucka, 'cause we ain't friends. Now I'ma ask you one mo' time. Where the fuck is my little brother?"

Julius' hand twitched. He could feel himself on edge, anxious to spill Robert Tassiano's blood; payback for his disrespect and indiscretion. A feeling rushed through him, sending a tingling sensation through the fibers and muscles of his trigger hand and Tassiano started to tremble in fear. His gun was still pointed at Tassiano's head when he bent down in front of Tuffy and whispered with tears still flowing freely down his cheeks. "Tell me what I want to know and I'll let you live. If you don't tell me I'm going to make you watch me kill him and then you're next! Now tell me where my little brother is. Where is Charlie Boy?"

"Fuck him Tuffy! Don't tell this shine shit!" Robert Tassiano cried.

Without warning, Julius lowered his pistol to Tassiano's dick and pulled the trigger. A thunderous clap was followed by a shrill scream escaping from the pits of his tortured soul and then silence. Death had not come for Robert Tassiano as of yet, but silence was his only reprieve from the searing pain that coursed through his body. "The next bullet is yours unless you tell me what the fuck I want to know!" Julius whispered.

Barely able to speak because of the fear that gripped him, Tuffy muttered something about a cabin on Lake Michigan.

"What about Lake Michigan, Tuffy? Speak up!" Julius demanded.

"They have him at a cabin in Benton Harbor that overlooks Lake Michigan. As far as I know there's only one, maybe two people guarding him!" Tuffy squealed.

"You, you're...a...fucking...rat!" Tassiano whispered in agony.

Julius stood and looked at Robert Tassiano. Shaking his head, he grabbed the man by his cheeks forcing his mouth open and shoved his pistol in his mouth. "No Robert, he's smart!" Julius said as he sent a bullet into the recesses of Tassiano's skull. The top of his head exploded in a mess of blood and skull fragments.

"You see that Tuffy? This kid isn't playing around, so you'd better hope that the information you're giving is accurate. We need an address, or a map or something, capische?" Jimmy Galici asked, removing a knife from a nearby toolbox and cutting the tape from Tuffy's hands.

With shaky hands Tuffy drew a make shift map with written instructions on how to get to the cabin.

"We'll check this out Tuffy and if it pans out, we'll let you go, but your name is no good here anymore. So, I'll offer you this reprieve. Since you've taken money from these boys toward your house, you'll sign over the deed to the

Gage boys and then you're going to board a plane back to Italy. If you ever step foot in the United States again, we will hunt you down and cut off your balls, do you understand? This isn't optional, it's law. I'm going to put the word out that if anyone sees your face after you're banished, they have the greenlight to rip you to shreds and you and I both know that you have more enemies than friends!"

Tuffy nodded his understanding. His plan had always been to collect the money from Otha Lee and Eugene, make a little money from helping Tassiano seize power and then retire to Italy anyway. So everything worked out the way he'd planned, with the exception of the money. Instead, he'd be going home with the money that he'd banked over the years, but it was more than enough to give him a leg up in the old country. Hatred would be his fuel and he'd make sure to tell his nephews, nieces and any other family members of the disrespect that he'd suffered at the hands of Jimmy Galici and the Gages. Once he was safely away from them of course.

CHAPTER 29

Eugene and Otha Lee walked around Tuffy's compound making plans for their lavish future, while Julius and Jimmy Galici sat in the dining room trying their best to come up with a plan of attack. They'd left Tuffy in the basement with Gina and had given her instructions to wait for a phone call. If they called without Charlie Boy, she was to kill him and they would dispose of the body later. In all actuality, his brothers were getting on his nerves, especially their lackadaisical approach to their baby brother's dilemma. The situation was due in part to their selfishness and they were still displaying the same behavior.

*****

In a corridor off the lower wing of the house, both Eugene and Otha Lee huddled in a small room, whispering. "Man, that nigga put his gun in my fucking mouth bruh!" Otha Lee whimpered.

219

"This shit is getting out of hand. That black motherfucker acts just like daddy! I guess we're gonna hafta kill him too huh."

"I wouldn't go that far Gene. He's our brother, not some common nigga on the street!" Otha Lee said.

"That's how he treats us, shit! Like we some nobody ass niggas on the street!"

"So, we just supposed to murder him? What about Charlie Boy? Jimmy? We gonna just kill everybody?" Otha Lee asked, shooting Eugene a scathing glance.

"If necessary! Look, it's me and you. Charlie Boy probably already dead and Galici is an old man."

"Shut the fuck up man. You're losing your goddamn mind! I love you, bro, but sometimes you're the one who acts like daddy! You're willing to kill anybody that stands in your way, huh?" He asked.

"You motherfuckin' right!"

"I guess that includes me too, huh?" Otha Lee asked sadly.

"Nah nigga, we family!"

"Do you listen to yourself? Charlie Boy is our baby brother Gene! Julius is our oldest brother man! I'm not finna have this conversation with you." Otha Lee turned to leave.

Eugene grabbed his arm and spun him around. "Don't turn your back on me nigga! Keep this shit to yourself unless you wanna have problems with me!"

"Otha Lee, Eugene! Y'all down here?" Julius screamed. His voice was getting closer as they emerged from the small room.

"Hey bro, we were thinking about making this room in here like Charlie Boy's study room. It's away from all the noise and everything!" Eugene lied with a fake ass smile plastered across his face.

"Yeah, I hear you, but right now we need to get with Mr. G to finish figuring this shit out," Julius snapped.

*****

By the time that they made it to I-94 in route to Benton Harbor, it was a little after 4 pm and their ride was nearly three hours long. Julius was sitting in the front seat with Jimmy Galici, anxious to get to his younger brother. It seemed as though the weight of the world was on his shoulders and the lack of sleep was starting to take its toll.

"Why don't you close your eyes for a few Julius? You look like shit and you need to be fresh if we're going to pull this thing off," Jimmy suggested.

Julius nodded. It was true and he had to look like shit, because he felt like shit. Instead of closing his eyes, he stared out of the window as they passed scenery that all looked the same. The snow had begun to melt underneath the bright gaze of a midday sun. Spring was fighting to make her appearance on a musty and dreary frontier. Dirty snow and greyish brown slush littered the landscape and Julius found it nearly impossible to keep his eyes open.

After they'd found Otis begging in front of the haberdashery, he'd spent as much time as he could with him. They talked about their childhood; both good times and bad.

Their last conversation wouldn't let Julius rest. "I know I'm not what I'm meant to be bro, but you have time to become whatever you want! The restraints we had in Arkansas don't apply here. Shit, I done seen niggas with mo' money than white folk here!" Otis had said.

"I'm exactly what Nathaniel made me. I'm a killer, I'm good at it *and* I make a lot of money doing it."

"It's not about what daddy made you bro. It's about what God's plan is! Look at me. I stink, I'm dirty, I'm broke and I'm a junky, but you know what? I'm at peace with myself, because I know no matter what happens, God still loves me." Otis smiled with his brownish yellow teeth.

"How can you say God loves you? If he loved you, he'd pull you up out of this shit!"

"It ain't about that. This world doesn't matter anymore. We all make our own decisions and sometimes those plans are contrary to God's will. He gives us free will to go this way, or that way and when we choose that way instead of his way, then we have to suffer the consequences. Once I get to heaven I'm guaranteed a rich man's payday," Otis said.

"So, niggas have to wait until they get to heaven to see riches? No thank you. I'll take mine now."

"You can be rich right here, but it depends on your definition of rich. Money is a myth man. Yeah, you can have it and do shit with it, but true happiness comes from knowing that our God is with you regardless. Money can't buy salvation Julius, remember that!" He'd said.

Now as Julius sat with his head propped against the headrest of the van, his heart felt heavy. There were voices in his head nagging him, telling him to just call the police, yelling at him to not go, but there was no turning back. People didn't call the police in the lifestyle that he lived. No, they handled things with their own brand of street justice. He felt himself drift in and out of a semiconscious state until he finally fell asleep. In his dream, he was sitting next to his mother overlooking the stream where he and his brothers had played on so many occasions. To his left he could see Otis and Charlie Boy fishing, while they laughed and joked, but to his right stood Otha Lee and Eugene. Their faces were contorted into grisly masks of pain and envy. Gertrude's face was washed in a bright light as she spoke to Julius. "Julius, hard times are coming baby."

"Whatcha mean mama?"

"Watch for the signs. You see this?" She asked, removing one of her breasts from her dress, covering the nipple. "From one of these feeds righteousness," she said, replacing the breast. She pulled out the other one, but that time she didn't cover the nipple. It was dried and haggard, nearly torn from the skin. It leaked a greenish, yellow puss filled substance. "From this comes malice and hatred." She said. In the dream Julius heard both Charlie Boy and Otis scream and it drew his attention from his mother. He looked toward where they had once been standing and saw them both running toward a large mountain in the distance being chased by two large black dogs. He looked to his left where Otha Lee and Eugene had been standing, but they were gone.

A puddle of the same poison that had filled his mother's breast was in the place where they had once stood and as the dogs ran they dripped trails of the sludgy mix. He stood and turned to his mother, but she was merely a pile of bone and dust. Otis had picked Charlie Boy up and started to ascend the mountain while below them the big, black dogs had been joined by smaller, paler dogs. One of the big dogs turned to the smaller dogs as if communicating with them and the smaller dogs tried to ascend the mountain. The second black dog turned and walked away as if disgusted by his partner's use of outsiders. The smaller dogs barked and nipped at the feet of Otis while he carried his little brother to safety. "Julius! Julius help me!" Charlie Boy screamed. "Julius! Julius! Oh my God! Julius!" He continued to scream.

"Julius!" Eugene said, finally rousing him from his slumber. "Goddamn man, I thought you was dead! I been calling your ass forever! Wake up, we almost there."

"Shit, I thought you were Charlie Boy. He was calling me in my dream," Julius said.

Darkness was upon them and the temperature had dropped, probably due to their proximity to the water. The street lights illuminated the streets of the small town of Benton Harbor as they pulled into the parking lot of a Phillips 66. Jean Klock Park was less than five miles away and they needed to get ready for war. "I'm going to go pay for gas. You boys need to load up because we'll be there in about ten minutes." Jimmy Galici said.

Benton Harbor was a sleepy little town on the coast of Lake Michigan that was home to less than 20,000 residents.

Whirlpool Corporation and Bendix kept the mostly black population working while their white counterparts chose to live in neighboring St. Joseph. They were often called the twin cities, but Julius understood why the Chicago mob had chosen to hide Charlie Boy in Benton Harbor. The blacks of Benton Harbor very seldom were caught out in Jean Klock Park after dark and if they were, they were probably doing wrong themselves, so they would mind their own business. Unlike Benton Harbor, if they were caught with a black man in bondage, the conservative whites would more than likely turn them in to the authorities. Whereas, the blacks of Benton Harbor were more than likely afraid of the Italians, but the ultra-conservative whites of St. Joseph looked at the Italians as niggers also. They were just one rung above the blacks in their neighboring city. The young whites of St. Joseph had made it a common practice to come down to Benton Harbor to keep the blacks there in line. Young blacks in Benton Harbor had started to form small pocket gangs in an effort to protect the only home that they had ever known and the white business owners in return began to pull out of the city for fear of an impending race war.

"Are we ready?" Jimmy Galici asked.

"About as ready as we'll ever be!" Julius said.

The night sky was pitch black as if everything in the universe had retreated and hidden from the Gage brother's fury. The moon was hidden by thick mounds of clouds and if there were any stars in the sky, they refused to shine. They pulled into the entrance of Jean Klock Park and parked their van near the abandoned guard shack. They would hike the short distance through the marshland of the park to keep the element of surprise. They trudged through the ice cold swamp waters under the cover of darkness, hidden by the tall, pine trees. The larger than life sand dunes to their west shielded them from any late night skinny dippers, or campers who were braving the elements. Julius saw a small cabin in the distance with a constant flicker in the window. As they got closer the glow grew stronger until Julius realized that it was the fireplace. Eugene and Julius would take the front of the cabin while Jimmy Galici and Otha Lee would circle around back and survey their surroundings.

Chapter 30

"So Charlie Boy, you're seventeen huh?" One of the mobsters asked, then continued, "So you had some pussy yet?"

Charlie Boy didn't answer. He just eyed the men who had kidnapped him. There were three of them, but the one that they called Marcel was nowhere to be found. They had busted Charlie Boy's lip, but hadn't done much damage as far as he was concerned.

"You don't hear Tony talking to you moolee?"

"It's okay Vito. I think the kid knows he's gonna die. Hell, I'd be pissed too if I was gonna die before I got my little tallywhacker wet!" Tony said with a chuckle.

The third man was completely quiet. He hadn't said much since they'd arrived there. His only concern was the amount of puffs he could get in on his cigarette before the cold overtook him. He opened the door and stepped out onto the porch. After flinging the rifle strap across his shoulder, he cupped his hands to light his cigarette. Julius took aim with his sniper rifle with the silencer and focused the scope.

227

From the corner of his eye, he saw Eugene turn his rifle on him. He locked eyes with his brother and the dream that he'd had on the way there made sense. Eugene had the same look in his eyes in that instance that he'd had in the dream. Julius turned his head and stared through the scope of his rifle. The tip of the Italian's cigarette glowed a fiery, reddish orange. He blew out white, smoky clouds that seemed more exaggerated, because they'd been mixed with the mist and steam of the cold. Julius lined his crosshairs with the center of his forehead, between his eyes as he inhaled a deep, tasty, lung full of satisfaction. Then he pulled the trigger. The Italian's body barely convulsed, but his 6' 6'' frame crashed to the ground like a large oak tree that had been cut down in its prime. The noise from his body dropping drew the attention of the other kidnappers inside.

"Vito, go check it out. Tell Frankie to stop fucking around!" Tony said.

"Got it boss!" Vito said. As soon as he opened the door and stepped outside, Eugene let a shot go that pierced his neck. Vito grabbed his neck to try and stop the bleeding, but stumbled back inside of the cabin, collapsing in front of the fireplace.

"Uh oh, here come them Gage boys! If you let me go right now, I might be able to convince them not to kill you!" Charlie Boy said triumphantly.

"Shut up! What's to stop me from putting a bullet in your fucking head right now?" Tony asked.

"Nothing, but why die? You can go home to your fat, hairy wife, and lay up watching Dick Clark, while you feed

228

the fat bitch linguine, or some other bullshit!" Charlie Boy teased.

"Tony...help me amico!" Vito begged hoarsely. He reached a bloody hand toward Tony, trying desperately to scoot his body across the wooden floor.

"Uh oh, two down, one to go!" Charlie Boy laughed.

"I swear, if you say one more word I'll do you right here, right now!"

Julius and Eugene had both made their way to the front of the cabin now and were looking inside at the exchange between Charlie Boy and Tony. Julius picked up a large stone and threw it to the other end of the long porch that bordered the cabin. Tony's head jerked to the right in the direction that the noise had come from. He discharged his pistol in that direction and shot through the window. Eugene burst through the door with his rifle trained on Tony. "Drop the gun and we'll let you live homeboy!" He yelled.

"Fuck you! How do I know you're going to let me go?"

"You don't, but if you don't let my little brother go, I can guarantee that you won't walk out of here alive!" Eugene said.

"My boss will be here in a little bit and when he gets here there is going to be hell to pay!"

Julius walked through the front door, dragging the smoker's body. He dropped him next to Vito's bloody body. "We're already two for two, now be smart. You wanna join these two motherfucka's, or do you wanna go home and play grab ass with your wife?" Julius hissed.

By the time Tony had finished contemplating Julius' offer, Otha Lee and Jimmy Galici had slid into the house undetected. Otha Lee crept up behind Tony and put a bullet in his temple. His body dropped, spraying blood onto Charlie Boy as he slid to the ground. "Goddamn ol' messy ass nigga. You got his blood all over me!" Charlie Boy spat; half joking, half serious.

"Let's get these bodies piled in the other room and wait for his boss. Charlie Boy, call Mama Gina and let her hear your voice bruh. She's worried sick. Make it quick though, because we don't know how long it'll be before ol' boy shows up!" Julius said as he untied him.

His mind was still trying to process the fact that his little brother had drawn down on him, but that was something that he would have to deal with later, hopefully much later.

*****

Marcel Franco had yet to hear from the Galici camp and he was tired of playing with the smart mouthed young, black kid. No matter how much they tried to intimidate him, he wasn't swayed. He gave banter for banter and it was starting to irritate him. When he got to the cabin they would kill him, and set the cabin on fire.

Marcel pulled up in front of the cabin and saw the shadows of movement inside. At least Frankie wasn't outside huffing those stinking cigarettes like he usually was. He left the car running so that he could not only have a quick getaway from the fire, but to keep the heater blowing while he was inside. If they could get it over and done with in a timely fashion, he would go down to Rosetta's Place in downtown Benton Harbor and gawk at the black girls who frequented the place with their tight leisure suits and large afros. Two in particular had caught his eye. They sang together on stage and each of them were as beautiful as the other. Naje and Starlet were both superstars in Rosetta's, keeping the audience captivated for hours on end with their syrupy soul stirring voices. Neither of them seemed to notice the young Italian who threw money around in hopes of impressing the young women. He quickened his pace toward the cabin with the added motivation of a horny man anxious to get to his prize. He opened the door and for whatever reason entered with his back turned. "Let's kill this little fucker so we can go to Rosetta's. I wanna see if I can finally get that little regazza nera in the bed at least once!" Marcel said as he locked the door.

"What little black girl is that?" Jimmy Galici asked.

Marcel fumbled with the door lock, trying to escape, but Julius grabbed him and spun him around. "You ain't killing shit today playa!" Julius said, patting him down and taking the small caliber pistol from his waistband.

"Come on fellas. I know you guys can understand. It was just business. My bosses wanted the man responsible for the priest, that's all!" Marcel pleaded.

Charlie Boy whispered something in Otha Lee's ear and Otha Lee smiled a knowing smile. He cocked his pistol and handed it to Charlie Boy, who in turn stepped to the front to face Marcel Franco. "Do you have brothers Marcel?" He asked.

"Yeah, two."

"Where do you fit on the food chain Mr. Franco?" Charlie Boy asked.

A look of confusion washed across Marcel Franco's face.

"You look confused, so let me ask that a different way. Are you the youngest, the oldest, or are you in the middle?" He asked.

"I'm the oldest."

"Ohhhh, that explains it. See as the youngest child I'm often underestimated and left out. My dear brothers here don't believe that I'm capable of handling my own business. So, I'm left always fighting to prove myself; to prove my love. They believe that since I'm the youngest, I'm privileged and needy. I'm always put in a positon where I'm constantly trying to impress men that deserve no impressing. Much like your little brothers, I'm sure. They look up to you, so they're willing to do just about anything to gain your respect, right? Right!!??" Charlie Boy screamed.

"R-r-r-right."

"That's better, don't be rude. So, I said self, and myself said yeah, Charlie Boy. I said what can I do to prove to my brothers that I'm the baby boy, but I ain't no baby...boy and myself said kill the son-of-a-bitch that caused your family so much of an inconvenience. Mr. Franco, I don't think you're a very nice person and I do believe if we were to let you go today you'd try and hunt us down, so with that in mind, I bid you a farewell!" Charlie Boy said.

Marcel Franco fell to his knees and began to beg and plead for his life. "I have kids Mr. Gage please. My little Nancy is only five and my Michael is only two. Please don't do this."

"I don't even have kids yet, but you were going to kill me before I even finished high school. So fuck you!" Charlie Boy barked.

Marcel Franco opened his mouth to contest, but before he ever uttered a word Charlie Boy jammed the pistol into his mouth and emptied the clip of Otha Lee's gun. Marcel collapsed into a puddle of his own blood and brains. Charlie Boy turned to Eugene and Julius, then to Otha Lee and Jimmy Galici. "I love each of you with every breath in me, you included Mr. G, but any of you ever test my gangster again, you'll meet the same fate as Marcel Franco! Can you dig it?" Charlie Boy asked, wiping Marcel's slobber from the pistol before handing it back to Otha Lee.

CHAPTER 31

Spring had come whipping into Detroit with a crisp vengeance. It had melted away the snow and melted away the quiet anxiety that nagged at Julius' soul. The Gage boys had continued to do jobs for the Detroit outfit, but there was something different. It was almost as if Jimmy Galici was moving into another realm of the business. His reign over Detroit was as solid as ever, but he now had *friends* in New York and as far away as Texas ringing his phone for *favors*.

With Tuffy gone and the deed to his estate signed over into the Gage brothers' names, they'd settled in comfortably, utilizing the vast amenities that they had enjoyed and trained in under Tuffy's tutelage. Eugene had taken it upon himself to commandeer Tuffy's old room with its king size bed and larger than life living space. He was lying in his bed with his arms folded behind his head, with his eyes closed. Both he and Otha Lee had taken up with two local girls named Elizabeth and Emma. Eugene was enamored with Elizabeth and he spent every waking hour that he wasn't working, or training with her nearby. As Julius walked into Eugene's room, she lay naked with her arm draped over his chest.

"You awake bro?" Julius asked.

"Yeah, I'm awake. What's going on?"

Elizabeth stirred slightly, but didn't wake up.

"I need to speak with you in private man," Julius said, moving toward the door.

"Whatever you gotta say to me can be said in front of Liz. We don't keep no secrets from each other."

"Man, I ain't tryna talk business in front of your broad. Get dressed and meet me in the parlor downstairs," Julius huffed, tossing pants in Eugene's direction.

"She ain't no broad as you put it, ol' disrespectful ass nigga."

Julius didn't say a word. He eased Eugene's door shut and went to the next brother's room. He kept it up until he had informed all three of them about the family meeting. They all met in the parlor, still waiting for Eugene to make his grand entrance. Nearly a half hour later, he finally traipsed down to the parlor with Elizabeth Miller in tow.

"This is a family business meeting. I don't think you should be having no females join!" Charlie Boy snapped.

"Shut up little nigga, and stay outta grown folk business!" Eugene countered then added. "Julius put a leash on your puppy man!"

"Nah, you put a leash on your bitch nigga. Don't put no leash on me punk!" Charlie Boy snapped, removing the pistol from his shoulder holster.

Eugene in turn did the same. "Call her another bitch nigga! Go 'head say it!"

235

"You two done? Goddamn, can we ever have a moment where somebody isn't trying to kill each other? Elizabeth baby, would you be so kind as to leave and call Eugene a little later? We have a little family business to attend," Julius said in his smoothest voice.

Elizabeth shot Charlie Boy a hateful glance and kissed Eugene deeply. "Yeah no problem Julius and thank you for being a gentleman, unlike some people in the family. Eugene baby, I'll call you later."

Elizabeth strolled out of the parlor in route to the front door. Her expensive high heels clicked and clacked and it wasn't until Julius heard the front door open and close that he began to speak.

"Gene man, I'm tired of fighting with you man. You're like a little kid with this shit!" Julius argued.

"Kill that shit. Liz don't seem to think I'm no kid!" Eugene said, rubbing his crotch.

"Yeah, that little piece of pussy got your nose wide open too! What the fuck you see in her anyway?"

"In addition to what Mr. G here sends us, her daddy and Emma's daddy sends us plenty of work. Them niggas got dope from here to New York City. The list of rivals that they need taken care of is endless because everybody wants to be the smack king!" Eugene said proudly.

"Well, for future reference, if we have some business to handle, let's keep it between us," Julius advised.

Jimmy Galici stood and waved his hand as if to calm the volatile conversation. "It won't be long until Charlie Boy walks across that stage and gets his diploma and that's something that we can all be proud of, but there is chatter in the street about that thing that took place in the woods," Jimmy Galici said. He knew that he had their full attention then, because no one was moving or talking. "Those Chicago boys are going to be trying to find a way to hit hard and make their presence felt, so we have to be on our toes. I honestly think it would be best if you all left for a little while. In your business you can set up shop anywhere," he said.

"That's actually not a bad idea Mr. G," Julius agreed.

"I know. I have some connections in the same town that that thing happened in and I also have a couple of little jobs in Dallas that need to be handled. When things cool off bada bing, you're right back here like you never left," Jimmy Galici explained.

"I like the idea, but what do you guys think?" Julius asked his brothers.

"Fuck that shit! I ain't scared of them linguine eating muhfuckas man. Why we gotta leave? Naw, I ain't going nowhere!" Eugene said.

"Yeah, me neither man. This our home, and this where we run our shit! Fuck Texas and fuck raggedy ass Benton Harbor!" Otha Lee chimed in.

"I'm with you Julius. Shit, home is where you make it and I ain't tryna die no time soon just for a pretty ass house and a hairy snatch. Besides, a change in scenery might do us good!" Charlie Boy said.

"It's settled then. Next week after Charlie Boy walks across that stage, we're leaving. First stop Benton Harbor, next stop Texas. You boys sure you can hold down the family name while we're gone?" Julius teased.

"Shiiiiiit, by the time you niggas come back, the Gage name will be the most feared in Detroit. The mere mention of our name is gonna make niggas piss themselves, trust me," Eugene assured him.

*****

Gina stood in the middle of Charlie Boy's room facing him with tears in her eyes. She straightened his tie one last time, licked her thumb and smoothed his eyebrows. She let her soft hand caress the sternness of his jaw and turned to leave. She had sacrificed so much for the boy that family and friends didn't seem to understand. They thought she pitied the young boy and that she did it out of some hidden, deep seeded obligation. They thought that Gina was trying to replace Ernesto, but she couldn't, she wouldn't. True, Charlie Boy had come into her life when she needed him, but her goal had never been to replace Ernesto. Her argument had always been that, if a parent lost a child, should that lessen the parent's love for the siblings? No one understood that though, not even Albert. Less than a year after Ernie's death, Albert picked up and left town. No warning, nothing, he just vanished. He'd skipped work at the deli one day because of a stomach ache, but when Gina had gone to check on him after the lunch rush was over, he was gone. Empty drawers remained opened and clothes hangers were strewn about the room as if Albert had left in a hurry. The only

238

remnants of his presence was a note that he'd left behind in his elementary scribble scratch that rambled on about his embarrassment and how their friends saw them. How she had not only replaced Ernesto, but him as well. How she hadn't touched him in months, blah, blah blah. In Gina's mind though, those were just excuses; a way for Albert to shirk his responsibilities as a husband. Gina had been crushed, but if he couldn't see how amazing Charlie Boy was, then it was his loss. That was more than eleven years earlier and now he was graduating from high school. She had intentionally never remarried because she refused to explain herself, or her relationship with Charlie Boy. As she left the room Charlie Boy trotted after her, "Mama Gina?" He said.

"Yes, my love?"

"Thank you for not giving up on me. You know, for being a mother to me and my brothers. Thanks for having my back all the time, no matter what. When I walk across that stage tonight, that diploma will be for you!" He hugged and kissed her.

"No baby. That diploma is for you and your bright future!"

Charlie Boy held out his arm, Gina hooked it with her own and they descended the stairs.

Julius stood at the bottom of the stairs swollen with pride. Seeing as how both Otha Lee and Eugene had dropped out of school, opting for the lucrative world of murder for hire, Charlie Boy would be the first Gage that Julius knew of to graduate from high school. Behind Julius stood nearly thirty people, some of whom Charlie Boy knew, but others not at all. "What's all this?" Charlie Boy asked.

"Just a little precaution against the Chicago boys. But, don't worry about all of that, damn man look at you!" Julius said, bear hugging his little brother. Then he added, "Mama would be so proud of you bruh!"

"She'd be more proud of you for keeping us together bruh!"

"Man enough of this kumbaya ass bullshit! Y'all can hug and kiss after the graduation. I got shit to do!" Eugene sniffed.

"It don't matter whether we get there now, or get there later, the graduation still gonna start at the same time, so pipe down!" Julius countered.

*****

When they pulled into the parking area of the graduation, Charlie Boy's entourage looked more like a presidential caravan than a senior high school graduation. A procession of limousines and luxury sedans all corralled around one vehicle; a black Lincoln Continental. Charlie Boy stepped out of his brother's car and was surrounded by some of the heaviest muscle that the Detroit mob had to offer. If Marcel Franco's people had any ideas about retaliating, they were more than prepared to handle it.

Once inside, Mafiosi spread out into different parts of the auditorium, watching the parents and spectators closely, just in case someone was trying to blend in with the crowd.

Name after name was called until finally they heard it. "Charles Boyd Gage," the principal said.

Julius, Otha Lee, Gina and Jimmy Galici all erupted into raucous cheers, but Eugene, not surprisingly, barely clapped. He applauded his brother more out of obligation than genuine congratulations. As soon as Charlie Boy received his diploma, he headed for the door with the mobsters following close behind. The move came as a total surprise to Julius and the rest of the family, so they all scrambled to catch them before they made it outside. Mama Gina caught up to him first and took him by his hand. "Charlie Boy! Why would you leave like that?" She asked.

"Ma, I got what I came for! Why hang around until they make it to Z? Most of these people dislike me, because they can't get like me. So, I have no interest in staying here and pretending like everything is hunky-dory you know? I'd rather go home and party with my family."

"I understand baby. We can do whatever you want," Gina said.

They all emerged from the auditorium in high spirits, excited about going back to the Gage compound to party. A black sedan pulled into the parking lot mere feet from them and came to a stop. The mobsters formed a protective barrier around the family and drew their weapons. Seconds later a trusted, but somewhat loud and low level hoodlum named Tony No Nuts emerged from the driver's seat. He was a little too ambitious in Jimmy Galici's eyes and he would do just about anything to fit in. He was all bravado and swagger with very few brains. He had no idea what tact, or diplomacy was, so it came as no surprise when he blurted out to Jimmy Galici, "Boss they bombed the deli!"

"What? Who?!" Jimmy Galici asked.

"Those Chicago assholes! I got a few guys from the neighborhood coming down and we're gonna handle this for you boss! I told them, I said, the boss will be grateful for you's guys stepping up! I told them, the boss doesn't take kindly to assholes messing around on our turf. We all know how much you loved that place!" Tony No Nuts said.

"So you're speaking for me now? Do me a favor and shut the fuck up! Don't ever assume that you're qualified to speak for me. I've forgotten more than you will ever know!" Jimmy Galici snapped. Tony No Nuts slinked away quietly without so much as an acknowledgement that he understood. Jimmy Galici turned his back to the man and conferred with the crowd that he was traveling with.

Back at the Gage compound, Jimmy disbursed his soldiers to go and keep an eye on his other properties while he assigned four of his most trusted Mafiosi to guard Gina at her home. The only ones to remain were Jimmy Galici, Crazy Vinny, Joey Craps, Sammy Bags and the Gage brothers.

"This shit is about to get real ugly!" Jimmy Galici warned.

"We're ready to go to war! We're family Mr. G and as you've always said, cut off the head and the body is useless! Give us the word and we'll go straight to the source," Julius huffed.

"No!" Jimmy Galici screamed, surprising most everyone present, but he softened quickly as Crazy Vinny took the floor.

"I think what my friend is trying to say is that you're not invited to this party, fellas. He can't risk you boys dying, or getting hurt. He'll also lose Gina in the process. We've set aside some cash and things for you boys to sustain yourselves until you get settled and we can get some work coming your way!" Vinny said.

"So fellas, this will be our last night together," Jimmy added.

"If that's what you want Mr. G, then we'll respect that and leave," Julius said.

"I ain't going no muhfuckin' where! This is our home, our house, so nah count me out! Julius, you gon' just tuck your tail and run when the family needs you?" Eugene smirked.

"I don't understand why you're so much like Nathaniel Gage, but be clear, I ain't never ran from shit! If Mr. Galici says to stand down, then that's what we'll do."

"Well, I'm with Eugene! Where else we gonna find a house this nice? So, I say we stay and fight," Otha Lee insisted.

"This is my fight and if you choose to stay you will stay out of it! Capisce?!" Jimmy Galici ordered.

"That's even better! Shit," Eugene said sarcastically.

Jimmy Galici put his hand on Eugene's shoulder and lightly tapped him on the cheek with his other hand. "Good boy. We'll let you boys say your goodbyes. Come on fellas," he said to his friends, turning to leave.

After Jimmy Galici left and it was just him and his brothers, Julius addressed Eugene. "What the fuck is wrong with you man?" He asked.

"What you mean?"

"That's even better? What kinda disloyal shit is that to say?" Julius asked.

"Loyalty? Man I'm loyal to the money. Tuffy was loyal to them muhfuckas and where he at, huh? They put him on a plane back to Italy like he wasn't shit. You see this house? You see these bad ass threads? Shiiiit, why should I fight, or leave and risk losing it all?" Eugene snorted.

"Man, fuck this house, this is brick and wood. Fuck them ho's you love so much, fuck them clothes, fuck your little expensive ass shoes, fuck all this shit! This is material shit, it comes and goes, but family is forever! Besides, you wouldn't have this house or fancy clothes if it wasn't for Mr. G!" Julius reminded his brother.

"No nigga, fuck you and that family over money bullshit! A broke family ain't shit!" Eugene shouted, jumping in Julius' face.

Julius hit Eugene in the stomach with such force that he knocked the wind out of him, doubling him over in pain. As Eugene knelt there gasping for air, Julius let his knee crash into his face, sending him sprawling to the floor. Julius pulled out his .45 caliber pistol, cocked it and pointed it at Eugene's head. He looked at Otha Lee who immediately threw his hands up in surrender.

"I don't want no trouble bro!" Otha Lee said.

"You little niggas need to remember that I'm still the same amount of years older than you as I was when you were born! I'm still the oldest and ain't shit slick to a can of oil. Y'all got these little flunky niggas out here fooled, but you and me both know who the killer is in this family. Try me again and I'ma remind you!" Julius hissed.

Nobody moved and no one spoke. Eugene had always known how to push Julius' buttons, but in the same respect, he knew when his brother was serious and Julius was deadly serious.

"Okay bro, you win. I quit! You ain't hafta hit me like that!" Eugene said between forced breaths. Tears streaked his medium brown cheeks, more so from embarrassment than pain. Instantly Julius felt guilty, as he watched Eugene struggling to get to his feet, pouting, looking pitiful. He could only see the face of that little frightened boy that had been through just as much as himself. He saw the hunger and the uncertainty that they'd faced and he understood, but he needed to be taught a lesson. He replaced his weapon and helped Eugene to his feet. "I'm sorry man, you just need to learn to let shit go sometimes! Look, y'all already made up ya minds so, ain't much to discuss. I'ma take Charlie Boy with me. When we get settled, we'll call and let y'all know," Julius said.

The Gage boys took turns hugging one another. That would be the first time that any of them would be without the other and it scared them primarily, because although they didn't always see eye to eye, they had always depended on their familial connection and the ability to feed off of one another.

CHAPTER 32

In the wee hours of the following morning, Julius guided his Lincoln onto John C Lodge freeway headed toward I-75 South.

"Well big brother, where to?" Charlie Boy asked.

"I figure we'll give Dallas a try since Mr. G said we have friends there."

"Cool, baby cool!" Charlie Boy said.

They had become men on the streets of Detroit. True, they were southern boys to the heart, but city slick thanks to the city of Detroit. For hours Julius drove and just before dusk they pulled into a small gas station in Little Rock, Arkansas. The homecoming was bittersweet for Julius. He missed the simplistic country living, but racism was still alive and well in the south. The gas station proudly displayed a sign that read *No Coloreds when white folk are inside the store! Management.* It was a stark reminder that regardless of what money a black man was able to amass, he was still considered a nigger in the south.

"Stay here Charlie Boy. I'ma go pay for this gas. Hopefully I won't have to slap one of these honkies!" Julius said. He tucked his pistol into the waistband of his slacks and got out of the car. The bell clanged above Julius' head as he entered Hackney's General Store.

"What you want boy?" The store clerk asked.

"Gimme three dollars on pump one. Anywhere to get food 'round here?" Julius asked.

"Not for no darkie, lessen you finna drive to the bottoms. They got some places down there that might serve your kind boy," the clerk said while dragging Julius' money off of the counter.

"Why you gotta be so nasty man? I'm just asking you a simple question," Julius countered. He intentionally bent over to retrieve two bags of pork rinds so that the clerk could see his pistol.

"I don't want no trouble boy! Just pay for your shit and git!" He said. He put one hand beneath the counter in an attempt to bluff Julius into believing that he had a weapon stashed there.

"Yeah, me either." Julius said, throwing a crumpled dollar bill onto the counter. "Keep the change peckerwood!" He added as he left the store. The clerk removed his hand from the beer bottle beneath the counter and sighed in relief. Julius was still smiling as he made it to the car.

"What's so funny?" Charlie Boy asked.

Julius tossed him the pork rinds and continued to smile. "Honkies man, honkies."

*****

"You ever thought that you were meant to do something other than the shit that we do bruh?" Julius asked.

"Num, smack, smack, num, uh huh."

Julius looked over at Charlie Boy and hadn't realized that he'd fallen asleep. They'd be pulling into Dallas in less than an hour and Julius' heart felt heavy. His heart was heavy due to loneliness, but not physically and not for a woman. It was hard to explain. Something was missing. It was an emptiness that no amount of sex, booze, or blues music could fill. Whatever it was that he was missing, he hoped that it was in Dallas, because he hadn't found it in Detroit. He understood that with new beginnings came new possibilities. He was aware of that, but it didn't feel like a new beginning. If you lived by the gun, you died by the gun, that much was true. If he ever had sons, he would insulate them from the path that he and his brothers chose. He wanted to set a solid foundation for his children to flourish. Julius smiled as he pictured himself the father of a tiny, chocolate baby girl with pigtails. Julius considered himself one of the good guys when it came to women. He'd only been with two women, neither of whom happened to be what he was looking for. One was an admitted alcoholic, who preferred to drink her breakfast, lunch and dinner. The other was a control freak who felt the need to control every aspect of their relationship, from the clothes that he wore to how he spent his time. His thoughts were interrupted by the sound of a monstrous boom and then the sound of lightning crackling that illuminated the sky. Large raindrops pelted the windshield and then the sky opened up, showering down torrential rains, making it nearly impossible for Julius to see. He considered pulling over and waiting for the rain to let up, but he was tired and needed a good meal and the comfort of a nice, soft bed. The hard rain didn't last too long, almost as if it was only raining on one side of the road. Through the lifting rain, Julius saw a sign blinking ahead of him in the distance. Clara's Kitchen shined brightly from the highway as Julius exited. He reached over and shook Charlie Boy awake. "Hey, you hungry playa?" He asked.

"Shiiiiiit, is pig pussy pork? Hell yeah, I'm hungry! Where we at?"

"We in Dallas bruh," Julius said.

"Oh shit, I was sleep that long?"

"Hell yeah and your breath smell like you was sleep longer than that! Let's go in here and see what's on the menu," Julius said as he exited the car.

The inside of Clara's Kitchen was brightly lit, but its patrons looked like street workers. It reminded Julius of some of the haunts that he and his brothers had frequented in the ghettos of Detroit. Girls in short miniskirts and thigh high boots danced and giggled in the middle of the floor, while their young pimps with colorfully coordinated outfits cheered them on. Julius and Charlie Boy took seats at the counter looking over the menu. When Julius looked up from his menu, an elderly black woman was smiling at him. "What can I get for you handsome?" She asked.

"Yes ma'am, can I get a cup of coffee and a BLT, and whatever my little brother wants."

"And for you baby?" She said to Charlie Boy.

"Yes ma'am, I'll take fried chicken, collard greens with yams and cornbread. Sweet tea to drink please."

"I'll get that right in for you," Clara said. She snatched the ticket from its pad and hung it in the opening for the fry cook to take. She turned back to the Gage brothers. "You boys ain't from 'round here are you?"

"No ma'am, we from Arkansas by way of Detroit," Julius said.

"I can tell. You two dressed all up like you got a little sense. You see how these boys dress with these clown colors and big jewelry? They make their living off the backs of these little stupid girls. Sleeping with any Tom, Dick, or Harry willing to pay 'em. I hope y'all ain't like that!"

"No ma'am, never had no aspirations to be no pimp," Julius said politely.

"Good! Now what brings y'all to Dallas?"

"Just wanted a change of scenery and tired of cold weather," Charlie Boy said.

"It gets pretty cold here too honey. I don't think y'all gon' have no problems keeping warm baby. These girls gon' be all over you two!"

"Why you say that?" Charlie Boy asked.

"Nicely dressed, smooth, chocolate boys like you? Hell you're both so handsome, you're borderline pretty. Watch how they flock to you." She winked.

Clara turned, grabbed their plates and set them in front of them. "Eat up babies, before it gets cold. What's your names?"

"I'm Julius and this here Charlie Boy."

Before Clara had a chance to respond, her attention had been drawn to the loud couple that came stumbling through the door. Julius followed her gaze and noticed a girl with a white waitress's dress and apron on, strolling arm in arm with a man about his age. His white suit with its large yellow lapels matched perfectly with the yellow lizard skin shoes and yellow fedora with white band that he was wearing. He smacked the girl on the ass and kissed her on her neck. "Yellow Shoes, what's up baby!?" One of the pimps shouted.

"You know how it goes playa. Breaking these ho's, checking that dough! Purse first, checks next. If a bitch break bread we might have sex, ya dig!"

Julius turned away from the men and dug into his BLT.

"Chele you're late...again!" Clara said.

"I know Miss Clara. I lost track of time, that's all."

"Baby, losing track of time is coming in ten, or fifteen minutes late. You're three and a half hours late, sugar." Clara huffed.

"I got a reeeeeal good reason this time Miss Clara. Guess what?"

"I can't wait to hear this one. What Chele?" Clara inquired, rolling her eyes.

"Look what Yellow Shoes gave me! We just got engaged!" Chele said, excitedly, holding her finger out for Clara to see.

"How you gon' marry a pimp baby?" Clara asked.

"That's just his job Miss Clara, but he loves me!"

"A job huh? A pimp don't love nothing but a purse and what's in it baby, but you can believe what you wanna believe. Now get these young men their drinks. One coffee, one sweet tea," Clara said.

Chele looked toward where Clara was pointing and nearly fainted. She felt her coochie twitch and then moisture. There sat two of the most handsome men she'd ever laid eyes on. She felt guilty because Yellow Shoes had just proposed to her and here she was lusting after another man. Her hand trembled as she placed the drinks in front of them.

"Can I get you anything else? Anything?" Chele asked, letting that last *anything* linger and slither out of her mouth like a personal invite. Yellow Shoes from his perch across the room noticed her fondness of Julius and seized the opportunity to degrade her.

"Aye waitress, aye bitch, get me some coffee and a slice of pie, ho!" He screamed.

As Chele scurried to get his coffee and pie from the back, Yellow Shoes made his way to the counter. "How's it hangin' baby? I'm Yellow Shoes, ya dig? Did my bitch give you any problems?" He asked.

"Nah, she was a sweetheart, but congratulations on your upcoming nuptials," Julius said, sarcastically.

253

Yellow Shoes, threw his head back and laughed sadistically. "You mean that ring? Dig these blues baby, that ain't shit, but a dime store trinket playa. I got a drawer full of 'em at home and a stable full of bitches just like her out in the street!"

"Wow!" Julius said, feigning admiration.

"Indeed, so if you ever need a bitch, or two, or a favor just look me up!"

"I'll keep that in mind." Julius smirked.

"Mama Clara, here you go!" Yellow Shoes said, peeling three five dollar bills off of a huge wad of bills. "Their meal is on me. By the way I didn't catch you playa's names," he added.

"Julius and Charlie Boy Gage," Julius said.

"Gage huh? I like that shit! It's gangsta as a muhfucka. Enjoy your meal playa and welcome to Dallas. Gage, I like that," Yellow Shoes said as he walked away.

Clara watched him. She couldn't stand the young arrogant pimp, but he tipped well and threw money around freely. "See they already know you're not from here baby. Be careful of that one though," she whispered.

Julius leaned in. "He might need to be careful of me!" He said, winking at Clara.

"He's envious of anybody that's doing good or that he feels like don't need his ass, but somehow I get the idea that you can take care of yourself handsome," Clara said.

"I do okay. So let me ask you. Are there any hotels around here?"

"The nice hotels like the Adolphus, the Belmont and the Magnolia won't even let you through the front door baby. They still don't allow blacks in there unless you the help." She chuckled and then continued, "My friend Delores has a big rooming house not too far from here. I can call her and see if she got some rooms open if you want honey," Clara offered.

"That would be great ma'am."

Miss Clara stepped into the kitchen and put in the call to her friend Delores, explaining that she had some nice presentable young men fresh into town and in need of lodging. All the while, Chele kept tugging at her apron string, trying to get her attention. After the call was over she addressed the young girl. "Whatchu want chile?" She asked.

"Who is them men? Where they from?"

"They from nunya," she said, rolling her eyes.

"Where that's at?"

"You ain't never been to nunya bidness? It's up by get back to work and across the border from if you late again, you fired! Don't nan one of them boys want you child after you done come up in here with a doggone pimp." Clara laughed.

Clara went to Julius and scrawled the address and directions onto a napkin. She told him not to be a stranger, to watch out for snakes in the streets of Dallas, Texas and bid them farewell. Julius agreed to stay in touch as he and Charlie Boy moved toward the door. He didn't notice that every pair of eyes in Clara's Kitchen were on the two newcomers, especially Chelle's. She was devising a plan to

255

get away from Yellow Shoes and make Julius her man, if he'd have her.

CHAPTER 33

For days Charlie Boy had tooled around south Dallas, unimpressed by what he saw. It was more the same like Detroit, especially the street life. He could always tell the hustlers from the pimps and the whores from the square women. They moved a lot different, maybe not to the naked eye, but he could tell. He walked from the rooming house to Clara's Kitchen, grabbed breakfast and sat in the park across the street from rooming house. It was just after 9 am and the streets were busy with activity. Most working class people had already made it to their destinations and the only ones on the street were those involved in illegal activity. A junky that he'd met named MC ambled over to where he sat. "Gage, my brother how you feeling slick?"

"Whatchu want MC?" Charlie Boy asked.

"Who says I want something?"

"Only time a nigga walk up on you that friendly is when they want something, so whatchu want?" Charlie Boy asked again.

"Man, I got this nice piece of change coming in later on this week, but I'm sick right now mane. I just need me a little taste to knock the edge off."

"If you can't afford to put that shit in your veins, you might need to change your habits bruh. I'ma let you hold $10, but I want my goddamn money back MC. Don't make me hafta look for your ass!" Charlie Boy said, peeling a ten from a wad of bills.

"I promise man! You'll see. Shit, I might give you $20 back, you never know."

"Uh huh." Charlie Boy smirked. MC scurried off in search of his next fix. Days later Charlie Boy would learn that MC had been given a bad dose of heroin and died foaming at the mouth in an alley just off of Grand Ave.

"That was so sweet," a voice said behind him. Charlie Boy turned around to see a beautiful, young white girl staring at him with a smile on her face. She looked different from the white girls in Detroit, with their poodle skirts and bobby socks. She wore a form fitting dress with very high heels and no stockings. Her legs were shaved smooth and she had on very little makeup, but Charlie Boy had seen her kind before. She was a whore. He was willing to bet his life on it.

"Yeah well, I try. Whatchu doing out so early. You ho-ing?" Charlie Boy asked with a knowing grin on his face.

"You said that like it's something wrong with it?"

"Hey, if selling your little pussy is what you're into, who am I to judge?" He shrugged.

"I guess you could say I do what I have to do to survive. I'm Mel by the way." She extended her hand.

"I'm Charlie Boy. Now run along because it's too early for me to have to fuck up some pimp behind his broad!"

"I don't have a pimp, thank you very much! I sell me for me. So, I can stop whenever I want!" Mel said.

"So, why don't you?" Charlie Boy asked. He'd never been attracted to white women, especially coming from Arkansas, but being around the Galici's had definitely opened him up to different possibilities.

"If I had a reason to quit, I would. A pretty black man like you could make a girl change for the better!"

"I'm not trying to have niggas laughing at me for being with no ho! You probably done been with most of these niggas over here anyway," Charlie Boy said.

"I stay off Gaston with my brother. I don't work over here. I just come over here to score my reefa. All of my tricks are either picked up downtown, or in west Dallas. South Dallas is off limits, because my brother patrols over here."

"Patrols? Your brother a pig or something?" Charlie Boy asked.

"Yeah, unfortunately. Can I ask you something?"

"Yeah."

"What's the difference between you getting involved with someone who has a past that you know about and getting involved with someone who hides their past and you find out about it later? I guess what I'm saying is, okay, I'm not a virgin, but so what? I doubt if you'll find a virgin in south Dallas anyway. Or are you just a prejudiced asshole who doesn't want to give a white girl a chance?" She asked, sliding onto the bench next to Charlie Boy.

"Fucking with a white girl in these days and times is suicide baby girl. What makes you think that you're worth the trouble?"

"I may not be worth the trouble, but there's only one way to find out. We can be friends if you want. We can just fuck if you want. We can do whatever Charlie Boy wants," Mel said. She had a pained look on her face as if pleading, almost campaigning for a spot on his team.

"If I did agree to fuck with you on some relationship shit, you can't ho no mo'. If I find out you're ho-ing, or that you stepped out on me once, I'm done! I shouldn't even be considering no shit like this, but I like you."

"As of right now, I'm done whoring!" Mel declared. She reached inside her purse, retrieved a large wad of bills and handed it to Charlie Boy.

"What's this?"

"It's my choosing fee. In the pimp and whore kingdom, it's customary to give a dowry to your new man!" She said.

"I ain't no pimp, but dig these blues. Take that money, go get enough lids of reefa to sell and let's make money. The same streets you ran to sell pussy will be the same streets you run to sell that reefa. Same streets, different product."

Mel stood and took Charlie Boy's hand in her own and kneeled in front of him. "I promise to make you happy baby, or die trying. Just like you told me, just don't cheat on me. Men have taken advantage of me my whole life. Maybe we should start slow, but I don't know how to start slow. So, from this day forward I'm fully committed to you and only you!"

Chapter 34

Julius stood on the porch of the rooming house and stretched, trying to get the cobwebs out of his head. He'd made contact with Jimmy Galici and he'd set up a meeting with some very influential "friends," so Julius was anxious to get his day started. He saw Charlie Boy sitting in the park eating breakfast, talking to a shapely young, white girl. He didn't know whether it was from instinct, or paranoia, but he looked both ways frantically searching for the cops. The last thing that Julius needed was to have to kill a cop for rousing his little brother. At any rate he didn't want to pull him away from his conversation, but they were slated to meet their "friends" at 10 am downtown and Mr. Galici had emphasized not being late. The white girl was kneeling in front of Charlie Boy when Julius whistled. Charlie Boy immediately looked toward the rooming house and waved his acknowledgement. Julius walked back inside, loaded his pistols and put his blazer on. He passed Delores in the hall on the way out the door and she winked at him. When Miss Clara said she had a friend with a rooming house, he had naturally assumed that the woman was elderly like Miss Clara, but he'd been wrong. Delores was maybe five or ten years older than him and she was sweet on him. She wasn't married and she didn't have any children. She and Julius talked a lot, mostly about what he wanted in a woman. That was a question that he found rather difficult to answer. She was a Christian woman and had nearly begged him to go to church with her, but Julius was sure that God didn't want to have anything to do with him, so he continually declined her offer. "Your voice, your words and your testimony is powerful Julius. The Lord can use you baby," she'd said.

"The Lord don't need, or want no nigga like me Delores, and neither do you."

Now as they passed each other in the hall, she winked, smiled and brushed his hand with her own. That was her subtle way of letting him know that indeed, she did need *and* want him. If everything went according to plan with their new friends, maybe just maybe, he'd bed her tonight...Maybe.

*****

Julius and Charlie Boy drove downtown and parked at the curb on Commerce St. near the meeting place. He was intentionally a few minutes early so he could scope out the place. No matter how good of friends they were supposed to be, the only person in Dallas that he trusted was sitting next to him. There was little movement near The Carousel Club when Julius and Charlie Boy exited the car. The brothers walked into the club and were immediately impressed by the opulence of the small establishment. Half naked girls walked around the burlesque eyeing the pair of blacks that stood near the front entrance. In the back of the club sat five men. Four of them were sharply dressed while the fifth man looked somewhat disheveled. As they made their way to the table all of them stood and invited them to sit. One of the men extended his hand to Julius.

"You must be Julius? Have a seat, fellas. We've heard a lot about you boys. Our good friend Jimmy G speaks very highly of you and your skills. I'm Joe, Joe Civello. This is Carlos Marcello, Santo Trafficante, this is Jack Ruby, he owns the joint and this is Lee Oswald. You're among friends. Have a seat please, sit. Would you boys like a drink?"

"No thank you, nothing for us. I'd prefer to get right to it," Julius stated bluntly.

Charlie Boy didn't speak. He watched intently though, content with letting Julius handle the business.

"Right down to business? I like that. We have a problem that needs to be taken care of. We have some very influential friends who are willing to pay top dollar for this job," Joe Civello said.

"Who's the target?" Julius asked.

"The son-of-a-bitch that you're hitting is making life very uncomfortable for us and our friends. His fucking family has had their hands in the pockets of the outfit for years and we're sick of it!" Santo Trafficante huffed. He was Tampa's most feared and only standing mob boss. Carlos

Marcello was a boss as well, reigning over New Orleans' underworld with an iron fist. He nodded his head in agreement with Trafficante.

"Okay, so if you all agree this guy is a problem, then who is it?" Julius repeated.

"You ask a lot of questions," Carlos Marcello said tersely.

"Maybe I'm asking the wrong question. Let's try this again. How much is this job worth?" Julius asked.

"If the job is successful, all parties involved will receive $250,000. So, between you and your brother, that's a half million smackers," Joe Civello said.

Julius' eyes bucked with excitement. He had never done a hit for more than $20,000 and those had been very influential people as well. "With those kinds of incentives gentlemen it's nearly impossible for me to say no, but I will walk away if someone doesn't tell me who the mark is! This is too much money for a common mark," Julius said bluntly.

"The mark is John Fitzgerald Kennedy! Does that make a difference?" Carlos Marcello asked.

Julius didn't know how to answer that question. Most black people saw Kennedy as their savior, like he loved all things black, but Julius knew better. To him he was just another white man who'd been smart enough to capitalize off of making the black man his ally instead of his enemy. Anybody with a half-ounce of common sense realized that a move toward the black vote was an almost assured win. Some white folk in their prejudice couldn't put their hatred aside long enough to see the bigger picture. "Do you have a plan, or do I need to construct one?" Julius asked.

The man that they had introduced as Lee was sweating profusely and seemed edgy and uncomfortable. Jack Ruby spread a large map of downtown Dallas across the table. "You and your brother will be positioned here at the Texas Book Depository on the 7th floor in a corner office. Lee will be positioned in the same building, but on the 6th floor. We have another man coming in as insurance by the name of Joseph Milteer. He couldn't be here because of his racial views, concerning you people. He'll be positioned in the old county jail on the 5th floor. He has a man inside of that jail that will get him into position. We also have a few men inside the Dallas Police Department that will take position on the grassy hill on Elm St. Just for extra security, I have a few friends on the force that I can rely on just in case things don't go as planned," Jack Ruby said.

"Sounds like you have everything worked out. Can I have a few days to think about it?" Julius asked.

"We need an answer soon. He's slated to be here next Friday," Santo Trafficante said.

"I'll get back to Mr. Ruby within the next two days," Julius said. He shook hands with all of the men present. However, when he shook hands with Lee Harvey Oswald, the man's hands were clammy and his handshake was limp. Julius locked eyes with the man and felt a cold chill run down his spine. He had no way of knowing it then, but he was locking eyes with a dead man.

　　　*****

"You know that's a setup right?" Charlie Boy asked.

"Yeah, I know, but these aren't the type of men that you just say no to. Nah, we have to handle this the diplomatic way."

"Man, we get caught up in this shit and not only will we be on death row, but we'll be hated by every black person in America. You know how niggas feel about Kennedy!" Charlie Boy said, with a chuckle.

"Yeah, I hear you," Julius said, but in truth, he wasn't listening to his brother. The mob was offering them life changing money for less than an hour's worth of dirty work. Charlie Boy was right about one thing though, assassinating the President of the United States was indeed a death sentence and not by the government. Julius was nobody's fool. He was well aware that the mobsters had no intentions of parting with that much money. It would be cheaper to kill them and make it look like an accident, or kill them in an alley and stuff their pockets with $100 worth of smack. Yes, Julius felt it, he knew it deep down inside that he and Charlie Boy would end up patsies in a plot much larger than either of them.

CHAPTER 35

Eugene lay in bed staring at the ceiling in deep thought, listening to Elizabeth with her rhythmic wheeze. Something about the things that Julius had said to him ate at his very core. His big brother knew him better than anyone and if he said that Eugene had been acting like Nathaniel, there had to be some truth to it. The last thing that he ever wanted was to be anything like Nathaniel Gage. With Elizabeth pregnant with twins, he would have to make some changes. Not only him, but Otha Lee would need to as well, because Emma was expecting too. Pretty soon there would be more Gages running around and he had some hard choices to make. Now that Jimmy Galici had basically given them the okay to step away from the business, he could either get a square job, or throw himself wholeheartedly into the business. Eugene sprang from bed and ran to Otha Lee's room, not bothering to knock, or announce his presence. He just burst in. In full sight was Emma's round, firm, chocolate ass hiked in the air with her perfectly, pink love slit exposed for the world to see. Her head bobbed up and down on Otha

Lee's shaft while Eugene watched lustfully. He cleared his throat to finally announce his presence, and although Otha Lee looked around her voluptuous ass, Emma never missed a beat. She plopped Otha Lee's phallus out of her mouth and climbed on top of it, letting Eugene see her insert his brother's hard piece into her soft moist crevice. The entire time she kept her eyes trained on Eugene.

"The fuck you want nigga? Standing up there watching with your freaky ass!" Otha Lee barked.

"We need to talk bruh."

"In case you haven't noticed, I'm a little busy right now!"

"Ugh, ugh, ugh, ohhhh daddy, ugh, ugh. I'm gonna cum daddy, ugh!" Emma moaned, throwing her hips in a vicious circle until she collapsed on Otha Lee's chest. She let his stiff, sticky member slip out of her as she raised her ass to once again show her slit. She climbed off of him and walked toward Eugene. "Now y'all can talk and why is your dick hard Gene?" She teased, referring to the stiffness jutting through his pajama pants. Her smooth, chocolate body was beyond perfect. The areola and nipple of her breasts were the same dark luscious hue as her lips. Her breasts were perfectly round and bounced playfully as she sashayed past him. The perfectly coiffed bush between her legs matched the kinky, well put together afro on her head and the sway of her hips was like watching a snake charmer seduce a cobra. She was poetry in motion, with no music.

"I'm a man. I see pussy and my dick gets hard," Eugene said.

Emma giggled as she passed and he smacked her on the ass.

"Nigga, keep your hands off my bitch and what's so important that it would make you disturb my nut?" Otha Lee asked. He had grown irritated by their meaningless conversation and playfulness.

"I think we need to get with Mr. G and get his connect for the hits."

"Why? He keeps the business coming in steady, so why worry?" Otha Lee asked.

"Because he's an old man. I think we need to branch out and do our own thing."

"And what did Julius have to say about that idea?" Otha Lee asked.

"I ain't talked to him about it yet, but he's the one that said we need to man up right? So, I don't see him having a problem with it," Eugene said.

"If Julius gives us his blessing I'm with it, but you think the old man will give up the connection?"

"Either by choice, or by force, but he'll give it up one way or another! Get dressed, we gon' go see if he's with it, or if I'ma hafta kill him!" Eugene said. His hollow laughter boomed throughout the bedroom and poured out into the halls, bouncing and dancing against the mahogany walls.

CHAPTER 36

Jimmy Galici was sitting on his back terrace when his housekeeper, Polly informed him that Eugene and Otha Lee were there to see him. "Good, I'll be right down." Jimmy wanted to talk to them anyway. His plan was simple. After he got his revenge against the Chicago mob, he was out. He was tired of playing the game and would cede power and control of his family over to Crazy Vincent Finazzo. After that he would turn over his hit list connection to the Gage brothers. Hell, he wasn't getting any younger and a few of his associates had already retired and gone south to Florida. As he ascended the stairs he could feel his brittle bones pop and crackle.

"Moving kinda slow there ain't you old man?" Otha Lee asked.

"Yep, I'm about ready to retire son. Let's step into my office." They adjourned to Jimmy Galici's where he told them of his plan to step away from the business. He told them that he no longer wanted to be involved in the day to day and that they would no longer have to answer to anyone.

They were free to do as they pleased. He handed Eugene a small black book. "What's this Mr. G?" Eugene asked.

"This is everything that you will need to make you and your brothers very rich men! Call these people, introduce yourself and they will handle the rest."

Eugene's eyes lit up with excitement, because as much as he hated to admit it, he had been prepared to do whatever was necessary to extract the information from the old man and there he was handing him the keys to the kingdom. "Are you sure about this Mr. Galici?" Eugene asked.

"Absolutely son."

"Nice, now I don't have to kill you for this information!" Eugene said. They all laughed, but Jimmy Galici had no idea how serious Eugene was.

*****

Jimmy Galici bid the boys farewell and went back to his office. He pulled some brochures from his desk and leaned back in his high backed leather chair. The first one showed Boca Raton, Florida with its sandy beaches and endless golf courses. In the center of the trifold brochure a bikini clad blonde was holding a beach ball with a huge smile on her face. In the background were huge mounds of sand and sapphire blue waters. Above her head was the caption: *Discover the fountain of youth at Boca Grande!*

It seemed that the other brochure had missed the mark in marketing to their targeted audience. For whatever reason they had chosen teenaged beach goers, happily frolicking in the water as their signature photo. Even on the inside they showed more teenagers on the beach playing volleyball in the sand. *Home is just a few steps away*, it read. Jimmy Galici grimaced. He could only imagine the youthful horror that living in Ft. Lauderdale might bring. The phone on his desk rang and when he picked it up he heard Julius' voice on the other end.

"Are you alone?" He asked.

Jimmy Galici dropped the brochures. Something wasn't right with him. He'd known the boy for many years and something in his voice didn't sit well in his gut. "Yes, I'm alone. What's going on son. You don't sound right."

"I think I'm in trouble Mr. G!" Julius said.

"What happened? Are you down in Texas making babies like your brothers?"

"Wait, what? No, this is serious!"

"What's wrong son?" Jimmy asked.

"I need you to listen carefully. That new job at the fish market stinks," Julius said.

"Why is that? I thought you liked working at the fish market."

"I do, but they want me to chop the head off of the kingfish," Julius said in code.

"Really? I thought that it was just guppies and perch, maybe a few catfish. You should just quit."

"I want to, but I'm afraid that they will try to make sure that I never work again," Julius said anxiously.

"You let me worry about that. Meanwhile, call Mr. Red and tell him you're no longer interested in the position and I'll handle the rest from my end. I'm sorry son. I didn't know."

"I know," Julius said, as he hung up the phone. Moments later Jimmy Galici was on the phone with Santo Trafficante.

"Pronto?" Trafficante answered.

"Aye Santo, it's Jimmy. How you's doin'?"

"I could be better, I'm okay for an old man, I guess. What you need Jimmy?" He asked.

"I need a favor Santo, friend to friend."

"You name it Jimmy, anything you want," Santo replied.

"I need for you to find another dry cleaner."

"Why? The owner going out of business, or something?"

"Nah, he just doesn't have the experience for a job this size, you know?" Jimmy asked.

"How do I know that if I switch dry cleaners, he won't get sour and burn my suits? He knows how I like my shirts starched, how I like my pants creased and the whole nine."

"I'll take full responsibility. If that happens, I'll replace the suits you lost!" Jimmy Galici said.

"Okay Jimmy, you got it, but you owe me one! Arrivederce."

"Arrivederce," Jimmy replied, hanging up the phone. He had staked his life on Julius' morals. Jimmy had all but raised the four boys and most of his teachings had been on the unvirtuous act of being a rat, but that was big. Even if Julius never opened his mouth, if the plan was botched in any way, not only would Santo Trafficante cash in on Jimmy Galici's promise, but he'd kill Julius and Charlie Boy on general principle.

CHAPTER 37

Julius had watched the news in horror and shock as they recounted John F. Kennedy's assassination. The man that he had met by the name of Lee Harvey Oswald, with the clammy hands, had been arrested for the murder and then subsequently gunned down himself by the club owner Jack Ruby. Julius couldn't help but think that he'd dodged a proverbial bullet by calling not doing the job. He hadn't talked to Jimmy Galici after the ordeal for months, waiting nervously for the mob to come. He was waiting to walk out of one of the juke joints in south Dallas and be gunned down, but they never came. Jimmy Galici had been true to his word and *took care* of it. Dallas was taking a toll on Julius. It was a different type of beast and after a few years of living in the sprawling metropolis, he was ready to move on to greener pastures. He was sitting on the side of his bed in his boxers when he heard a light tap on his door, pulling him from his revelry. "Who is it?" He asked.

"It's Chele, Julius."

He opened the door and she rushed past him, placing two glass containers on the table. He stood in his boxers, lean and sinuous, watching as Chele went into her oversized purse and removed a plate and silverware. She made herself comfortable in his small place and in essence made him more uncomfortable than he already was. "I brought you some of Miss Clara's famous meatloaf, some turnip greens, some candy yams and some lemon cake. I woulda brought you some hot water cornbread, but the lunch rush wiped it out. Now hurry up and eat. I wanna take you to Joskes to get you a new suit!" She said excitedly.

"What are you doing Chele?" Julius asked.

"Whatchu mean?"

"You come up in here like we're together, or something. You got food, you want to take me shopping. What's all this?" Julius asked.

"Miss Clara said a woman needs to care for her man if she wants to keep him around."

"I'm not your man, so where did that come from?" Julius asked, resisting the temptation to laugh.

"Because you fucked me!"

"Yeah, and I told you before we even did it that I wasn't interested in a long term relationship and we couldn't be together."

"Who is she?"

"What?"

"Who is the bitch that's keeping you from me?"

"Ain't no other woman Chele. I just don't want to be with you."

277

"Is it because I work at Lady Love?" She asked sadly.

That was part of the problem, but truth be told, Julius didn't trust Chele. She'd been, according to Miss Clara, robbing the old lady blind just to keep Yellow Shoes flushed with cash. Miss Clara hadn't wanted to believe it, that is, until she caught her red handed. Soon after she caught her, she'd fired her. Chele, being desperate for money, had allowed the pimp Yellow Shoes to put her to work in the strip club. "If that's not it, then what is it? Ain't nobody gonna love you like me Julius."

"Listen, that was a onetime thing; a mistake," Julius clarified.

"Let me make you feel good baby!" Chelle pleaded, reaching toward Julius' crotch.

"No girl! Stop and get out of my room! I'm sorry if it seems like I'm being mean, but you need to leave."

"I'll never love another man the way that I love you Julius. If I can't have you then I don't want nobody else. You're everything I want in a man," Chele whined.

Julius felt bad for Chele. He didn't want to be mean to her, but the only way that he could make her understand was to be perfectly honest. "I'm never going to love you Chele. We're just not meant to be," Julius admitted.

"Look me in my eyes and say that."

"I…am…never…going…to…love…you Chele! Now please if you don't mind, can you get out of my room? I have shit to handle!" Julius said sternly.

Chele dropped her head and shuffled past him. She looked back one last time and blew him a kiss. Julius had effectively crushed her dreams, or so he thought. After Chele left Julius showered quickly and dressed even quicker. He left his small apartment and knocked on Charlie Boy's door three apartments down.

"Come in."

Julius walked in and saw Mel standing in the full length mirror, putting on her earrings. "Can we chat for a few ticks Charlie Boy?" Julius asked.

"Yeah, hell yeah. Mel was leaving anyway. Hold on bruh," he said and turned to Mel. "Mel, don't forget to pick up that money from Bon Ton, then go over to Dixon Circle and get that money from Moon. He's expecting you."

"What about the money from Pine and Colonial and over on Grand Ave?" Mel asked.

"Yeah, hit Grand Ave, but I'll get that money off of Pine and Colonial. I don't want you over there without me. The nigga Yellow Shoes done already disrespected you once," Charlie Boy said, smacking Mel on the ass as she exited the apartment.

He turned back to Julius. "Now what's up?"

"How's everything going?" Julius asked.

"Everything is good. Business is booming like a muhfucka. I got Mel on my ass about getting a place together, so we can start a family and shit," Charlie Boy said as he moved to the bar to make a drink.

"So, what did you say? You ready for that?"

"I didn't say much of shit really. I told her don't be letting Emma and Elizabeth get in her fucking head with that baby fever bullshit. They sit on the phone for hours bruh.

Those long-distance charges high as hell and they just cackling like hens," Charlie Boy complained as he downed his drink.

"I can dig it, but listen, I'm thinking about going home, or at least close to it."

"Why? Is everything okay?" Charlie Boy asked.

"Yeah, I'm good bruh. It's just that with this bitch Chele borderline stalking me and this nigga Yellow Shoes looking upside my goddamn head, I'ma end up in jail. Shit, the other night I went to The Bus Stop lounge and him, Rabbit and that nigga Booty Green was all in there. They was staring at a nigga so hard I had to ask them what the fuck they was looking at!"

Charlie Boy threw his head back and laughed until he heard himself snort. He could see his brother with that Gage scowl on his face as he confronted them.

"What did they say?" Charlie Boy laughed.

"Rabbit tried to buck up and get smart, but I shut him up real quick when I asked him wasn't he supposed to be out on the stroll with the rest of Yellow Shoes' bitches?!" Julius chuckled. "That nigga turned beet red."

"What did Yellow Shoes say?"

"Not shit about that. He laughed in the nigga's face and then started talking in them bullshit pimp riddles he always reciting. Sounding like goddamn Dr. Seuss and shit!"

Both brothers laughed at the sight of the clownish pimp reciting what he believed to be epic lines in his pimp lingo dictionary. "So when you thinking about leaving?"

"Soon man. Shit, you got the reefa and bootlegging going on. You got Mel and even though I don't agree with that mixing shit, she's a good girl. It's time for me to move around. You grown now baby boy," Julius said.

"I can understand that big bruh. Have you talked to Gene and O about coming back and getting back in?"

"Nah man. Those cats are up there making babies and starting a family. I don't want to interfere with what they have going on, you know? I'll set up shop around Benton Harbor, but I'll do my dirt out of Kalamazoo, Joliet, Chicago, places like that. It'll be small work, but it'll be enough to keep some cash flowing. You sure you don't want to do this little job with me?" Julius offered.

"I'm sure man. I'm just not cut out for that constant killing shit. You be killing muhfuckas, then go home and have cornflakes. I try to eat after that shit and no matter what I eat it looks like brains and blood so, um, no thank you. On another note, you know we gotta party like a son-of-a-bitch before you go right?"

"Nah, no parties bruh. Let's just get together, have a nice quiet dinner and then I'ma slip out of town, no muss no fuss," Julius said.

*****

Sherman, Texas was sparsely populated and no place for a city slick black man to be caught after dark unless he was sneaking in and sneaking out. The old ways of doing business as far as Julius was concerned was over. He no

281

longer received his jobs from the mob, but every now and then Mr. Galici would throw him a bone. Mostly small ones to keep him afloat, but that particular job was massive, and would bring Julius a whopping $100,000. That was more than enough to relocate and start anew. From the information that he'd got on the job, there was a land owner who refused to sell his 1,200 acres of prime real estate that happened to be nestled between the I-75 and I-82 corridor in Sherman. The oil companies had offered him ungodly amounts of money to allow them to perform fracking on his land. He'd insisted that there was no oil on his land, but the oil tycoons knew better. They had secretly sent soil testers and his land, the land that they had to have, was rich with crude. Philip Lassiter was staunchly against selling the land that his father and grandfather had passed on to him, but his wife Rebecca saw dollar signs. No more horse manure, no more slopping hogs and no more driving sixty miles south to Dallas just to find a decent hair salon. With the amount of money that they were offering, they could move to Dallas and live like normal people. So, when she was approached by a stranger pretending to represent the oil company's interest with a solution to her *problem*, she was all ears. She'd arranged for their two bratty daughters to have a sleepover and she would conveniently be their chaperone. While her husband was having his face blown off, she, her daughter and six of their acne faced friends would be eating pizza and giggling about some random, freckled faced boy.

Julius watched from his car as Philip stumbled into the Dizzy Donkey Saloon, obviously already half drunk. The parking lot was dusty and littered with rusted pickup trucks and motorcycles. One lone light barely lit a corner of the lot and Philip's truck just happened to be in a very dark place. Julius got out of his car, went to the trunk and removed two large pillow cases. He crept across the parking lot and climbed onto the back of Philip's truck. A pair of headlights neared the saloon and Julius had to lay flat to go undetected. His pulse quickened, his heart pounded and he felt sweat beads running down the creases of his neck. A vehicle parked near Philip's truck and he could hear the sound of a woman's voice scolding her man about the idea of urinating on the side of the saloon instead of waiting until they got inside. "Why don't you just wait? That's plain nasty Clyde!" She yelled.

"Aw, can it Mickey Jean. I couldn't hold it no dadblasted more! If you shut your yap, won't nobody know 'cept us!"

Julius heard the door open, then close and then silence. He rose to his knees slowly and looked around. The night was still and quiet. There was only him and the devastation that he held in the pillow cases. Julius tried the back sliding glass of the truck, but it was locked. He removed a spark plug from his jacket pocket and tapped the glass a few times until it shattered. The porcelain against the glass was a volatile mixture, but a quiet solution. He took the first pillow case, untied the string holding it closed and tossed it onto the floor board of the truck. He repeated it again and smiled at his handy work. Altogether, Julius had just dumped twelve diamond back rattlesnakes and six large cotton mouth water moccasins in the floor board of Philip's truck. He went back to his own car and waited, albeit, somewhat impatiently, he waited nevertheless. Nearly two hours later Philip fell through the door of the Dizzy Donkey.

"Fuck you goddamnit! You can't cut me off, I'm not sdhhrunk. I'm tipsy, but I'm not sdhhrunk!" He slurred. The bouncer, a thick necked white man with an extremely long beard, slammed the door in Philip's face as he fumbled with his keys. "Goddamn motherfucking assholes, put me out! I'm too sdhhrunk (hiccup) to keep sdhrinking (hiccup), fuck them! Go home, fuck my wife, look at (hiccup) some of these perky tittie little girls (hiccup)," Philip slurred.

He opened the door and climbed into his vehicle. Julius watched in amazement as Philip started his truck, backed out of the parking lot and headed west on State Road 56. He swerved and weaved back and forth. Suddenly his truck sped up, swerved violently and then came to an abrupt halt. Philip's door opened and he fell to the ground. Julius pulled close enough that his headlights were shining on Philip and his truck. He lay prone in the middle of the highway while snakes slithered around his dead body in an attempt to make their way to the prairies lining both side of the road. Philip's lifeless eyes gazed out at Julius as if knowing who had been responsible for his demise. His pink face was swollen and beset with multiple puncture marks from the strike of the snakes. The toxic poison from the reptiles had done exactly what Julius wanted and that was to kill him without a trace of foul play. Rebecca Lassiter would collect the money from the oil barons *and* the insurance money from her husband's death.

CHAPTER 38

Julius had managed to stay afloat in Benton Harbor for the last couple of years by doing a few jobs, but nothing major. His heart was wavering and he wasn't sure if that was what he wanted to do anymore. A few times he'd ventured into different churches and he always felt like the preachers were talking to him directly.

You can't run from the Lawd forever! When he call you, you gots to go! Can I get an Amen? See, we can run the streets, we can sleep with loose women, we can drank and smoke, but God don't care 'bout none of that. He wants your soul, see he already know your heart! He wants your soul! The bible says come as you are people. There ain't no sin too great for the Lawd to forgive. Come to Jesus today! The preacher would say.

Julius didn't know if Jesus would forgive a murderer or not, but if the preacher said he'd forgive all sins, then who was he to second guess. Julius sat at Jean Klock Park; the same park that he and his family had rescued Charlie Boy from years earlier, wondering where his life was heading. He wasn't getting any younger and he had yet to start a family. Between Eugene and Otha Lee, they had made four more Gage boys. He tossed the beer can, drove back to his small wood frame house on Pavone and dialed Eugene's number. "Hello?"

"Gene, what's going on bruh?" Julius asked.

"Man, I was just about to call you."

"You crying nigga? Elizabeth finally left your whorish ass?" Julius asked playfully.

"Nah, bruh. They got him man. They got him and Mama Gina!" Eugene cried.

"What? Wait, what? Who bruh, how? When slick, who the fuck?" Julius couldn't think. His mind was racing and his heart hurt. He gripped the phone so tight that he could feel his pulse in his fingertips. The tears began to fall, as he thought about Charlie Boy. How could he tell his little brother that the woman who had been the closest thing to a mother that he remembered was gone?

"All I know is that shit has been all over the news. They're calling it a gangland hit. Mr. G and Mama Gina were supposed to go to Ernie's grave yesterday, but when they got in the car it blew up. The whole car didn't explode and bystanders said that Mama Gina was screaming, trying to get out. When the bomb first went off, it moved the car so her side was pinned against the car next to them. Them muhfuckas sat there and watched her burn to death! They were basically reduced to ashes bruh!" Eugene cried.

"What's wrong daddy?" A little boy asked.

"Nothing baby, I'm okay. Go find your mama. Daddy's okay," Eugene said to his son.

"Damn man, how the fuck are we gonna tell Charlie Boy?" Julius asked.

"I don't know bruh. I don't know, but these muhfuckin' Italians being real closed mouth about the whole scenario and I'm not trying to call that nigga without some facts. He be trying to play innocent, but he crazier than all of us."

"Yeah, I know. Fuuuuuuuuck!"

"Besides this fucked up bullshit, how is everything in Benton Harbor for you and Starlet?" Eugene asked.

"Ain't no me and Starlet. We're just, you know, doing our thing. She doesn't particularly care for my lifestyle," Julius explained.

"You told her what you do for a living?"

"Hell nah fool ass man. I'm not stupid. For whatever reason, she thinks I'm like a pimp, or a drug dealer." Julius laughed. "So what are we going to do about Mr. G?"

"Ain't too much that we can do, because we don't know exactly who did it and the Feds are all over this shit. This shit is so fucked up on so many levels, but that's life," Eugene said.

*****

Julius called Charlie Boy and Mel answered the phone. "Hey Mel is Charlie Boy available?"

"He's been in bed all day. He says he doesn't feel good. You want me to see if he's up to talking?" Mel asked.

"Yes, please."

Seconds later Charlie Boy spoke into the phone hoarsely, "Hello?"

"What's wrong bruh? You okay?" Julius asked.

"Man, I'm glad you called. Something is wrong Ju. My stomach been in knots all day. I think it's something wrong with Mama Gina man."

In the background Julius could hear Mel whispering excitedly, "*Tell him Charlie Boy, tell him!*

"Tell me what?" Julius asked.

"Aw man, she wants me to tell you she's pregnant and shit."

"Yeah? That's good news right?" Julius asked.

"Yeah, yeah it is. I just can't shake these blues man. Hold on bruh," Charlie Boy said. Julius heard him in the background, telling Mel to run down to the store and grab him a pack of Kool filter kings and almost immediately the door slammed.

"Hello? Yeah I'm happy man. It's just her brother, this old crooked ass cop named Patrick Sweeney, is always up my ass. He already don't like me because I'm black, but he won't really get out of line, because he doesn't wanna piss off Mel. That shit done already put a little wedge between us."

"I got some news of my own." Julius said.

"Starlet pregnant?"

"How the hell you know that man?" Julius asked.

"I don't know. You just never start your sentences off like that I guess."

"Yeah, she's pregnant, but she isn't really fucking with me like that, you know? She said she ain't raising no baby in the life. Whatever that means. Listen bruh, there's more," Julius said, his voice taking on a somber tone.

"What is it? Why you sound like that?"

"You know why you're fucked up right now? Sit down man," Julius said. He was trying his best to prolong a conversation that he was dreading having.

"I'm already sitting down man, so say what you gotta say!" Charlie Boy said.

"Somebody killed Mr. G and Mama Gina man! They tried to blow up the car, but ended up burning them alive!" Julius blurted out.

Julius heard a gut wrenching scream and then the sound of the phone dropping to the floor.

"Noooo noooooo mamaaaaaa, oh my God, mamaaaaaaaaa!" Julius heard his youngest brother screaming. The sound was faint as if from a place very far away. "Hello? Hello?" Julius screamed into the receiver, but Charlie Boy was too far gone emotionally to speak. The sound of a door opening could be heard as Julius pressed his ear to the phone.

"Charlie? Charlie Boy, what's wrong baby?" Mel screamed. She picked up the receiver and spoke into the phone, "Hello? Who is this?" She asked.

"It's still me, Mel. Listen, take care of him for me. All I can tell you right now is that there's been a death in the family. When he's ready, have him to call me. Tell him I love him will ya?" Julius said, disconnecting the call. His heart hurt for his younger brother, because he knew the feeling. When Gertrude had died, Julius had experienced the same bout of physical and emotional distress. It felt as though God himself had reached in and snatched out Julius' umbilical cord. He was hurt, angry and sad all at the same time, so he most definitely understood. He'd felt lost and abandoned and searched for something to fill that void. Sure, Gina Galici wasn't Charlie Boy's biological mother, but his love for her and her love for him was as biological as it could get without him passing through her birth canal. No sooner as he'd hung up the phone, it rang again.

"Hello?"

"Is this Julius Gage?" A muffled voice asked.

"Yes, this is Julius Gage, who am I speaking with?"

"That's not important, what is important is whether you want to make $1,000,000?" He asked.

"Doing what?"

"What you do best of course. Taking care of small problems."

"$1,000,000 is a lot of money for a *small* problem," Julius said, in disbelief.

"Well, let's just say that I have enough money for that $1,000,000 to be a very small drop in the proverbial bucket."

"So, what are the conditions?" Julius asked.

"Go to the bleachers at Benton Harbor High School, go to the middle row, eight rows up and look underneath the seat. There you will find instructions on what needs to be done and how to pick up your money after you've completed the task. One more thing Mr. Gage."

"Yeah, what's that?" Julius asked.

"Since I'm the type of man that doesn't believe in putting all of my eggs in one basket, you're competing for this job. The first man to perform the task will receive the money and no need to worry, I'll be watching."

Click, silence, dial tone...

CHAPTER 39

Julius had gone to the high school and retrieved a large paper sack full of newspaper articles. One of them had been put inside of a zip lock bag with three, type written pieces of paper. As Julius read the newspaper article, he understood what the call was about. A few years earlier a young girl named Betty Mackle had been kidnapped and in the article her mother had recounted the harrowing ordeal play by play.

Betty Mackle was a precocious teen and the daughter of a wealthy real estate mogul from Florida. The girl was enrolled in a prestigious all girls' school in Decatur, Georgia, a suburb of Atlanta. She had taken ill with influenza days before Christmas and her mother Lucy had driven up from Coral Gable, Florida hoping that she might feel better so they could drive home for Christmas. They had got a hotel room, because the infirmary at the school was packed with girls suffering from the same illness. Sometime, during the early morning hours of December 23, there was a knock on their hotel room door and when Lucy answered, she was set upon by a large man with a shot gun. He demanded entry and Lucy Mackle obliged. He tied Lucy up with the cord from the hotel room's venetian blinds and gagged her with duct tape. He knocked her out by pouring chloroform on a towel and when she came to, her daughter and the kidnapper was gone. George Deacon had taken Betty Mackle to a wooded area just north of Valdosta, Georgia where he had inserted a plywood box in a shallow grave. Inside of the crate was a fan, a bed pan for bodily functions, a blanket and a flashlight. Betty was put into the crate and then the top was screwed on. It had two tubes inserted at the top for ventilation. Lucy Mackle, after waking up, had banged on the wall with her feet, but no one ever came. She'd managed to open the hotel room door and hobbled down to her Pontiac Firebird where she beat the horn with her head. The property manager had come out of the office and upon noticing her dilemma called the police. Joseph Mackle had been notified as well and immediately flew in to be with his distraught wife. They'd spoken with local authorities and then flew home to Florida. The kidnappers had demanded $500,000 in non-traceable $20 bills. They instructed the Mackles that if they contacted police, they would kill their daughter. They also stated that if they wanted proof that she was still alive, they should check near their mailbox. There they found an opal ring that she always wore and a Polaroid picture of her bound and gagged. They were instructed to leave the money on a small strip of sand in Biscayne Bay. Just by chance, when Mr. Mackle left the money the night that the kidnapper was supposed to pick up the money, an off duty cop saw a small motor boat zoom into the inlet. Because there had been a rash of waterfront break-ins, he felt the need to investigate and when he did, he spooked George Deacon. He was caught two weeks later boarding a plan for the Cayman Islands, but because their evidence had been circumstantial, his case was dismissed and he walked.

Julius shook his head. It was a sad story, because they'd found Betty Mackle's body less than two weeks later, seemingly sleeping peacefully, but dead nevertheless. The typed papers gave Julius George Deacon's last known whereabouts and instructions. They wanted it cleanly done, but they also wanted it known that he had been murdered. Attached to another piece of paper was a safe deposit box key and underneath it was the caption: TO BE UNLOCKED ONLY AFTER THE DEED IS DONE. DOING SO BEFOREHAND WILL FORFEIT YOUR CLAIM TO THE REWARD...JM

According to the letter Julius had forty eight hours to complete the mission, or it would be passed on to someone else. The letter was explicit. They wanted George Deacon killed on Betty Mackle's birthday.

Julius went back to his home, put his M40 sniper rifle in its case and got on the road to Chicago. Two hours later, he was pulling into a parking lot in the Cabrini Green projects. At the corner of Locust and Sedgwick was a well-known haunt called Libby's Pool Hall and many had coined the intersection as Death Corner. An old girlfriend of Julius' still stayed in Cabrini Green and it would be from her apartment, on the thirteenth floor facing Death Corner,

295

where he would snipe his victim. He removed the case from his trunk and climbed the thirteen flights of stairs. Julius knocked on Jeanette's door and she opened with no hesitation, no who is it, or anything. "Girl you better start asking who the hell it is before you just swang your door open." Julius said.

"Heyyyyyy baby, shiiiit ain't nobody worrying about me. How you been lover? You come to give mama some of that good chocolate lovin'?"

"Nah baby, this here is strictly business." Julius handed Jeanette ten crispy $100 bills. He walked inside of her apartment and looked around in amazement at the art that littered her space. On one wall was a velvet picture of an afro sporting black woman sitting on a black panther. Another that was also velvet showed a group of militant young black men hanging a white man by the neck. On the ceiling was a net hanging, with album covers inside and in a far corner was a wicker throne with two spears and a shield hanging on the wall behind it.

"All I need to do is take a shot. You don't need to know who, or why Jean."

"Nigga you just handed me $1000, so you can assassinate Moses in this motherfucker if you want to!"

Julius kissed the woman on the lips and set up his M40 on a small table in front of the window. He brought his scope into focus and then waited. Nearly a half an hour later, Julius saw the man known as George Deacon enter Lizzy's, and five minutes later he was coming back out. Julius touched the dial on the side of the scope to get a more precise shot and as he brought George Deacon into clear view, he saw Eugene and Otha Lee approach the man. They exchanged words with him briefly and then they both opened fire. They yelled at the men on the corner as if addressing everyone and then Otha Lee removed a large wad of money and threw it on the ground. Julius was furious and proud at the same time. Furious, because they had beat him to a $1,000,000 payout. After all, the man on the phone had told him he'd be competing for the job. But, Julius was proud because they had handled it like mob bosses. They'd made a bold statement where murder happened so frequently that the police wouldn't bother to investigate. Julius packed up his rifle and trudged back to Benton Harbor. He milled around his place until the silence was maddening. He wanted a nice cold drink, some good music and a piece of pussy if he could get it. After all, it wasn't every day that a man lost $1,000,000. He showered and dressed in his favorite eggshell white leisure suit with gold buckles. Honey colored crocodile loafers and an eggshell white Dobbs hat with a honey colored band. He splashed on a dab of Pierre Cardin cologne and brushed his goatee. Julius looked at himself in the mirror and curled his lips to reveal a snow white, radiant smile.

He pulled into Rosetta's place, parked, took a deep breath and exhaled slowly. He had always promised himself that if he had children, he'd be there from birth, but Starlet didn't want that. She was convinced that she could raise the baby alone and she was adamant about it. Now he was at the same juke joint where she and her friend Naje' performed. He would have to face her and her judgmental eyes probing him, searching for answers. He stepped inside to hear the sweet melody of Naje' singing her rendition of Curtis Mayfield's, *People Get Ready*. She smiled and waved in Julius' direction as he took a seat at a table near the back. He nodded back in her direction and tried to manage a smile. As her set ended, she exited the stage and stopped near her sister Shirley's table. "Giiiiiiirl guess who just stepped in here?" Naje' asked Shirley excitedly.

"Who? Julius' black ass? I'm gonna get him as soon as Starlet says she's finished with him."

"You're out of luck baby girl. I'm going to protect him from your little slutty ass honey!" Naje' said.

"Bitch, you ain't fooling nobody. You just want him for yourself, don't you? What makes you think he gonna want your ass with all them little bad ass kids running 'round?"

"Child, did you see him? Any black ass man that can wear a white leisure suit and make that shit look good like he do can have *all* of me. Starlet might have just missed out on this one. That nigga is too pretty and chocolate to be alone!" She said to her sister and then turned toward Julius. "Hey sweetheart, mind if I buy you a drink?" Naje' flirted as she moved in Julius' direction. He was everything that Naje' had ever wanted in a man and if he'd have her she would do her best to give him as many children as he wanted and die trying to make him happy... She wanted and needed to be a Gage!!!

Dolores - Nathaniel's mother (son)
Nathaniel Gage (Juanita/Otis)
Rufus Gage - left house to Nathaniel
Joseph Gage - father of Rufus & Phillip
Joseph left house to Phillip
Phillip left for NY City & left house to Rufus

Indians
Gertrude Running Deer / Gary Fox / Matilda (grandmother) (father) (brother) cook / baby sitter

Nathaniel's sons
Otis / Julius / Charlee Boy / Eugene / Otha Lee

Annette (train station) → Uncle - Roman

Jimmy Galici - bakery / daughter - Gina / Albert / Vinny - friend
Robert Tassejano / Domenic Aljueta / husband
Erosemo - Black Sam / AKA - Joey Chops / Salvatore - Sammy Bags (herbene)
Ernesto - Jimmy's grandson / Carlo Tuffy → gambling